A City Solitary

A VIKING NOVEL
OF
MYSTERY
AND
SUSPENSE

Books by
NICOLAS FREELING

Fiction

LOVE IN AMSTERDAM
BECAUSE OF THE CATS
A QUESTION OF LOYALTY
VALPARAISO
DOUBLE BARREL
CRIMINAL CONVERSATION
THE KING OF THE RAINY COUNTRY
THE DRESDEN GREEN
STRIKE OUT WHERE NOT APPLICABLE
THIS IS THE CASTLE
TSING-BOUM
THE LOVELY LADIES
AUPRÈS DE MA BLONDE
DRESSING OF DIAMOND
WHAT ARE THE BUGLES BLOWING FOR?
SABINE
GADGET
THE NIGHT LORDS
THE WIDOW
CASTANG'S CITY
ONE DAMN THING AFTER ANOTHER
WOLFNIGHT
THE BACK OF THE NORTH WIND
NO PART IN YOUR DEATH
A CITY SOLITARY

Non-Fiction

KITCHEN BOOK
COOK BOOK

NICOLAS FREELING

A City Solitary

VIKING

VIKING
Viking Penguin Inc.,
40 West 23rd Street,
New York, New York 10010, U.S.A.

First American edition
Published in 1985

LIBRARY OF CONGRESS CATALOGING IN PUBLICATION DATA
Freeling, Nicolas.
A city solitary.
(A Viking novel of mystery and suspense)
I. Title.
PR6056.R4C5   1985   823'.914   84-48839
ISBN 0-670-80607-2

Printed in the United States of America by
R. R. Donnelley & Sons Company, Harrisonburg, Virginia
Set in Times Roman

'A City Solitary'

– Quomodo sedet sola civitas plena populo.

(V.i., 1.i. of penitential psalm known as the Lamentations of
Jeremiah, forming part of the old monastic ritual of Tenebrae.
The wording of the Authorised Version runs:

– 'How doth the city sit solitary, that was full of people.')

PART ONE

Chapter 1

Nine o'clock is not late. In the countryside perhaps, there one might say 'nine at night' where in a town one would say 'nine in the evening'.

There is a French expression, 'the end of the evening': it applies, for this is a French countryside, one of the innumerable dales that mount winding from the broad and fertile river valleys, narrowing among the foothills, becoming crankier and more crooked as the high Pyrenees loom closer. A busy river, much given to flooding when the snows melt, shrinks to a still busy stream, a stony bed fouled by slimy old motor-tyres, stained plastic bottles, a floodmark of cans, of ragged carrier bags hooked into stubs and brambles, still shouting slogans. Every tiny factory along the streamside happily throws overboard wastes and oils, the bleaching agents and used lubricants; a long and dismal list of prohibited toxic chemicals. Let them worry about that down where the water will carry it all; to the Garonne in the end, past Toulouse. The Préfecture knows all about it and would like to slap the offenders with punitive fines. But what are you to do? – nearly all these are wretched, marginal tiny businesses. Which do you put first? The revolting, negligent, antisocial and egoist pollution? Or the continued employment of half a dozen men, ten women? We must wait, and hope, for better days: little sign of them is to be seen, and apathy predominates.

The rich have leverage. They can always turn the key in the door, declare themselves bankrupt: their personal fortune remains intact. The poor have always been so, and should be used to it by now.

Higher still the stream is just a rocky mountain brook. Less polluted, since there are fewer people. That pollution more organic; the village sewage. A festoon of lavatory paper or the guts of a rabbit, caught in the chink between stones.

A mountain economy: everything above three hundred metres is a mountain economy. 'Modern' agriculture is impossible. The fields are too small and steep, the cereals too thin and late to ripen. A few sheep and a goat or two; little gardens. In the sunnier valleys hay for cows. It is all much like the Tirol or the Valtellina. There are tourists in summer. High up, some villages are prosperous with winter sports and lower down many abandoned cottages have been tarted up as weekend nooks for townspeople. There is a sort of precarious prosperity. Nobody now wants the traditional berets or espadrilles but there is a trade in Pyrenean wool, fake antiques, objects of wood and metal, tourist phonies like shepherds' crooks and Spanish leather wine bottles, plastic rosaries and virgin-marys for the bondieuserie booths of Lourdes: there are flinty white wines and good cheese.

The people inevitably are dour and harsh-featured, close of mouth. Often open and kindly, hospitable and quick to laugh. There are many different bloods here, between the Basques of the Atlantic and the Catalans of the Mediterranean. What are Gascons? – Celts and Visigoths and heaven knows what. They are not at all French: opinion must differ as to whether this is to be counted to their credit. There are many strange religious beliefs as well as many superstitions. Much of this is Cathar country, taking a low view of Popes and, where Catholic, decidedly rebellious towards pious dogma. Bishops in former episcopal seats like Pamiers, or St. Bertrand de Comminges, of old so inquisitorial, would today be lighter of touch, more attentive where they put their feet.

One meets other people too up here; artists and ecologists and all manner of oddity. Some do not understand the world in which they live, and some despise it. Some are earnest, others quicker to mockery.

It is an April night, and raining, and in the hills it has long been dark. The road is rough and narrow, much black-patched but certainly not black-topped, full of pools, rivulets and loose stones. It leads along the streamside, through the village, going nowhere but to another, even tinier village higher up. By nine few people are astir: after the evening meal country folk tend nowadays to rivet themselves to the television set. Still, the sound of a car would attract no attention, for in the high village –

a population of perhaps thirty – there is now no café. There is a house with flaked faded sign-painting, once ornate in the antique style, across the façade. The words 'Café de l'Etoile' can just barely be made out.

In this village stands a house distinguished from the others by a tiny bell-tower, built of wooden shingles and perched above the roof tree, that once called the children to school from the outlying homesteads.

In one of these houses lives Walter, at this moment sitting before a dying log fire in the 'studio': the barn is part of these little mountain farmhouses (and the animals were stabled beneath). It is as big as two large rooms, and the attic space above added; a large airy work place. A French window has replaced the primitive wooden shutter through which hay was loaded, but he has kept the wooden bridge to the steep hill-side meadow behind. The rest of the house is shuttered and bolted, for only laziness or lethargy has stopped him from going to bed, but the French window is not locked, for Sylvie, his wife, is out and may be late, having 'gone to town'; and it is a long drive back from Toulouse. The children too have a way of dropping in as the spirit moves them, and often in the middle of the night; and they also will 'slip in through the back'. There aren't any burglars round here, for heaven's sake. The pickings would be too thin.

Walter, who is daydreaming, raises his head for a moment as the dog below in the kitchen barks. Stupid animal, barks at anything, even the most innocently botanical of tourists, even a car on the road below whose note he does not recognise. Walter sits back, crosses his legs, ankle resting casually on knee, throws a cigarette end into the embers. Ian Fleming once remarked that only an Englishman sits this way and is thus instantly recognisable as such. Walter perhaps is not quite an Englishman. Plenty of English blood but in any case a northerner, with the long skull, the floppy fair hair that will never part properly, the tallish bony figure stiff-jointed and awkward, the long lippy face full of features. Hair now the indeterminate between mouse and grey, a lot of lines in the face and around the sea-grey-blue eyes, for Walter is well into middle age, but the body still slim and light: much walking over hillsides has kept him healthy. The face looks undistinguished enough – a lot of forehead, chin and nose, but nothing to catch the eye, save that he had been too lazy to shave that morning. No doubt an observer, if asked to make the effort, would agree that Walter's face has interest, character, intelligence; but nothing startling. Even around here these fair-haired Norman-looking types attract no attention – they pop up anywhere.

The local people, while sensitive and suspicious, and indeed intensely resentful of any foreigner who were to give himself airs of superiority, accept Walter with placidity. His accent amuses them, for both his French and his Spanish sound stilted and literary, but he dresses as they do in faded overalls and darned jumpers, they like his way of seeing a comic side to bread-and-butter happenings and they appreciate his polite, old-fashioned manners. What harm does he do? He's an 'artist', and all southern people quite enjoy having one (however vague and disreputable this obscure calling) in their midst. The faintly exotic air that clings about him, a whiff of northerly seas, easterly steppes (la mère Prat claims he's a Russian) disconcerts them less than might be expected. Perhaps there is a buried memory that their forefathers too, long ago . . .

Bed would be the logical place and why hang about? Sylvie might not be home for hours. He had no idea what she was doing and no wish to enquire. She liked to see people; to have fun. She often went to the town. It was anyhow a point of honour to say "Well, enjoy yourself" at her going and a "Had a good evening?" on her return. No questions . . . It's perfectly normal even if there's a long story behind it. Walter likes this lonely, rustic corner: it bores her out of her mind. He is on the whole unsociable and loathes parties: a scrum is to her a physical need . . . He lives very largely in a world created and peopled by imagination: Sylvie has beauty, intelligence and wit; as much imagination, says Walter coarsely and at times impatiently, as a pot of yoghurt. But she lives with him, alone for the most part since the children have grown up. They must endeavour to respect one another, and the lives the other leads . . .

Sleepiness thus, for Walter keeps country hours: the early morning is his best time for work; while Sylvie, a night bird, grumbles when after reading in bed for an hour or so he wants to turn the lights out (from – habit? – they still share the enormous old fruitwood bed where an ill or unhappy child has often been tucked in and plenty of room over for two adults to sleep undisturbed without playing sardines – the bedside lamps are three metres apart but Walter's eyelids are sensitive to light, while Sylvie can sleep happily in the middle of the ring at Madison Square Garden). Absentmindedness. And, very often, a sapajou-like slowness of reaction. Like many people quick in the wits, Walter can be as dim as any sloth.

The dog begins to bark furiously and he only regrets that it is too far off for him to say 'Oh shut up, do' and poke its ribs with the nearest shoe.

Like a good many of us, perhaps most of us, Walter will ask himself (both 'out loud' and loudly) how he could have been so stupid, in an exasperated wail and banging his hand upon the table: and it will be Sylvie who asks 'But even if you had been less stupid . . .?'

For like the mother of the little girl in the rhyme
'Who stood on her head
On the little truckle bed' – you think it is the boys. One had come in through the kitchen window only the week before, masked in helmet and goggles, in a long leather coat, and done a Karloff, lurching menacingly towards the dog, who retreated terrorised and growling under a chair: much merry laughter. And when the French window opened quite quietly, five paces from where he was sitting, it took Walter two, three slow counts to perceive anything abnormal, to stop the phrase 'Didn't recognise you for a moment.' The one lamp switched on was in another corner. The tall figure in the leather jacket was not masked; simply in shadow.

"All alone then?" A quiet voice, though harsh and mocking. Walter heard only that it was a strange voice. It was also sarcastic, and above all confident. And that makes a total of six adjectives, and they are quicker written down than assimilated by ear. "All sad by the fireside?"

Indignation, and no fear. Country folk do tend to walk straight in: as though into a mill to buy flour. And the young have never any manners.

"And who the hell are you then?" Two more figures have edged in, one a girl. Even at this stage Walter thinks either that they've lost their way in the hills or run out of petrol: irritated.

"Stay as you are. No need to get up!" Parody of a social

manner. The hand by the side was brought forward; a pointing finger two feet long.

A machete. A forty-five centimetre blade, the back straight and heavy, the business side curved and wicked. Walter had one himself: no sugar cane on his terrain, but plenty of tall weeds . . . He thought it a lot more frightening than a gun. A bullet can go anywhere, but a sabre . . . Walter's mind, so slow, is also rapid. He sees the moment when the cavalry of the British Army, a joke for a hundred years, caught a mob of Boers in the open. Lancers, Dragoons, blade or point: once is enough. Walter understands the 'arme blanche' – the bayonet, the knife. He has only his wits, and sits back in the chair. Much good may they do him, but one might as well be comfortable. He recrosses his legs, folds his arms. The way they strolled in! On some pill perhaps; speed or whatever. Probably a car parked quite openly – nothing furtive.

"Nobody else here then? No women? Children?" Walter shakes his head. He is pleased. He may behave well, or badly, but he is on his own.

The young leader – they are all twenty-one or -two, the ages of his own children – tucks the machete under his arm, strolls about. Downstairs, the dog's barking and growling has reached a paroxysm. "Take a look then," he says to the two. Looks around. "Books – what use is that?" In passing he snicks the telephone cable, the way a housewife heads a dead flower. Just tidying.

The trouble with writing, as Walter, a writer, has found, is that there are too many words. Thought is much quicker than action, but takes longer to say. One believes in non-violence but in defence of the home . . . The ancestors, one may believe, would not have been unduly impressed by a cutlass: all in the day's work. Given maybe a walking stick, one could have a go. None was handy, and he was meditating this but had no more than uncrossed his legs when the voice said idly "Come on hard, you'll sure as hell find me come on harder. To show you, like." The little hearthside poker was too small. He stretched his legs, both frightened and unfrightened. He is recalling a detail from Dumas, in character if apocryphal – Charles I at his trial, tapping the axe with his little cane. 'Heaven help us, these people think I have no more courage than a butcher. I strike you,

12

waiting patiently for you to return the blow.' Walter tenses such muscles as he has and the other turns around, points the sabre.

"Take it easy, and I'll do you no harm." It almost sounds human. "Lost our way on these goddam roads. Hungry, as much as anything."

The other two came back, with sour faces.

"Nobody else. Poor pickings." The man, or boy, carries lengths of ripped material, recognisable as net curtains from the downstairs living room.

"We'll see. Look in the cellar? – find a few bottles. All right, Charley, we'll tie you up, so's I can digest me dinner in peace. That chair'll do," tearing stuff lengthways.

"You poor or something?" asked the girl contemptuously. "Looked a good house, from the outside." His arms and feet were held, without violence. It is not worth the trouble to gag him: the next house is a hundred metres away. They will be sitting snug and warm there and the television on full blast. Perhaps in mockery, perhaps because she likes to show her power, perhaps even liking to inflict pain, the girl taps him lightly, painfully upon the temple with the big flashlight – his – she is carrying. They walk out then without a glance back; he no longer exists. It is only then that he notices – the dog no longer makes a noise. And he realises that they kill. It is bad, then, to have imagination and Walter closes his eyes.

One must try to think. They wear no masks, they leave footprints and fingerprints everywhere. They don't care then – it means that they are going to kill me? But their traces will remain, plenty for identification. They feel thus the certainty that the slow, stupid police will never overtake them? Or they just don't care? How does one come to grips with this? They are not Arabs, blacks, Turks. They are French children, indistinguishable from mine. City voices, speaking an argot language which is that of an entire generation. Illiterate? Many children at universities, and with degrees, are illiterate: it suffices now to be numerate. It is very likely that they decided schools were a waste of time. My own children came to the same conclusion. Yet these rob, break, and kill. Where does the difference lie? Asking this sort of question is surely also a waste of time. And stamping them out . . . likewise. For one stamped upon, a hundred more are waiting, ready. These are the Ecorcheurs, the mercenary soldiers of history, who were out of a job – or had not been paid. Their numbers are growing . . .

Walter is aware that this kind of thinking is perfectly futile.

It is again the leader who comes back. The other two will be downstairs, ransacking. He is surprised that he is unfrightened, that he does not care. Close up, there is a smell of food, of wine. They didn't find anything wonderful. No foie gras, no vintage Bordeaux.

"What happens when you get old?"

"I'll help old ladies across the road. All right, Charley, let's get to business. Safe? Gold coins? Jewellery? Stamps? Tell it easy, or tell it with your socks off." As he had thought. Foot burners. One must try.

"Use your brains. I can see you've plenty. Think I'm a bourgeois? I own this house, I got it cheap, I make a living. The door is open. No alarms, no radar, no safety locks, and no safe. What would I put in it?"

"Tell me then." The young man has used his foot to hook a little table, handy for appurtenances of comfort; a wineglass or a coffee-cup, an ashtray: he perches on it. He has picked up Walter's lighter, and clicks it on and off. Annoyingly. He turns the little wheel to stretch the flame higher. Walter concentrates upon keeping his voice level. Steady if it can be managed. The flame has the elegant, even pretty shape of an assegai's blade. It leans inward to the back of Walter's bound hand, reaping a swathe of the fine hairs that grow there. Done with such neatness that his skin has felt no more than warmth.

"You can make me scream. But that won't bring anything here that you'd fancy. Books as you said yourself. And what use is that?"

Walter has closed his eyes. He is thinking of pain he has suffered – twice in his life he has had stones in the urinary tract, and numerous accidents, including burns: he knows his pain threshold to be low. No doubt but that more pain awaits him, before his death. Unwanted comes the passage from a book of Malraux – the Chinese thrown into the firebox of an old steam locomotive. *The Human Condition*, is it not?

The lighter snapped off.

"You think I'm the Gestapo or something." The tone is reproachful. "I'm a business man, Charley. I want full value,

14

and giving nothing. Since that's business, right? Okay, won't waste time decorating you. The stereo set's all right. Camera? – everybody's got a camera. Got to cover our expenses."

"Look for yourself, Christ." Tasting bile in his throat, trying to unclench.

"Wetting y'self, Charley?"

"You never have?" Walter heard himself ask. "You will."

It got a laugh that surprised him.

"Maybe, mate; that may be." There is no longer contempt in the voice. "Thanks for the thought. Sorry, no time for the big discussion." Walter has shut his eyes again because pain is now sharp in his belly. And instead of an image it is a phrase that has come into his mind. Where does it come from, and what does it mean? 'Are you hungry, are you cold?'

From below there is a noise of shattering china. From the volume it will be La Flamenca's party dinner set. Limoges porcelain, hand made and hand-painted. Twenty thousand francs to replace that now. He simply feels weary, surprised how little he cares. These are only objects.

It is the phrase of the general who, to teach his son discipline, has had him put in the military prison and left overnight; and realises in the morning his own impotence. Epitome of pathos, and one is sorry for him. The son looks at his father, and says nothing. Are you hungry, are you cold?

I am no business man, thinks Walter. Thank god, or heaven, or whatever. My biology is odd: I pay back, for my robber ancestors. It is my point of honour to give full value, regardless of what I may get back.

He looks. The Bang and Olufsen has been disconnected. Another twenty thousand francs. Perhaps I will make a big television sale, and then I will buy it all new. And a Porsche car. He can afford to laugh, because the back is turned, searching his bureau.

The other two came back, poormouthing.

"Some art shit. Pictures 'n' the like. Damn books everywhere. These candlesticks, though. Bit o' silver." Are they sophisticated enough to understand hallmarks? The things are in fact plate, if of excellently thick and heavy quality as well as of degenerate Victorian design.

"Plate – worth a few thou though," says the leader.

"You won't get value, fencing them." A mistake of Walter to have spoken, a mistake to have even a suggestion of irony in the voice. The leader looks at him.

"Think of going into the business, do you?" But Walter has been stung. More painful to him than the rest, however expensive, is the sight of the girl. Her thievish picking little fingers have been going through Sylvie's clothes. She has found nothing – La Flamenca being twice her size (ratty bony thing it is) – but a silk scarf. Beautiful, and to be sure expensive. Does that cause the twinge? Or seeing it now around her certainly dirty neck? Or that it was a birthday present from himself; a wound now to his vanity.

Not much of a haul, these few pieces of silver and the rest (he has not even a camera), so that he feels fear of their trashing the house seriously, from spite; setting even the house afire. In these other two he recognises the violence of stupidity, the need to destroy anything they cannot comprehend, themselves enjoy. The leader, it is to be hoped, is more of a professional. He has tossed Walter's chequebook on the floor – these things lead too easily to identification.

"Whip that lot down and stow it away then. Making a lookabout, and I'll be with you." Silence: this one was cat-footed in movement where the other's boots had resounded on the stairs: there were no more sounds of breakage but some other form of defilement was at work?

He came back though; stood unhurried, looking at Walter. Disappointed?

"I did tell you," said Walter sadly. "No desirable objects, nice and portable. Hoffmann Laroche bearer bonds, Bons du Trésor that slip into the pocket. I don't have any."

"A poor fellow," said the young man. "Middle-aged, going grey 'n' all, hasn't anything. What is it you do – write? With that?" gesturing at the table. "Christ, mate, forty years old, it's an antique. Buy y'self a computer, get into the world. Living up here in a hole like this, telling y'self stories." He reached out with the machete, inserted the sharp-ground tip under the corner of the typewriter, sent it sprawling on the floor upside down.

No insult, no damage could have injured Walter more. A blow direct in the face had hurt less, humiliated none but the giver.

The exaggeration had been small; the machine was thirty years old: with the little Olivetti portable of his beginnings it was his working life. Harder to bear than the silk scarf. Something of his effort to hold his face together showed, for the young man smiled, at last satisfied.

"All right, so you aren't a criminal. Think y'self too grand like, to dirty your hands with money. Tag along after, to pick up the crumbs, taking no risks. Half smart. Thinking himself clever. Bourgeois in your little mind. A collaborator, we call that." He smiled: he had an idea. "What we do with that, we scalp it a little bit."

He stepped forward, gathered the longer hair above Walter's forehead: the bitter edge of the machete scythed through. "Little souvenir, Charley. But for you, not for me," dropping the hair teasingly on his nose. "To remind you. Don't be in a hurry, running down to the gen-darm-erie," drawing out the syllables with contemptuous amusement. "They won't do you much good, as you'd find out. I might be back, and next time take your ears with me. Remember that. 'Bye now. And *sois sage*." As one might say to the children, when going out to an evening party. You can look at the box awhile, and be sure you're in bed by half-past eight.

At the terrace door, a slow look around before leaving. There should be a masked head that sweeps from side to side, eyes coldly burning in an unseen face, a paralysing breath of ice and terror. Like one of Professor Tolkien's Black Riders. But what utter nonsense. This was no spirit of evil. Nor was it any loutish mercenary out for nothing but vulgar loot. Something in between. Like himself, half-intelligent. He had said it – half-smart. Self-proclaimed the enemy of a corrupt society; a self-appointed scourge. Listen to them all talking about right and wrong – you hear me, Charley, these things no longer exist. Never did. Inventions of the curé, propaganda spread by the vicar. Property is theft, cousin, and theft keeps the machine juiced. For what I lift from a supermarket, you think that worries them? You think they send the gen-darm-erie running after me? Know a better trick than that, cousin. Add the percentage on, and it's paid by the stupid herd like you.

The scalp bristled and prickled. It hurt too, with a burning pain, though no blood came trickling down over his forehead:

the wetness came from lower down. He heard the car start, sounding to his sharpened ears nearer than it was. They had not even bothered to gag him. He was fast bound with the strips of curtain but could yell.

Would he yell? He had a fine resounding yell, and the ceiling in here would be a good sounding board: there had always been a good acoustic (would one ever again listen to music, in this room?) Yelling would in the end penetrate the neighbours' television-dulled eardrums. And would that do him any good? Had that young man (what point was there hanging adjectives on him as though upon a Christmas tree? Would they make him less dreadful, less horrifying, less vicious?) – had the young man not put his finger very neatly on the flaw in bourgeois protection? The injury to their vanity. Giving the neighbours a good gloat. Swallowing the knowing grins and half-hearted enquiry of the local police: themselves bourgeois, for a few gold ingots, or master paintings, they might consent to take their hands out of their pockets. For a pitiful handful of silver (just for a ribbon to stick in his coat) – they'd shrug, go through the movements. Type up a few forms.

Since the little clock had been taken he had no means of knowing the time. Latish – but not yet late. Sylvie might be many hours yet. The fire was out and the wet April night, raw at this altitude, beginning to make itself felt. He had lost sensation in the hands and feet: the blood was not circulating. The time would be long and painful.

Long? Painful? You'll still have to swallow it, cousin. So chew away bravely. Secrete saliva. Masticate. Your mind is free, and you can set it to the service of this stupid bound and crippled body. Your trade is to perceive, to apprehend. Having done so, to remember. Every little experience has its value. You've never been left tied up, before. You were never locked in the coal-hole as a child, either. Punishments of that kind did not come your way. Pain you learned about, having been whacked, sometimes most unjustly, by your raging mamma in the hottest of blood, using whatever came handy; an umbrella (incompetent) or a kitchen wooden spoon (alarmingly competent). For her time and social origins Ma had been an enlightened person. Never punish a child in cold blood. Never withdraw love: that bourgeois punishment.

18

Bourgeois he called me. From where he stands, the outlaw, that is what I am. He throws the commonplace insult, usable for anything that is different to himself. That I too am an outlaw would not occur to him.

And isn't it a stupid, worn-out word! Burgherdom is respectable. The burghers of Carlisle (woken in our childhood by the red glare from Skiddaw) were probably pusillanimous, but honest: the burghers of Calais, offering their lives to redeem their burgh, are noble. And we have found no better word for the parasite class, knowing no interest but their own, servile to the powerful and arrogant towards the humble. It seems unfair. We should have found new words for the unproductive, who create nothing, who buy cheap, and sell dear. Something better than this stale Marxist vocabulary.

Chapter 2

Tears have dried on your cheeks, a salt estranging sea becomes a sandy desert: the eyes are those of the third class carriage that has sat up all night, Paris to Marseille, the old steam train days and not any Blue Train neither. The face is a mask of filth. No amount of wrinkling, blowing, grimacing, shaking the head which is all you can shake has succeeded in getting rid of the hair on your nose. The terrace door is one of those with the bad habit of opening again unless firmly latched: a moist chilly draught plays around your neck; around your legs too, if you could feel them. To talk of summoning up courage: there is not much to summon. Like the spirits from the vasty deep – will they come, when you do call for them?

Walter has tried to summon – for example – King Charles I. By no means a favourite character of his, the ingrained double-crosser forever borrowing money on the strength of charm, which he hadn't the least intention of paying back. But as already seen, the flash of Dumas' genius shows him at his best. It had been a sharp January morning – was snow falling? Charles trembling a little, not from fear. 'You might give me my dressing-gown, would you?' And 'Will my hair disturb you?'

politely, of the executioner. 'It could be tied up with a ribbon.'

Still, they had allowed him to die with dignity, like a gentleman. Taking his time, moving freely, 'saying a word' (he was able to speak in normal quiet tones, with no difficulty in salivating). Saying his prayers and giving the signal for his head to be cut off. To do them justice, it would never occur to them to do otherwise: he was still king. Coming to the wooden billet and the sharp edge, the devious, dishonest, sly and selfish man had behaved as a warrior, as though all his life had been saved up for this moment.

Indeed examples abounded of bad and corrupt men accepting execution with noble serenity. Danton's joke would serve for all. "One does not conjugate this verb in the passive, since nobody says 'I have been guillotined.' "

It made apparently no difference to have been bad or good: one did what one could, with style if one had it. The Carmelites had walked up the steps singing, as though in their choir; the voices falling one by one silent nowise altering the pitch and intonation of the last as she knelt in the sharp metallic smell of blood. What had they sung? The plain chant of the monastic office for the appropriate Hour? Who will find better than the lovely cadence of the 'Jam lucis orto sidere', the hymn to dawn? For them it was a day like any other. Or at eventide (what had been the hour, the season?) the splendid bounding rhythm of the 'Salve Regina'.

The train of thought was evident, identified as soon as it came. A schoolboy, scarcely to be distinguished from a crowd of solemn, Spanish, brilliantined schoolchildren, allowed to attend on occasion the church of the monks, near by (in Valladolid no shortage of religious orders). There he had heard sung the 'Salve Regina', the five syllables ringing out in a tenor solo theatrical as Siegfried ('Coveted sword' . . .) and the deep chorus answering. And, more moving yet, the singing of Tenebrae in Holy Week, for Jesuit-trained children a reward for good behaviour. There he had heard the first terrible slow line from Jeremiah. 'Quomodo sedet sola civitas plena populo.' How doth the city sit solitary, that was full of people. The last clear embers of beechwood had long slipped and settled into grey fluffy ash. His dog was dead. He had told himself that it was not so, but he knew that they had killed it.

To find courage Walter must go further back. The clock was gone, the little brass carriage-clock that had been his mother's, and her mother's: it still keeps – kept – perfect time. Of his mother not much is left. Her grave is far away and graves are to Walter no very strong focus of filial piety, for too many are unknown and unmarked, his father's among them. But the clock had been one of the last symbolic anchors. Wherever she paused, in vagabondage, she carried out a ritual, and whatever she threw away, for 'lightening the ship' was a favourite slogan, these she clung to. Where there was a living room, for the generation to whom central heating was a vulgar invention, belonging in hotels, there was a mantelpiece, not always dignified by the name of chimneypiece. In the centre hung a pretty italianate looking-glass, with the clock in front of it, and around this were grouped 'the ancestors'; four small portraits in chipped gilt frames. The adolescent jeered at these atavistic practices: the adult – after setting new records in vagabondage – did the same.

Valueless? – if a hundred years old or more, even an ugly and worthless object has now commercial value. Walter cannot feel sure that he would not prefer them to be gone altogether, rather than find them defaced and trampled. This thought hurts more: how foolish. And Walter turns again, away from these pains towards his physical discomforts, by now considerable and one particularly prominent.

There is a fine example of ironic humour in a memoir of some seventeenth-century lady: is it Madame de Sévigné laughing heartily at the misfortunes of a duchess she does not greatly care for? Invited, rare and tremendous honour, to share the King's coach during a lengthy, indeed interminable, journey. It was common knowledge that Louis Quatorze (himself the most self-controlled man in his kingdom and today, however detestable we find him, we have respect for this: he endured the barbarous agony of medieval surgery without a sound or a movement) would accept no frailty in ladies of his acquaintance. A duchess leaping out to crouch in the hedgerow would not be well viewed at all. Her efforts at courtly conversation while her bladder is simply killing her are described with glee: it could happen to any of us.

Not going to happen to me, thinks Walter. Pee and be done.

None of this can be called suffering. You have not been tortured. You have not even been beaten. You have lost neither wife nor child nor even home. Your crops were not burned. You are not threatened by famine, plague, or exile. You have been momentarily deprived of a few comforts to which you are accustomed. You have lost a number of trivial possessions that can neither feed nor clothe you. You have lost your dog. High, it is true, in the scale of nomadic man's treasures, but neither cow nor horse.

It is time to show yourself a warrior. 'Don Juan' or 'Genaro', walking in and finding him tied like this, would be holding his sides laughing. He has a novelist's fellow feeling for Carlos Castaneda's clutch upon the lifeline notebook, the need to scribble it all down on bits of paper; the earnest and humourless self-importance of 'methodology'.

Perhaps one could even try to silence the infernal chatterbox, the interior dialogue.

This is not an easy path to follow. Walter fails: he always does.

From far away he heard, and with extraordinary clarity, the contented purr of a small car's motor in a humid atmosphere, and the development of a familiar pattern; the grate of tyres on the roadway, the turn and roll back on rough grass, the squeak of the handbrake as the motor dies. La Flamenca. His dear wife.

A longish pause of a female nature: she is collecting handbag, umbrella, basket (high-heeled shoes, cardigan, headscarf). He sees, as though in a flashlit photograph, this woman as she rummages.

Fairly tall, in harmony with heavy bones and the musculature of Flanders. Her hands are short, and rather ugly, but her feet are small and well shaped, and her legs are still beautiful. Her movements are neat and competent – why, just at this moment, does Walter recall the innocent clumsiness of Manuela's gestures?

The doors of small cheap cars must be slammed to get them shut, but it is a clack, no more – Walter would have slammed it twice, massively, before seeing that the seat belt was stuck in the opening.

Light quick feet upon the terrace. Manuela's step had been heavier and slower. The door is open and the light is on. Sylvie's intelligence takes the scene in, in one quick indrawn breath: she wastes no time.

"Can you talk?" she whispers. "Are you all right? Is there a knife in your pocket?"

"Yes to all three," between clenched teeth but his voice surprises him; sounds quite natural.

"Is there someone here?"

"No." The quick hand wriggles in his trouser pocket. She feels the wetness, pays no heed, has understood.

"I'll have you free in no time." She uses the knife skilfully: the right force at the right point. "Can you stand?"

"No," sliding helpless, on to knee and elbow.

"A hot bath? – or would that hurt terribly? Shall I rub gently? Some eau de cologne?" Her hands are usually gentle, always skilful. Manuela's hands, long and bony, always cold, had not been skilful. They had been instinct with understanding.

Among other characteristics (the stain of ink on the inside of the right hand's middle finger would now be counted a museum piece) writers can be recognised by a vicious enjoyment of debate about the meanings of words even while rocking and hissing with pain. Can a nuance be established between skills inborn and those acquired by lesson?

Walter feels the warm tide of gratitude flood his heart while fighting pain. Sylvie is a good nurse, quick and unflustered. And very experienced. He has complained angrily and bitterly, in open or in secret, of her inner coldness; but now she is spontaneous. She loves him.

"Do you want some whisky or anything? Always said to be a bad idea but if you feel it would do you good it will."

"I'd be surprised if there were any left. I don't know how much there is of anything left. Have you been in the kitchen?" Sylvie covers her eyes with her hands and speaks between them.

"I thought tea would be a good idea. I went to put a kettle on. I did, but I'm afraid I couldn't look at anything else." She takes her hands away, resolutely, but cannot stop nervously twisting her ring. "I'll make the tea though."

"No. I'll go." A numbness still but he can stand, flex his arms and legs.

"We must phone the police."

"Police indeed – wouldn't even come, this time of night. And if they did what good would that do?"

"They might catch these gangsters!"

"Even supposing they did, would it help?"

"It might help others," though with no tone of reproach.

"To them it'll be one more statistic. Think about it in the morning – is it already this morning? But I'll clean up my own sick. And since I don't want to go downstairs – now's the time."

She takes his arm and links it in hers; a physical solidarity that touches him.

He had not thought he would be sick, but he was. Once, before he mastered himself. Wiping cold water off his face he thinks that everyone has the right to be sick once. Policemen too, or medical students. Sylvie is not sick. He remembers a night far in the past. They had been poor, alone; a shabby room in a strange country: she had miscarried. Then, too, they had been totally together. He had nursed her. A miscarriage too is violence. But less wanton.

The dog had been cut down by a blow from the machete upon the kind skull, at the point where he had been used to place his hand, stroking down hard and playing with the ears, while the dog pressed back, looking up with love and faith, showing the whites of his eyes. One could only hope that the single blow had sufficed.

The man – since so one must still call him – had then put the blade parallel to the ribs, and thrust the point right through, in wantonness. Professor Tolkien had written a noble passage: could one call it a syllogism? Many live that deserve death; and many die that deserve life. Can you give it them? Then be not eager to deal out death in punishment.

It was Sylvie who thought of the groundsheet from an old tent the boys had had when little, and went to get it from the attic. Walter goes to the cellar, for spade and pickaxe. He expects to meet pools here too of blood from the half dozen bottles of expensive wine that is all he keeps and is surprised to find them intact. As though the fact were of any importance . . .

Sylvie leaves him alone to compose the shattered body, cold now and sticky. It is not from disgust that she stands back, but from tact. He curls the body in a sleeping position, on the blanket where the dog has always slept.

"I want to give him something." She nods. The daffodils are almost over, but by torchlight he finds still a few, and on the terrace border are irises in bud: he reaps them with his knife.

24

She has not moved; nods again when she sees what he has. Together they carry the four corners of the groundsheet, down the meadow to the streamside where the ground is deep and soft. It is still heavy work. He has not dug a grave before. One comes to everything in the end. Tell yourself you are planting a tree. I will come, in the autumn, and I will plant a tree, to shade you.

Sylvie holds the flashlight. It is unpleasant in the steady drizzle, sweating inside hat and raincoat. The subsoil is stony and one must get a good depth. He wants no marauders to plunder this final innocence. There are some big stones: he is going to heave them in the stream but stops in time. A small cairn is good. He is weary, and sobs for breath.

"Let me take a turn." Strong-built toughly knitted woman. Why not? But he shakes his head and she does not insist. They are bound by strong links. Blows of machete or pickaxe – there are worse and both have received as well as given – can forge as well as sever. They have taken a good few in common: the beast with two backs can be hit on both sides, equally sensitive to either.

He replaces the turves carefully, of the April grass that is alive with spring but has not yet grown. Now he feels the extremes of exhaustion, legs twitching and stumbling back to the house. Sylvie pushes him towards bed, switching his blanket on, helping him to undress. Passive as pudding he rolls heavily over and lies waiting for warmth and oblivion. Warmth comes fast, but oblivion is not to be hired. Not even from Electricité de France. From below he hears the jingling slide of glass shards into a dustbin. A man goes to bed, saying the hell with it, a shower of shit there may be but the morning will be time enough to tackle that: a woman will say sorry, sleep isn't possible with a pool of blood lying there. Resources still for thought. A step stirs his stupor, and a hand smelling of disinfectant fits a mug into his lax fingers, makes sure that he is gripping the glow of heat, the smooth solid contour. Tea. He has no sleeping pills. A murder does not often come his way.

But this is nothing. . . . Throughout the world war is raging. No second passes without the explosion, the flurry of shots: another skinny old man lying under the mattress and the cooking-pot he was running away with: another child with the flies thick on oozing eyes and lips: another woman with her bowels ripped apart. We could talk about the quota. The norm for the time of year. We get accustomed so very quickly. Blood and broken glass the most slipshod and casual of banalities. Hamburger and baked beans; cornflakes and fish fingers. The sound does not carry this far, to the sleepy stickiness of Europe. Little patches we might have here or there; pockets of infection – local difficulties. The fox got into the chicken run. Those people are only animals anyhow. Turn quickly to the stock-exchange page. There might be some broken glass there, but the blood doesn't show.

Only animals and, well, dear, they do massacre one another. Can't be helped. Natural selection, y'know; red-in-tooth-'n'-claw, 'n'-all-that.

The generation before mine, thinks Walter, was unusually unlucky. Two European wars, and Spain in between. I have known people who fought in all three, and what's more survived them all. Whereas mine was fantastically lucky. Too young for Hitler and too old now for any emotion but complacency. The odd bomb here or there is only Corsican folklore. Europe has become a monstrous suburb and the fox or the hawk are scarcely seen. Only the rats are still there.

Walter remembers the bird . . . Years ago. The year they had done the studio conversion, in the barn. The children had been little. They'd been cleaning up the builders' debris; dust and cement floating in the beams of evening sunlight. A small boy brought his canary in its cage, setting it in a window embrasure, saying 'He'll like it here.' They had laughed, gone to bed forgetting the bird, hopping and chirping in the sunset.

Walter had got up early, the next morning: a lovely summer dawn and a racket of birdsong: thrushes and what-have-you. He'd been loitering about enjoying it, while the coffee filtered. The cage was there on the sill, untouched? – at least unopened. There was no blood. And there was no bird. A few of the tiny, fine orange and yellow feathers still lay.

What was the point of Walter blaming himself for stupidity, lack of imagination, insensitivity? Who bothers that around a barn where hay has been stored, with animals below in a stable – however long ago – there will always be a few rats? Field rats. You hear them scuffling about from time to time. Harmless things.

Had the bird wakened at the slight sound, taken the head from under the wing – and seen the eyes at the bars? These little creatures die readily from shock: the heart gives one monstrous thump and explodes. He hoped that it had been so. For the desperate flutter, imprisoned in its own cage, torn to pieces alive . . . and how had those beasts passed the bars? Subtle, intelligent creatures.

What could one do? He cleaned the cage, set it away in the attic. My bird! said the child, indignant. But I'm afraid he died, my love: my fault, I must have left a window open and caused a draught: they catch pneumonia easily, you know. The child said nothing. But children are not fooled by a soapy voice, a hypocrite face. Adults are fooled because they wish to fool themselves. Why pretend that a fox never gets in the chicken run? Children are not sentimental. A year or so later a boy had been delighted at a bird's nesting in a wall-chink low enough to observe the progress of the nestlings. Good biology lesson: he had met it some ten days later carrying the nest, full of dead fledgelings. Cat got the mother, explained the child laconically. He had just had another biology lesson.

And he has not had a scratch. A dog. One is attached to a dog, as a child is to a canary. Man's best friend is Dog. Man's earliest conquests in a hostile and threatening environment were enabled through the help of Dog, and no other creature has so taken man's part, so openly chosen sides, with such perfect fidelity shown simple, unembarrassed love.

We like things simple and open, do we not? And women are so complicated, are they not? Are they not! – it is a fair guess that such would be the heartfelt chorus of the crowd.

Sylvie comes quietly though well aware he is not asleep. "I've done my best. The kitchen clean, at least. I hadn't the heart or the guts for more." She has had a shower, is naked under her dressing-gown. Her skin feels cool and still damp. She stretches her legs out, and he can at last unclench his tightly compassed ligatured body in her arms. Her body feels now burning hot. Facing the axes, next day, that have hacked into panel or commode; the sabre-slash into the canvas of pictures; they are grateful for these hours shared, for suffering. There have been others. The years of the past are long, behind them.

* * *

27

Walter was half asleep: the past became alive. He was perched upon the ridge of ground opposite his house, looking down upon the valley. A turfed hollow makes a seat; a bank the back-rest. Behind him march more ridges, climbing, becoming Pyrenees. In front of him the mule-track along the stream-side has been hammered over the years into roadway, pot-holed and wet in winter, dusty and stony in summer. Looking unreal in the clear light, two hundred metres off his house floats, aery. The perspective lends distancing, detachment.

He often came here: in the long sunny still afternoons of autumn his cigar-smoke rose untroubled, parodying the smoke from chimneys.

Doll-like upon the road and slow moved two or three village figures. Old Julot, small and bony under his greenish-black beret, marching with his looping ballooning walk, blown along by the wind, tethered to the ground only by the ballast of his rubber boots. Bruno plainly drunk; a stubby roughround mass quarried out of the subsoil, whose colorations are of Old Devonian sandstone, and the dark suffused purple of porphyry. And Jesus, a dignified, always leisurely saunter: his beret, worn in and out of bed for thirty years, is the colour of dust and ashes, of rainclouds, of prehistoric beginnings. His trousers appear hewn of limestone, his boots and his face granitic – beard-stubble a silvery sprinkle as though of quartz particles.

Walter thought about 'the upper class'. To which he belonged, if one could call it that: a fact with its tragical aspect as well as comic – but generally farcical.

It had of course all been swept away in 1914, and had then been out of date since the great liberal year of 1848. Even now there would remain, he supposed, a few fragments of flotsam and jetsam. Bleached and anaemic, too long upon the bosom of the waters, but tattered and discoloured labels still clinging, saying Earl or Viscount. Most, like himself, younger sons or disregarded daughters, free of the nonsense of titles though sometimes made painfully aware of it. Always an embarrassment, those daughters, making the wrong marriage or none at all, and in Europe taking to the convent a good deal; in England to drink, quite often, or drugs.

We were never trained for any sort of job, and never held any for long, even where eccentricity and incompetence were

28

tolerated and thought highly of – obscure corners of the British Empire. The difficulties in Europe were greater: younger sons of the French and Austrian nobility hung around distressingly, tending to become known to the police. From commercial enterprises we would by now have been, remorselessly, weeded out. Centuries of inbreeding has long bled all energy out of us and when did we ever know how to drive a bargain? As for countries now communist, an overdose of vodka where not of labour-camp would have exterminated us.

Walter remembered the one or two he had known. Disappeared – times are hard.

He had survived: there must have been others. At our core there can be a hard grain of talent, unexplained and unexpected. And a few genes surviving of the original toughness, transmitted through the generations. But would he have lasted this long without his wife? La Flamenca was a tough subject.

The sturdy, resilient woman – that Flemish bourgeoisie physically indestructible, rock-hard in the head, legendary toughness of fibre in the character . . . Something of that he too possessed. There was more to it than an old family. A talent or instinct for securing wives had been inherited: often before they had been sought far afield. Forestiers, outliers, and not so named without reason. In Normandy called the 'horsain' – the etymology is the same.

Walter's father had been English. He had never known these origins, never set eyes upon his English grandfather. The folklore of childhood was all that he had to go by; the ironic, self-deprecating jokes told by the grey quiet man who died in 1939, and considered that good timing.

A Norfolk squire of outrageous sort, even for that notoriously independent part of the world, sniffy about 'our German neighbours' (King George V at Sandringham). No title: who needed titles! They had held their land all these years – who could say as much? The Howards? (The hereditary Dukes of Norfolk were viewed with more respect than 'those Germans' – but not much.)

Saxons? Danes? They had, thought Walter, atavistic memories or instincts of the time when the North Sea had not been. However wholeheartedly they played the rôle of bloody-minded islander, and a much-quoted phrase had been 'Abroad?

- I've *been* abroad!', they had a deep feeling for Flanders, had often got wives there. Good solid marriages too.

Hardheaded and astute they had welcomed the Norman invasion and even married Plantagenet princesses. 'Female line boy, female line' – but royalty down to John of Gaunt (the town of Gand or Ghent in Flanders . . .) 'Not a praiseworthy character nor one to be proud of' – always that habit of irony. They had known how to lie low, through the abominable Tudor time. They had escaped assassination. Surviving 'the Welsh, the Scotch' – they had fought of course against Charles I – 'the Dutch and the Germans' (a sequence of mounting contempt). A well-proportioned view of English history. Since Richard the Third we have lived among crooks and canaille.

"Local education was good enough for us" – Gresham's School, Holt and King's College Cambridge; the irony again.

He had been struck while still at the University by rheumatic fever, an illness then little understood. It had left him with a heart permanently damaged, and bearded doctors had shaken their heads. Five years at the outside, was their forecast. He had lived almost forty.

Why else should he have committed so deliberate an outrage as to run away with a married woman, a Catholic, a foreigner? The triple condemnation had barred him from his home. To this day, Walter has never set foot in Norfolk. It was never spoken of, but Walter guessed that the old man had had strong religious principles of an intensely Protestant and even Puritan sort, and that some 'never darken my doors again' scene had been played. And we came thus to a situation (absurd) in which an English Walter, or more English perhaps than any other nationality, had never lived in England. The first few years in Germany, and then in France; and then in Spain . . .

It was in France that he remembered his father. Teaching the boy of seven to hold cards – a way like another of palliating pain and ennui. Old-fashioned games, piquet and bézique and even that old Spanish game long forgotten in which the master card is the Knave of Hearts and is called Quinola. Or those Victorian poker-dice (large, of yellowed ivory): 'we hold both a full house but mine is king high, yours is knave high; mine is master'.

"Why d'you call the jacks knaves?" asked his children when

he in his turn . . . "And this talk about deuce and trey." Brought up that way. But an act of piety, also. Sentimental of him, no doubt.

An Englishness, but of a time long gone by, of before the 'empire': a loathing of brag and smugness, cant and humbug and jobbery (an eighteenth-century vocabulary), and witness his derisory compounding of the word 'self'. Importance, praise, seeking, indulgence and satisfaction.

His snobberies were rare, though scathing. 'One would be chary of people who sent their children to Eton or employed a nanny'.

A marked feature was an extreme scepticism. Even Nelson, the rector's son from Burnham Thorpe (a neighbour, and a friend), one could be none too sure of. Again that wry irony – 'I should not choose to criticise him on grounds of adultery'.

With the French – he liked them, but was 'désabusé'. He enjoyed their wit; liked to tell the story of the judge – English as it happened – who when asked by some tiresome person whether he were married answered 'No, dear Madam, but I keep a loose woman in Edinburgh'. But the French had no humour; were incapable of it. Humour to him must always be self-deprecating: witness the dilatory craftsman who when asked, furiously, whether there was a word in his vocabulary equivalent to the Spanish 'mañana' drawled out "There is but it doesn't convey quite so much urgency." He could understand, he said, and forgive French avarice and vanity, but a people unable to laugh at itself . . .

Small wonder that he should so love Dickens's comic figures. Flora Finching and Mrs. Wilfer, Trabb's boy and Mr. Chadband – and of himself he would say that like Mr. Wopsle's great-aunt he had not quite yet managed to break himself of this unfortunate habit of living. Farce he loved, the more violent the better, and Americans were forgiven much for the strident humour of Sinclair Lewis: Doctor Almus Pickerbaugh he declared a masterpiece. He never took much to the cinema, but would go anywhere to see the Marx Brothers.

Whereas Walter's mother was a great cinema-goer. She went to see *Sanders of the River* five times because she was in love with Paul Robeson, but she went nine times (counted) to *The Scarlet Pimpernel* because she was in love with Leslie Howard

. . . An unabashed sentimentalist. No humour? None, his father would probably have answered. A sense of fun, and the best company in the world, but takes herself too seriously to possess humour. An incurable romantic. If his father went to the Comédie Française for *Occupe-toi d'Amélie* Mama-dearest went for *Cyrano de Bergerac*, and her great experience in finishing-school had been to see Sarah Bernhardt play *L'Aiglon*, and for Napoleon she had devotion, flying in the face of her German father (shocked) and her Spanish mother (horrified). "She must be a changeling," he had said indulgently. Walter never really knew his German grandfather, an exquisitely civilised liberal who went into the gunroom one day in 1934, at his country estate on the borders of Württemburg and Bayern, and did not come out again. Walter thinks that he was a romantic too, and more like his daughter, who had no sense of reality at all, than he cared to believe.

If his father had no vitality left Mama-dearest had enough for four. Her love-affairs, quite certainly all platonic, were as famous as her horses, her bicycle-riding, her ridiculous clothes: her eccentricity was perfectly English in its enormities and extravagance.

Not a beauty. But the strong determined face, the flying boyish hair, the sparkling intelligence and dottiness, the wealth of personality made of her a lass unparalleled. Very well educated (trust a German gentleman) by the holy Ursuline nuns in München, finished in Lausanne and in Paris, she loved France (Walter has not been quite able to break himself of loving France) and adored Italy. 'Oh Italy . . .' – Robert Browning is her favourite poet. Her English is fluent, with comic inventions. 'I'm afraid that mittagessen is rather moche today' and her ejaculations, which are numerous, have their exclamation marks Spanishly upside-down.

His grandmother he can remember, during wartime years, in a threadbare splendour, full of humour from which ageing has taken all trace of acidity: her company can be relished like the fine wine it is. Silvery, with traces of beauty; upright on the sofa. It was the generation that had been brought up straight-backed, and she looks remarkably like her contemporary the dancer Karsavina, so disciplined that she is now free of the dirtier little human failings. Envy or vanity cannot touch her and neither rancour nor remorse enters the room where she sits in a shabby high-ċeilinged Madrid flat that is the only thing left her, for she has not a penny: her relatives have seen to that, for her socialist sympathies in the Civil War, which never interfered with her fervent Catholicism 'but the Church that does these things has forgotten Christ'. Her daughter is fiercely Franquist, but such is her respect for her mother that in the old lady's presence she masters her tongue. The only time, thought Walter, that Mama-dearest was known to be tactful.

It must have been in the winter of 'forty-three that she died, simply from pneumonia brought about, it was said, by her obstinate insistence on opening windows. And by the end of the war his mother too had become old.

Europe was full of these ageing, pinched ladies. Obscure flats in twenty cities – only Dresden had altogether gone – with cracks in the ceiling, no gas or water, but which had survived bombardments; and among their polished shabby sticks, with their old fur coats over the still-solid tweeds, their clear old-fashioned English charming Welsh sergeants and American second-lootenants ('Why is he called that, d'you think, as though he were in charge of the lavatories?') They never complained. 'Rage is gentlemanly: complaint is not'. Phrase of his father's, after the occasional but violent moments when he lost his temper.

His father had stayed behind. If she was going to Spain it was on account of her child, of her mother, of – oh, all sorts of things. Papa had been rather more laconic. 'That is called fleeing'. And he would have nothing to do with that. Rumour, unreliable, spoke of his death in the harsh winter that followed – or had it preceded the hot harsh summer of 1940? Of the long-promised heartfailure in a Paris hospital but there was no trace; the archives were missing or muddled. An unmarked grave in exile, and Walter preferred it to any pompous funeral vault in the Père Lachaise.

A flat, quite a big flat. "So it will be a sensible arrangement, dear, and sharing the expense it will come less heavy," with dear-Edith in Bruxelles. Of all places.

Aunt Edie died of cancer in 1950. Mama lived on in the flat – in perfect comfort, to tell the truth – for another ten years, and another ten beyond that in a home, kept youthful by perpetual warfare with holy nuns: 'a sainted woman but of deplorable middle-class origins' and 'Reverend Mother has had all the corridors painted beige, really she is an impossible female'. Faithfully he answered her letters once a fortnight, with 'all the news'. She died at last, very peaceful, able to laugh to the last breath at what the chaplain had said to the Children of Mary. 'Thank God, dear, I haven't gone gaga: most of the old dears here are quite senile.' Still charming the pants off the nurses. "Pick up my glasses, dear, I've dropped them. Oh you are kind, thank you so much, dear child. And next time you're in the garden – pinch a few flowers for me, now do." "Pass me my red shawl, child, and I almost think I could have a window open." And at eighty "Give me my tin box" – the tiny morsels of cash, to buy stamps or envelopes. Handled with such flourish. As though the tin box were the very House of Rothschild.

As he reached the roadway, Jesus reached the same point. One never saw him coming; he possessed magical means for transporting himself unseen over quite large distances. This remark might contain seeds of misunderstanding: it must be said that in Spain the name is quite often given to the children of (presumably) pious parents. Or there is a well-developed sense of irony at work; in this instance, certainly exemplified by this skill at sudden appearances. Predictably, he was detested by the village, feared for a bitter tongue and his own fear of nothing and no one, but esteemed. Perhaps the village had secret pride in a probable witch, certain possessor of an evil eye, useful scapegoat for untoward and undesirable happenings like thunderbolts or a fox in the chicken run; and a foreigner, containable since poor and wretched.

A tall old man with unhurried elegance of movement, some seventy years on his back – but he could appear young, small, or awkward with simple methods; a change of hat or a wash, a number of teeth varying from day to day. He did no work, practised no trade. He lived in a large house, whose great beauty came from fine proportions but much more from a state of leprous ruin composed with great skill of patchwork repair in every imaginable material, of every colour and texture. Part of it was a barn – as with Walter's house – whose beams had rotted so that the roof fell in and now followed a wavy curve of startling rhythmic loveliness.

Within this house Jesus was said to have a wife, or keep a woman. Nobody had ever seen her – perhaps she was chained up, in the cellar? Walter however had seen her. But kept quiet about that. One must respect the magnificence, and dignity, of Jesus.

"Tardes, Don Suelto," shaking hands in a French way, but speaking Spanish. The old man enjoyed the subtle play of etymologies. This word, from the root soltar, meant skilful, and in some contexts free, as in flying, -wheeling and suchlike. A compliment? – with Jesus one could never be sure. Perhaps his way of greeting a kindred spirit.

"It goes – and as you would wish?" enquired Walter politely.

"As God and the Republic may please. La Flamenca is in health?"

"As far as is known. She will be honoured by your enquiry." He knew better than to enquire in return: the reply would have been 'What wife?', so "What is the news?" he asked instead.

"Good. That is, very slightly good. For the Republic, even the slightest is better than nothing. It is said that anarchists have assassinated a commissaire of the policia in a flinging of bombs."

"It is frequent, indeed normal, for bombs to be flung: by me however it is regretted."

"You are a distinguished gentleman, Don Suelto. With moreover artistic talents. Of moreover wealth and position. The behaviour of commissaires of the Republic towards yourself shows variations from their mode of conduct should I have the misfortune to find myself in their presence."

"It is true. But have we the right to assume that the assassin-ated one was indeed of bad disposition, and thereby to rejoice? Or have you an evil memory carried from previous acquaint-ance?"

"It is true that I had not. I have been guilty of malice and injustice. May it be forgiven me. May God, pardoning my bad disposition, receive the soul of this functionary, if indeed such have souls. But it is good news for the republic, for may not other commissaires, of other bureaucracies, be struck by fear, resolving to amend the evil they do?"

"We may be permitted to doubt it. The theologians moreover tell us that good will not come out of evil."

"They have safe jobs, those theologians, and await doubtless a heavy dinner, cooked for them by many pious but foolish

35

virgins. And a prolonged siesta, in ecclesiastical armchairs. I place little reliance in their sayings." And Jesus set off up the road, there doubtless to forecast meteors.

Their acquaintance had long been distant and formal. Walter had always made a polite greeting, returned in kind. Coming one day back from the baker, loaded with bread, shoelaces and electric-light bulbs, he saluted Dirty Jesus (as the baker's wife called him) in the usual manner, the old man standing, as was his habit, in the morning sunlight upon the doorstep of his house doing nothing particular. And instead of the usual Spanish commonplace (in no language is one more portentous about the day's weather) Jesus said, "Will you help me?"

"Certainly," trying not to show shóck.

"Administrations – a multiplication of printed papers. It would not molest you overmuch to glance at these abominations?"

"With pleasure." For indeed Walter translated jargon with glee, relishing the absurdities of the lettered illiterate. Jesus might not be able to read or write but was better educated than town-hall twits, besides having better manners.

"You would not object perhaps to stepping a moment inside?"

"It honours me," said Walter.

The second shock was a physical assault. The smell, of many goats cohabiting with many foxes, was a hammerblow. In a bed at the back of the room sat a woman who had been beautiful. Great eyes burned in a wasted face: long hair half black half grey fell unkempt about it.

"I beg your forgiveness, Madame, for the intrusion."

Jesus paid no attention. The papers lay orderly on a table; on them a scratched old pair of hornrimmed glasses. Of course he can read; like most of us, what is readable.

Walter could not now recall what it was all about: nonsensical complications of the official mind, diseased by pettifoggery. He gave advice, hoping that it was sensible but concerned only to be courteous and praying only to convey that he felt touched, truthfully honoured, for once free of false sentiment.

Jesus simply nodded, holding out his old hand. Walter bowed towards the woman in the bed.

"Au revoir, Madame, et au plaisir." She looked at him. It was impossible to know how far reached her paralysis – to the mind? She might be deaf mute. But as he reached the door she called out after him in a clear high seagull's voice.

"Thank you, Monsieur. You are a true gentleman."

Once in a blue moon perhaps, he thought, hurrying up the hill with his tin of sardines.

He has slept: it is morning.

It is cold comfort telling himself that things could be a lot worse. They could be a lot better. The four Persian rugs from the living room, worn but beautiful, were gone. Limoges porcelain and Baccarat glass were shards. And Walter had let the insurance lapse years before. Those were worse gangsters than any burglar; asked a monstrous premium and then when something happened found pretexts in the small print for wriggling out of settlement: was one to pretend the shutters of the terrace door had been closed? Fake entry marks on the wood? Knuckle down to their insisting upon ultrasonics or such claptrap?

Some of the furniture was hacked and scarred. A pity, a great pity, but antique pieces very often were. If you've ever had soldiers billeted upon you. They're country pieces anyhow: is it a Weisweiler commode, a Riesener bureau, an Oeben dressing-table? (very French, these French names . . .) A bit of fine sand-paper and some beeswax: it will patine over: in a year's time one will hardly notice. I do agree that it's odious and hateful about your tea-set and I can only hope the next book will pick up a good contract in New York and that the dollar goes up high, however unpatriotic that may sound; the Motherland is where the grub is. The nosh, dear; la bouffe. No, there's no contradiction. Faced with material considerations I get material-istic, very.

The immediate worry is trivial (we hope), an irritation com-pounded by these misfortunes into a thorn in the flesh, a rooftile on the skull. Walter has to go to The Town, for a brush with the law.

A formal piece of paper has arrived from the Tribunal d'Instance (civil court) telling him he was being sued for non-payment of a bill (damned bourgeois shopkeepers, adding insolence to incompetence – he is flabbergasted and furious).

37

He is under no obligation to hire an advocate and may if he wishes assume his own defence. But if he fails to appear at the hearing he is warned that judgment may be given against him by default.

Splendid word that, flabbergasted. Concise Oxford says helpfully that it dates from 1772 but funks, as too frequently, the issue with the parrot-squawk of 'etymology dubious'.

Dropping Concise Oxford heavily – Osbert Sitwell apologised charmingly for his copy having lost its cover 'on account of having been thrown frequently at a vulture' – Walter races for his files.

These are a sacred institution, in which he keeps all the business papers of the year before. After the manner of files, on the rare occasions when he has to consult these the relevant paper is in the wrong file when not missing altogether, but this time Wotan is Mit Uns. Account rendered, bill queried, a correspondence at first stately, becoming curt: all there and irrefutable. Walter congratulates himself, with much smugness, on his businesslike methods. But that was all a month ago, and today's the day. His stomach is uneasy.

Walter is not a great traveller now. To New York or Paris or London, once a year he stumps off solemnly for business purposes; and these centres of world culture or commerce do not much excite him. He pretends to be much older than he is and moves in grooves, complaining at the loss of familiar landmarks – a façade altered, a head waiter retired – and perambulating along streets he has known from childhood will put on an act of not knowing the way. As though, remark cronies of his, it were his first leave in forty years from an outpost of colonial administration. Back home, he says these places have got very provincial.

He prefers smaller cities, unafflicted by Losangelitis and where there is still a historic centre; 'where one can walk': Amsterdam or Edinburgh. 'Now Toulouse is a nice town'. And he likes to go there a half-dozen times in the year, given a pivot to revolve around: the occasional play or film, a nice opera or concert. One combines this with seeing something of the children, one spends the night in the flat, has a couple of proper meals, shops languidly for a shirt. All this unashamedly provincial, what Walter calls 'being up for the Chelsea Flower Show'.

38

After being poor for many years (the earliest car had been a Citroën deux-chevaux, really more fun than any other) he had gone through a bourgeois phase of pretty cars. There had even been years of a family car plus a girls' car for Sylvie. A long series of Lancias had come to an end when a brand-new one got totalled on a straight but bumpy Spanish road and he discovered belatedly that the insurance was only third party. A lesson has been learned from this episode. He has now no envy of anything seen on the road. They've all become ugly. Motorised supermarket-trolleys one and all.

Since it is still quite early in the morning, for Walter is a great believer in the virtues of an early start, there is room to park, behind the Palace of Justice. Reserved, according to a large notice, for officialdom: magistrates and advocates, of whom there are a great deal too many. I plead, Walter tells himself, therefore I am an advocate. Specialists in the more brazen and impudent kinds of legal fiction will claim that I am taking the bread out of their mouth, though judging by their cars they're getting on all right upon a strict diet of cake. Going in through the back door he passes these counsellors' changing-, dignified as robing-room, a sombre place full of metal lockers. A large notice enjoined the users to make sure their door was locked. That the robing room should be full of rogues does not surprise him at all.

It is a strange fact that the animal most closely associated with the legal profession should be the stoat, known when in its white winter fur as ermine. The backs of these creatures (celebrated for their appetite for warm blood) make nice bands, prettily setting off the black stuff of legal gowns. Their dear little tails bunch, in gay tassels, upon the more exalted, until the grander judges, and Public Prosecutors, are fair dripping with the stuff. Even on average, wherever robes gather there will be an immense assembly of stoats. Entering the Palace of Justice you feel yourself like Mole in the Wild Wood, beginning to imagine evil grinning little faces behind every toadstool.

He is early, meaning (being Walter) a great deal too early; a compulsive worrier, he is always at the terminus three-quarters of an hour before the train. The court room is empty but for three Arabs asleep on a back bench and a clerk; robed, but entitled to no ermine: poor him. He has nothing to do, but kindly consents to look at Walter's summons and write his name on a piece of paper.

"Monsieur Forestier, that's right, you're on the list – don't sit there! First two rows are reserved for advocates." There is no point in asking 'Why?' One might be tempted to ask 'By whose authority?' None whatever as Walter knows perfectly, but he doesn't. Meekness, or laziness?

The name Forestier is not uncommon: straightforward in etymology. Forester; woodsman. Quite right, and no occasion to consult the dictionary. If one does – like Walter – an interesting word comes to light. Foris in plain Latin means outside. In the medieval dog-latin this has become foranus, from which the French 'forain' and the English 'foreigner': in plain terms an outsider. The original has varied little in the countries of the Mediterranean basin – forastero, forestiero. 'Forest' began as silva forestis, the wood outside. The Wild Wood, dark and sinister. Concealed treestumps, slimy and sharp-edged. Nasty place and full of stoats.

They are by now arriving in numbers; drifting in with an air of having nothing in particular to do. Most stroll about with the confidence born of getting paid, even for doing nothing, but it's known as putting in an appearance. A few prowl, much like an animal sniffing round the perimeter of its terrain: one or two might be said to slink.

There are the elderly, stumpy and round-shouldered, with robes that are none too clean and briefcases like themselves, from which they produce papers they look at in a dilatory, lacklustre manner, wondering what this is all about before drifting irresolute back outside. In the wrong courtroom but would it, did it make much odds? A few, their hands in trouser pockets (those baggy suits would be unpleasantly smelly at closer quarters) leaned against radiators and looked cynical.

Some are bluenosed, shuffling upon painful feet, and one seemed not quite all there, tacking round wainscots as though about to sidle up to Walter with a hoarse whisper – 'Not got a cigarette about you, by any chance?'

As well represented is the tribe of Señor Speedy, brisk and shiny of shoe and briefcase, examining their dossiers with concentration and an impressive variety of reading-aids. Walter is first stupefied, then stimulated by the numbers:

40

counting those who have popped-out-again there are certainly forty. Whereas of the public there are eight, counting both the sleeping Arabs and himself.

More than half the advocates are women, also with interesting variations, from sparse grey locks shorn off straight and a haggard look (as of some elderly lesbian who isn't getting any) to brilliant blonde coiffures, sculptured and shiny; and a turned-on look, all set to confound Perry Mason. Many are young and pretty. Besides briefcases they have large handbags; manage all this and their robes with stylish ease. They stand like men, legs apart, exchanging the limp handtouch of a French good morning, or they sit, elegantly sideways with a practised flip of the robe and showy crossed knees, lighting cigarettes in defiance of ordinance. The clerk is saying to two more Arabs that the back bench is the place for them.

Things are hotting up: the legal chat has swollen to cocktail-party level, and the clerk has suddenly his big moment.

"The Court. If you please." Swelling forte, orchestrated by sleeves. "Up!" glaring at the Arabs. It is a single judge (this is the simplest of the civil tribunals) attended by his clerk, a young woman with the colourless face and hair that can be anything and generally spells competence. They sit side by side behind a simple table on a low dais: it is quite informal.

Twenty lawyers have made a concerted rush and are clustered before him like bluebottles on high meat. There is a list of cases, but the day's work is now improvised in offhand French fashion: sotto voce but one can follow the train. You first then, since this other fellow hasn't turned up yet, and your affair sounds complicated so we'll look to that later; and what's your trouble then? Got to plead before Grande Instance at ten? – we'll fit you in.

Nobody pays attention to the public, nor the clerk (plainly just an usher). I was under the impression, thinks Walter crossly, that justice should be seen to be done; likewise heard. This has all the air of a family game, country-house charades. We were called for nine and we'll all be here at lunch-time. Getting rid of nine out of ten lawyers would expedite matters.

But he catches glimpses of the judge, likes what he sees: an unfussy, unpompous man smallish in his big armchair, sidelong and head cocked, a bright bird. But is justice a matter of getting the lawyers suited?

Abruptly, justice starts getting done: the judge (and the usher is disregarded) raising his voice to professional pitch to call a couple. It is a dog-poor, dog-sad, dog-patient couple. The woman has a child on her hip, having nobody to baby-sit. "Come and stand here," says the judge kindly – lawyers make grudgingly space. And Walter admires justice at close quarters, and well timed: it is expeditious but the inarticulate, incoherent mumble is patiently heard.

It's an obvious one: they're out of work, the rent's not paid, and the owner wants an order to get rid of them.

"Well; you want time, and I'm prepared to give you some." A paternal tone, but no bullying. A malevolent lawyer is held at arm's length. Is this typical? wonders Walter – as justice goes it could be a lot worse. They leave looking less hang-dog. "And don't get into debt," shouts the judge jovially at their bent backs. A big silly woman pushes through the door past them (the usher has gone for a smoke) and bawls out, "Where's One-oh-four?" (this is one-oh-three).

"Not written on the inside of the door," says the judge conversationally.

"Now – Misters Abdul, Said and Mohammed – would you be so good?" punctiliously careful not to sound patronising, though the three sleeping Arabs are plainly a comedy act: they get up at leisure, slouch amiable and boneless forward, stand at negligent ease, totally unconcerned. They are dressed sharp, in spotless white and many colours, loose on top, madly tight at the crutch and desperately macho. The judge makes faces at the papers, perplexed. "Can't make out what these gentlemen are doing here at all."

A pretty woman explains, hardly able to talk for laughing. Presumably it had been less comic at the time. They have been condemned by the Criminal Court, for getting on a bus with no ticket, disturbing public order and tranquillity, making an affray, rebellion, and blows-and-injuries upon the person of a bus-inspector. Hilarious; all the lawyers are in stitches. The judge listens, and perhaps the Arabs do too, with this in common: they cannot see anything funny about it. A long list is read out of the improbable ways in which the bus was broken up as though by the Three Stooges: the bus company (lacking humour) with a persistent sense of grievance now pursues them in the civil court with a view to damages.

"I can't do anything at all: I haven't the report from the other court." Clerk mumbles, lawyer mumbles. "That's all very well; they shouldn't have been summoned when the paperwork wasn't done." He cuts the argument short.

"Now gentlemen, you'll have to come back, on let's see, the twenty-fifth of next month, have you understood? – Twenty-Fifth?" Helpfully, his clerk writes 2 5 on a torn-off piece of paper. Not a nod, not a word: an unruffled slouch away-out-of-this but it's all one to them. Perhaps the boneless back view does needle the judge a little since he launches, "And see to it that you do!" after the retreating army.

"Very well – mm – Monsieur Forestier please." And Walter is on his feet, not quite sure of them.

The lawyers part, as before, barely enough to give him room. This proximity bothers him. He would like to ask the judge to tell them either to sit down or stand well back. A man's dignity consists more perhaps than one expected in the physical space left clear around him: the more so when his privacy is invaded, which in court it always is. A smell of women wearing perfume, of men given to using too sickly aftershave, and by a long way too much animal warmth.

A lawyer is speaking. He has a nasty face and a nasty voice.

"My client has a claim for eight hundred and twenty-five francs in bills for services rendered. These have remained unpaid despite repeated reminders and enjoinders. My client in consequence demands a further hundred and seventy-five francs in damage-and-interest and sees no reason why the court should not so order."

And that's all. Walter is a little unmanned at the nastiness, more by the brevity. He feels hemmed in.

"Well, Monsier Forestier?" The judge is lounging back and has his eyes shut.

"Uh . . . may I say a word in explanation?"

"It's what you're here for," sounding sleepily amused.

"This is ridiculous – no case exists. I am an honest man."

"A universal claim," now sounding bored. O God, I'm losing my marbles. But the tiny flick of sarcasm is enough to make the

43

horse trot. The judge is separated from him by no more than the width of a table. He must concentrate on that and forget lawyers. One must speak conversationally, lucidly. He has written it all down! But that was a speech . . . he's not placed for a speech.

"May it please the court." And the formal phrase pulls him together.

"I can demonstrate briefly, easily. I have here the correspondence – including the original of a letter from the counsellor's client admitting a mistake in the amount. Three hundred and something instead of eight. And the carbon of my reply, ironising slightly over the mistake and enclosing my cheque."

"Nothing proves to me," interjects the lawyer harshly, "the existence of any of this." An idiocy, and will put the horse into a gallop. Walter turns to face him.

"With respect, Maître, that is ridiculous. The letter exists and the cheque was cashed as the bank will confirm."

The judge intervenes, polite and soft-voiced.

"You have the papers there? May I see them? And what's this?"

Walter is confused. The draft of his 'speech' – so very pompous and rhetorical; triple-spaced . . .

"And may I keep them awhile? We'll have them photostatted. Greffier! – in the lavatory again . . ."

"I'll see to it, and send them back to you shall I?" offers the clerk in her soft voice.

"I must ask for an adjournment," grates the lawyer. "I know nothing of these pretensions. They must be examined and verified."

"Rubbish, Maître," nicely warm now. "These are facts and the pretensions yours. You come into court on a frivolous charge, and badly prepared into the bargain."

The judge is reading Walter's answer to a threat of 'sending the bailiff to collect this debt'.

" 'Please don't send the bailiff because I've met him and his breath is so terrible but do beg him to see a good dentist instead.' " The judge doesn't even chuckle but a ripple of sniggers from the legal profession tells Walter his cause is won.

"I ask a continuance," woodenly.

"Smokescreen," snaps Walter.

"He needs to consult his client," says the judge gently. "A misunderstanding exists."

"May it please you, Monsieur le Juge, it is wasting the court's time on a trivial pretext."

"We see lots, much more trivial; you'd be amazed."

"But –" he is suddenly less sure of himself," – I'm accused of dishonesty; I've lost a lot of time working on this, and coming here. My time is worth as much as the counsellor's, or his client who doesn't even trouble to appear. He employs an advocate: I don't because I see no need." Too much of a speech.

"Monsieur Forestier, you too can ask for damages, you know; when the time comes, and if you so see fit."

"I wasn't going to. I'm accustomed to dealing man to man, and honest explanations. These chicaneries! – I damn well will see fit."

"Then we'll let you know, shall we?" Walter has a sensation of anticlimax. Where had he gone wrong? What! – a gentleman gives a pettifogging little lawyer a kick up the arse, and the judge doesn't back him up! Fuming his way out to the car Walter has written a scenario reading 'Not good enough, Counsellor: upon the plain face of the matter your application for a continuance must be refused, nor can cause be shown for further deliberation. Judgment for the defendant with costs and damages commensurate with his loss of income' ... expeditive justice, what! Walter is actually sitting in the car with his hand outstretched to turn the ignition key when a thought strikes him, leaving him fixed in this idiotic attitude, leaning slightly forward (clutching the key under the dash) and his face (an open-mouthed expression of persistent imbecility) near touching the windscreen, so that he resembles some fish seen in an aquarium that hangs motionless up against the glass with only its large loose lips expressing what must be a strongly-felt distaste for this strange staring creature on the other side.

The thought is this: that if a judge were to base his decision 'upon the plain face of the matter', he would have given an order for possession to that landlord against an improvident couple that failed to pay their rent. 'You have entered upon a contract there and are liable in law to be held to the terms therein – pay up or pack up'. A similar order would have been given for damages to the bus company against the Arabs.

What? – an open-and-shut case in the criminal court and the civil side hesitates to assign plain responsibility . . . outrageous! At this moment, quite likely, somebody purple in the face is banging his table shouting. The magistrates in this damn country are biased in favour of niggers!

There is thus a certain humour in Walter's indignation, and he has to laugh: how often has he not fulminated against filthy little bourgeois! The petty meanness, the naked self-interest with which they defend their hideous little privileges, fighting to the last drop of their caterpillar blood for the advantage acquired . . . And to find himself in those shoes . . .

He had thought of this episode as a tiresome and irrelevant interlude in the business on which he was engaged. And all the while it had been central to his decision. He has his answer! Through a direct experience.

Dura lex sed lex: the law is harsh but there's no getting away from it. One of the natural laws governing this planet is that law as man-made has nothing to do with justice.

And still less to do with honour. Honour is between me and myself (Walter is manoeuvring the donkey through city traffic, not always scrupulous about orange lights. 'Beating the red' is probably the most popular of French participation-sports). Other people cannot injure my honour but only my self-love, and my vanity – dura veritas sed veritas.

The fighting of duels was not intelligent. A humiliation, generally imaginary, caused by a scratch upon self-esteem was laved by a show – generally imaginary – of courage. Litigation one leaves to the bourgeois: justice one does oneself.

One does not, in any case, bandy either blows or personalities with shopkeepers and attorneys. One has them clonked by the servants and tipped in the gutter. In more modern – enlightened – days a more subtle vengeance can be taken, devised by Jeeves; something involving a massive shot of cascara-sagrada in the breakfast coffee. (Hitting the stretch of autoroute that will take him nearly half his way he sits back comfortable, floors the accelerator. The donkey is a horse, gallops, whips past these long plodding mule-trains.) Horsewhipping is a pleasant thought. Accords ill alas with pacifist principles – Walter tucks himself into the slow lane between two massive mule-trains, to allow a greater vulgar bourgeois attelage to rattle past at a fast clip.

Anyhow – where are the servants?

He is well accustomed to being put in a false position no matter what he does, as a consequence of being born in one. However, one can still find new aspects daily of this world that manages to be both turd and diamond. As he drives along these winding roads into the hills that he knows by heart, he is smiling to himself. He has remembered Uncle Pumblechook, upon whose turpitudes Dickens takes a characteristic revenge: for delinquents break into his house and – Walter is paraphrasing from memory – they ate his vittles and they drank his wine, and they tied him up, and they slapped his face, and (the touch that belongs to no other writer in the world) 'they stuffed his mouth with flowering annuals to perwent his crying out'.

He has made his decision; to say nothing of his adventure to anyone, least of all to the gendarmerie.

Chapter 3

Walter, at work and supposedly inviolable, became dimly aware of a noise still at a distance but coming steadily closer. Man and woman are placed at opposite poles of this problem: the male when concentrating upon a professional activity will often not hear the instrusive sound at all. It registers physiologically, but from there on the circuit is interrupted whereas a woman remains alert at all times to the signal from the outside world, an ability that can also be termed professional.

Sylvie, trained as a writer's wife, answers bells. Walter is impelled to look, for the time of day tells him that Sylvie is under the shower. And a glance from the side window tells him that the worst has happened. Indeed a mirror-cracked-from-side-to-side, because a dark-blue wagon of a kind familiar to him is parked, rather aggressively, bang in front of the door. 'The Doorbell Rang' is anyhow a phrase that evokes the F.B.I.

Ordinarily, Walter is upon civil if distant terms with the local law: in the context of recent happenings his feelings combine guilt, fear, and anxiety. Furthermore he has been wrong-footed. Keeping them waiting will have given them an impression, totally justified but for the wrong reason, that he is anxious to avoid them. Damn. There is no point in damning Sylvie, whose leisurely washing habits have been familiar to him for nearly thirty years. At any other time the damn would be a harmless reflex, similar to that when the soap slips out of one's hand when under the shower. Now it comes up from a lowish circle of the inferno because it is himself who is damned.

He wrenches the window open in a hurry, struggling with the catch, perfectly familiar but which he always manages to fumble: the moment is ill-chosen.

"Sorry, was busy first time and didn't hear. Be right down." Stop talking so much.

"Sorry, I thought my wife would answer but she doesn't seem to be around: were you waiting long?" This awful excusing of oneself, these unnecessary explanations and justifications. "Good morning, what can I do for you?" Over-polite. In itself that wouldn't matter for he always is and they probably know it, but now it's another suspicious circumstance to add to what they have already.

Two pairs of placid peaceful eyes are looking at him; two hands sketch embryonic salutes.

"Ah, Monsieur Forestier, bon jour, sorry to disturb you but like to have a word if it weren't too inconvenient." This too is over-polite and surely a bad sign.

"Come in, come in." An over-sugary bonhomie is characteristic of Walter's hospitality at all times: his unease is permanent. The gendarmerie's elaborate manners, taking their képis off and making a big thing of wiping their boots on the doormat, are simply professional – 'Give the public no cause for complaint' is in the handbook. They don't expect to be let in further than the kitchen. By bringing them to the living room, ushering lavishly, sitting them in handsome, slightly uncomfortable chairs, do you gain a slight psychological edge? Belatedly Walter remembers the scars. But Sylvie, working hard and unremittingly, has effaced damage to the point where you'd really hardly know.

"Now what can I offer you? – no no no," at the protesting outheld palms. Everybody in the countryside of France expects to be offered the classic *petit verre*: at the least this piece of bullshit will grease wheels. And gain time. And cool the fevered mind.

48

Why for example has the gendarmerie literary associations to anyone who has spent childhood years in pre-war England? It is the smart blue and black uniform with white facings. There used to be an advertisement, an enamelled plaque on the platforms of English railway stations, representing a big splendid ink-blot, and the simple legend 'Stephens Ink'. It would be a waste of energy exposing Walter to ink blot tests, assuming anybody still does: the answer would be railway stations. He is knocking about with glasses, fumbling around with bottles, arsing with the ashtray (so, at least, he expresses himself).

"The smallest drop." Gendarme, acting shrinking violet. And what would one call his own act then?

The elder has Sergeant's stripes, is glossily overshaved about a jaw that begins to menace jowl; has a smart black leather briefcase matching his gaiters, from which he has extracted documents. These are now arranged on the circular table, fanwise like a poker hand. The formal and meticulous papers of French legalism. Together with the feeling that there has been a lot of law about recently there is a sinking feeling on Walter's side that he holds no cards. In that little civil matter it was he who had all the impeccable paperwork. Is the nicely polished boot now upon the other foot? The younger gendarme sits and admires his boots. Both have the military haircuts that look faintly obscene (a sort of circumcised look?) when the cap is taken off.

"I am all ears," says Walter, drawing up a chair, crossing his legs, frigging about (he is the type of character to whom 'Be Prepared' means having in his pocket at any one time three or even four cigarette lighters). He is rather dirty too, and decidedly unshaved.

"Cheers," says the Stephens-Ink man "– um, good. Now we've got an enquiry afoot, rather complex. Just at present we're filling in gaps where we can. Possible that a point where we've a pencil line and a query mark you might be able to ink it in for us like, don't you know?" Even if the syntax is slightly astray the eyes aren't.

"From complaints received and informations laid . . ." A legal instrument in many copies. Signature and rubber stamp of a Procureur de la République. Ditto with ditto, a Judge of Instruction. Wheels that can take six months before turning (that traffic offence one had blissfully forgotten) had been whizzing speedily. This is not a piddling civil action, whine of complaint in the Tribunal d'Instance. This is, and Walter's lingering doubts have been dispelled, the Criminal Law, and not just the flags either (it is police court jargon for flagrante delicto) but conceivably the Assizes ... The Proc, looking at available evidence, decided on the blast. Misdemeanour, felony, or crime – something like the Richter scale for earthquakes.

Tar Baby, he don't say nothing.

"Traces of a gang. By a gang I mean three or four, we rather think only three, been about the district. Or simply through: of this we aren't quite sure as yet. Ripping off country houses. For the most part unoccupied. There may be exceptions to that." He is cooking Walter leisurely, turning him with a fork. "You've noticed nothing yourself on these lines, Monsieur Forestier? Like it might be breakage, an attempt at forcing a lock like?"

How much do they know?

"Mm. There's said to be a lot of that, isn't there? ... We're pretty peaceable up here I'd have thought ..." The Sergeant is very slightly overweight; nothing to speak of. Scratching the tip of his ear.

"We've some indication ... now it's quite a pretty little property you have here." Plainly, they knew. The bugger had laid his line gently – being tactful. But he was on a hook. And mightn't be clever to overdo the fencing act. They might turn nasty. If they have anything concrete. If. Walter is not much of a card player and is sensible about not playing for money. He makes a snap decision, towards frankness.

"Well. That's very smart work. If I didn't come down to see you, it was because this was really very trivial. Of course now that you take the trouble to come up here, to mention it ..." The Sergeant has a piece of paper ready, and a ballpoint to take him down: he has put this between his lips in an expression of utter disbelief.

"They paid a visit. Probably in a hurry, on the off chance, you know, of skimming off something portable and easy. But of course as you see – you've only to look around you – I've nothing much. You talk about a nice property but I'm not in the least rich ..." He is aware of floundering, as well as of not getting believed. Takes a sip of his drink. Bad, and shows up, but can't help himself. "Well, I've nothing to conceal. I'm afraid I'm a casual and often even careless person and I must have left a shutter unlatched. To some extent my own fault, you see: but uh, the kind of things I value, books and stuff I mean, have small appeal for these gentlemen."

"Perhaps you'd like to tell me what was taken, exactly."

"Some things which had sentimental value – a little clock. No great intrinsic worth. A pair of candlesticks that looked silver but were only plate. Gold coins or whatnot I simply don't have."

The Sergeant with hideous patience waited for the end of each long stumbling tale.

"Caused some damage, did they?"

"There was some vandalism," as though he had only just noticed it, "and the police you know tend to be not greatly interested in such things – tendency to say well you can't expect us to protect you when you haven't taken proper precautions."

"And you reported all this to the insurance company?"

"To be honest I don't have any: the premiums are too high." The impression of grovelling poverty thus created does not go down all that well.

"You understand, Monsieur Forestier, that one has a duty to report these things as a protection to other householders. If we don't have the data we're that much more handicapped."

"I do see this of course and I apologise; it was lazy of me."

"And you were away during all this?"

"Luckily, you see, my wife doesn't have a great deal of jewellery and most of that she was wearing." A skilful use of half-truth on which he is congratulating himself.

"You've no objection to telling me where you were?" The congrats seemed premature. The door opened and Sylvie came in. Sailed is not quite the word. She is majestic and she looks well, in a frock demoted by age and drycleaning to household occasions that suits her still admirable figure. Listening-at-the-door she has not been: no need. The gendarme's rumbly voice carries less than his own, of which she complains when unguarded remarks are made in public: 'That awful upper clas yap' . . . Sailing in is after all the word: hasn't she the sense to stay away?

"I hate to interrupt," indulgent and ironic, "but I really feel – please do sit down – obliged to set things straight. Out of belief

51

in his principles, and I know you'll respect that, my husband is misleading you slightly. The matter to him has no great importance but it has to me: this is my house." The gendarmerie is loving this! As for Walter, he has the red planet Mars where his eyeballs ought to be. He seizes the bottle to gain countenance: it trembles on the lip of the glass. There is no means of stopping her, short of a bullet.

"They broke in here, these swine, and swine is what I mean, let's have no mistake about that, I can talk frankly, at least. My husband is an artist and doesn't want to be the sort of hypocrite that has liberal opinions about the misfortunes of others and rages for vengeance when they are his own. So he won't tell you what happened because he's standing up for his convictions. Whereas I have ideas equally consistent which I'm not ashamed of.

"He was half asleep and he'd left a door open in case I forgot my keys as I often do, so that they could sneak in and jump him. He had no chance of defending himself."

"In defence of the home. Yes, I'd have thought of nothing; I'd just have fought. With a chance to use a gun I'd have used it (they never found the gun! But it isn't in any of the obvious places like under the mattress. Come to think I'm not even sure myself where it is . . .)."

Unable to bear it another second he ran away under pretext of the bottle being empty.

"My dog!" Sylvie is saying in a furious voice, and what point would it have, pray, to say that it wasn't her dog at all but his. He takes the new bottle and with courteous care refills the glasses, quite aware that he'll shortly be drunk. The Sergeant, busy taking notes, doesn't even notice. As for the young one, he's delighted! This is splendid stuff all round. "People who'll kill a dog like that in cold blood wouldn't hesitate to kill a person." Oh yes, the examining magistrate will be interested and the prosecutor much pleased.

The gendarmerie are professionals. They know a good deal of the grimy crannies in peoples' private lives. They do not have the time or the inclination for emotional considerations. They do not allow themselves pity, or sympathy – or contempt. It wouldn't do. Walter (it must be his own parallels with Uncle Pumblechook that lead his mind again to the book) recalls the lawyer, Mr. Jaggers, saying 'Now you get out – I'll have no feelings in this office!' So he sits quiet and composed, and showing no damned feelings. Much as one would long to give Sylvie a resounding black eye.

"Our only interest is to uphold the law," says the Sergeant, snapping the locks on his briefcase.

One's choice is to 'be a man and knock her silly'. Or to be a man and do nothing whatsoever. Or is one Pumblechook? – as monstrously bold in word as he is craven in action.

My wife for nigh on thirty years.

He has remembered a poem. Learned as a child in Germany. A German child! Nineteen thirty-four? – his German grandfather still alive . . . A seventeenth-century German poem.

'Annchen von Tharau ist, die mir gefällt,
Sie ist mein Leben, mein Gut und mein Geld . . .'

The gendarmerie has risen, and is settling its tunic.

"Right. That is all now clear. And if we should want a witness in court, Madame . . . ?"

"You won't find me lacking," says Sylvie, determined.

No reproaches are made.

"Au revoir then M'sieur-dame, and a good day to you both."

"I accompany you to the door," says Walter in his politest tone.

What is there to say? How formal can you be towards the woman who shares all you are and everything you have? He goes back to the chair and sits. Looks at her in silence. Goes through the rigmarole of taking a cigarette from a crumpled packet, straightening it out – it is rather a bent weak object – putting it in his mouth and taking it out to spit a fragment, moistening his lip, lighting the damned thing. Ray Chandler describes it well. 'All set?' asks Marlowe. 'Pulse and respiration normal? You wouldn't like a wet towel round your head?

Sylvie has got up without a word, lifts the ashtray he has been using and blows away a little dust, from the polished table.

As a child he was always word-perfect in poems while the others were still stumbling over the first couplet. It was arithmetic that left him foolish and helpless.

*

"Parlour, you!"

In jails and prisons the 'parlour', that fusty word redolent of

53

net curtains, unneeded tablecloths, unopened windows, has reverted to its original meaning: parloir, the place where one talks. A functional little room.

Only two kinds of people are interested in talking to jail inmates. One is the police, for detective work goes on, even after arrests. The other is the defence advocate, for the law states that the prisoner, before trial, must be given unimpeded access to his legal representative. The average 'inmate' is pretty indifferent on the whole. The police, behind an easygoing and generally friendly manner, is intent upon tipping you further still into the shit. The lawyer's attitude is of professional competence and helpfulness, but it's mostly of a fairly perfunctory nature. He 'sympathises', and it's the superficial sympathy you have with people who are part of your daily work and necessary to it. All the 'inmate' is really interested in is a break in the monotony. The classic illustration is the prisoner who informed that he was being taken to torture remarked 'Good, it'll make the time pass quicker'.

The guard might have said "A nice parlour you've got there; she's a looker, too." But the guards find Fernand a sullen young man. Far from giving him encouragement they find that his arse needs kicking.

A tallish young man, built long and light but with the web of muscle that shows country forebears. The physique is neither squat nor rawbone, but it looks and is durable. The facial bones are sharp, prominent. People who have been in prison any length of time put on weight or lose it; acquire the look of either passive resignation or an aggressive acridity. But Fernand has only been in jail a few weeks; just long enough to come to terms with his new situation, no longer kicking himself for being fool enough to get caught. He looks the way still he did outside; watchful, competent. Boredom is gaining ground, but his reaction-time has not been slowed.

He has good white teeth: a rarity at any time in any company, in France. The straight hair of the northerner. Sharp spitzy nose; a lot of jaw: he isn't 'good-looking', but the girls haven't complained. He is slouching as he walks, but that is only from idleness. He puts his legs astride and lifts his arms for the regulation body search. One has the right to privacy, with one's lawyer.

A surprise: it isn't the usual lawyer.

You have the right to the lawyer of your choice. You can demand a famous advocate, a 'tenor'. Naturally all the ground work, the basic preliminaries will have been done by one of the young 'pro deo' lawyers who round out their income devilling for the famous – so that the end result is largely the same. All the big names have contact-men in the provincial tribunals. And the younger, rising stars in the firmament, who happen to have a case afoot in one of these, are alert to anything in preparation that might sound of interest. Fernand, who has been affecting lack of interest in legal proceedings has only met his counsellor once and that was an introductory formality. Po-faced young man he'd thought him. Who the hell was this? At least – less po-faced. Youngish, and a woman. Well, Fernand has nothing against women. This is one you'd quite like to be up against, close up against, come to that. Long dark hair. Definitely a looker. The voice is a bit chilly, though.

His first impression isn't far out. Miriam Lebreton is regarded in the Paris bar as a speedy one, a comer, with a turn for sharp and original pleading in criminal cases. She doesn't get you off with spectacular rhetoric: this sort of acquittal against the odds is a myth. But she is both imaginative and tenacious, and is building a record for getting penal sentences that could have been a great deal heavier. She rather likes them nasty, rapists as well as rape victims. She doesn't belong to any of the big combines: a freelancer. Within her profession she is both liked and disliked, but with more intensity of feeling than is altogether usual.

She happened to be pleading down here. Saw somebody's case notes. Took an interest. To the local lawyer it's nothing one way or the other whether she takes it or leaves it. The fee gets split anyhow.

"Maître Lebreton." She gives herself her title only because she's in civvies and not in her robe: it saves explaining. "I thought we'd have a talk. I'm from Paris. Your counsel is willing to pass it on to me if it works out that way. You can keep him if you prefer. It's up to you." Fernand shrugs his shoulders. "Put some snap into it, man," says Miriam tartly, and his eyes open a little wider.

It's a challenge: no more. Nothing personal. Certainly

nothing sexual; he's a man, she's a woman; so what? Tja, there is that much more tension, edge would one call it, in a relation with the other sex, even the lawyer-client thing. But really it's just that life, that threatened to become highly boring for a stretch of time as yet undetermined, is of a sudden less boring. And that's of value to a chap in jug, no?

"So you invest a little time," says Lebreton taking a cigarette case from her handbag and offering it him, "and me a little time, and both of us a little effort if you so please, and if you don't please we've both lost five minutes, and there's an end to it: which is it to be?"

"D'accord."

"Agreed? Right. No hang-ups, about a woman pleading for you, that's jessie?"

"Don't see much about you that's jessie," says Fernand with the first sign of animation.

"Good." And she breaks out into a smile that is vivid and illuminates the dingy little parlour. "Let's go!" From her brief-case, a shorthand block, a silver pen, a lighter for two cigarettes. A bag of toffees. All prisoners like sweets; she always has some 'for her prisoners'. "Here, the guard will let you keep these, if you aren't on his shitlist. If you are, try to get off it. Get the morale up. I don't want to plead for any down-in-the-face hang-dogs. This is lesson number one. To get a current of electricity flowing. When we come into court, it's not going to be like a freshly killed rabbit hung up there skinned and limp. The judges take one look at that, and they're not interested. And that means round the siphon, into the drains. I don't take that. Innocent, guilty, none of that interests me much. That this is a human being, that human beings are important, they don't just eat and sleep and let wind. They think and they feel. They're valuable," putting emphasis in that. "No use my saying it, the judge has to see it, right from the start. I'll put ginger in you mate, you put ginger in me. We aren't lawyer and client, we're two live people. Any judge sees you as that much more cabbage he has to tunnel through, he's got another think coming. Right?" O yes; the percolator is perking. Fernand is sitting up already.

"Okay, here's lesson number two, this is the Assize Court. It's a very old rule in criminal pleading, better the deed, better the day. You're some penny slot-machine bandit, you're a yawn.

Commit a crime at all, make it a big one: if it's not big make it interesting, get a flow of adrenaline in the procedure. Three judges there and a row of jurymen or women, no odds, if they're bored out of their pants it's a lost cause; I don't mind them hostile, I don't want them indifferent.

"So I don't know exactly what they're charging you with yet. It's just this jewellery shop bust – that was a goddam stupid caper – that will not be very good news because it's a technical offence that leaves little margin for interpretation, and the nice thing about the Assize Court is that there should be and frequently is a good wide margin. You could be shopped for three, five, eight, but we've a chance for eighteen months, meaning less than a year unless you're the wild man. Do that standing on your head, you're half way before you're even tried.

"But if they tie you in, and this is a deal I can try and make with the prosecutor, on these private house busts, it's bigger, or looks so, but we've better material, more margin. Nocturnal breaking and escalading, assaults against the person, now we're getting something that makes them sit up and pay heed. That could be them. Who cares about some piddling jeweller? We'll see. Much of this depends on the kind of witnesses they bring against you. If it's just police and technical witnesses, it's thin stuff to work with. We can shake them on nothing but trivial grounds, little discrepancies, a ten-minute error, a frig-up in their procedure – feeble. But if they bring aggrieved householders into court, to snivel how you pulled their diamond necklace off, then they're being emotional and we'll make them regret that.

"Lesson three and that'll do for today. I take it, because it would be standard, they've blocked what money you may have, as from a suspect source, failing proof to the contrary you'd find pretty difficult to establish? Yes? It's catch twenty-two. And you've no family? No friends? Nobody to stake you to canteen and a few comforts? No? I thought as much. Well, mate. What's your name? Fernand? No need to look ashamed of it. Maître isn't any soup kitchen, nor is she a soft cushion to put your bum where it's hard. But we'll see if we can't find a bit of money for you somewhere to view as a loan against future winnings, we'll call them. I can't loan you money, it's illegal. Need a third person to act as go-between."

* * *

She's in too much of a hurry, thinks, but does not say Maître Bastien Piontek. For if he were to say it to her, the reply would come back tart and quick; you're not there to slow me down, you know. She hasn't quite learned the difference yet between being fast and being hasty. What will it take? An accident?

He is her partner, the 'collaborator' who with a couple of girls runs the office, and when Lebreton is on the move, which in his opinion she too often is, it is 'dear Bas' – the final s is pronounced – who interviews relations, verifies unlikely tales, and is generally seen in the 'parlours' of Fresnes or La Santé or Fleury-Mérogis; the big prisons, so oddly like big teaching hospitals, of the Paris area. He is very 'Parisien' besides being nearly sixty and as he calls it 'lazy', and it's as much as anyone can do to drag him as far as, let's say, Soissons or Melun. Pleading in Amiens or Nancy, known sarcastically as putting the show on the road, isn't at all to his taste: in fact he doesn't like pleading at all and does so, in a dry level voice, only upon necessity. Before striking up this partnership, which is fairly recent, he had had a solid but quite undistinguished career. Asked whether it suits him, to work with a woman half his age, he says he likes the money; likes his elegant car (English, with lots of leather and a well-mannered automatic gearbox) that will bring him to the Palace of Justice in silence and in comfort: says he couldn't afford that otherwise. Thanks very much, the red Ferrari or whatever-it-is, ridiculous thing that Miriam rushes about in, isn't for him.

'The rich arrive in style
And also in Rolls-Royces' as far as can be possible, in view of Paris traffic in and around the Ile de la Cité,
'They talk of their affairs
In loud and strident voices.'
"And that is a Cautionary Tale," says this easy-paced anglophile. He refers to himself as the Flywheel. "I stop her burning her bearings out, or whatever the technical term is." The Mechanic would be more accurate, if Lebreton is the Driver, for it is largely Uncle Bas' doing if she arrives well briefed in the courtroom.

She's a natural comet; she goes fast. Her ambition is to arrive in the exclusive club, the Formula One drivers: in fact she's on the fringe of that already. Comets arrive in a blaze –

"forgive this metaphorical way of speaking, dear boy" – and perhaps too, I'm no astronomer, they collide with other meteors and go whirling off in bits with sparks and a lot of dust into a black hole or whatever.

And Bas, if you aren't the man in Miriam's life, we presume there is one, and who?

"Perish the thought and it isn't to me, my dear, that the question should be put. She's the kind of woman who is perfectly capable of burying three husbands." Doubtless a man would be a steadying influence, thinks Maître Piontek, but that has nothing to do with me. Her work is her motor right now, and probably always will be. It would indeed take a remarkable man to be the preponderating influence in Lebreton's existence. I know nothing about it, but should imagine that hitherto men have been and are a convenience, an amusement, a distraction or relaxation; but nothing that touches her closely.

"I've picked up what may be an interesting little number in Toulouse," she says, coming into the office, hanging up her hat (she has taken recently to dotty hats, manages somehow to get into that absurd car without knocking them off).

"Oh dear."

"No, it has features."

"Horrid ones, no doubt."

"Rather an odd boy – is there a cup of coffee, Jeanne, in the little macchina? – the usual type on the surface, sour and sullen, butt here's something about him even if I'm not quite sure what.'

"Threw a hook into your tender heart, did he?"

"I have no heart as you know, but what I do have is a knack for getting alongside interesting people and I think this will prove no exception. A boy who would become, I think, an interesting man. P'raps I'm just being maternal, poor me. May I just indulge a moment Jeanne, standing on the hearthrug warming my behind, while you read me what's in my diary?"

"A judge of instruction at ten a.m., and will you please be on time because it's Alain Verneuil."

"Oh help, and is it that rather tiresome woman who goes to bed with her brother? – ask Bas to go instead."

"Not on your nelly," said Maître Piontek. "You get into these things, you get out again. My day is anyhow much worse; somebody wants me to go to Versailles – where is Versailles?"

It isn't an affectation; he has no very good sense of topography further out than the Bois de Boulogne, 'and they're forever changing the roads round'. "Is it that horrid tunnel underneath Saint Cloud?"

* * *

Walter's working table which is large, rectangular, austere, is spread with the encrusted, haphazard accumulations of filth in which a writer lives and is happy. Not for the writer the beautifully composed and structured nest, exquisite, draught-free, luxuriously lined with moss. Consider rather storks, who choose uncomfortable windy platforms, throw a few nasty sticks about and consolidate with an accretion of the most disgusting débris which one would not care at all to examine at closer quarters. Out of this comes an image of domestic bliss and cosy maternity; disconcerting.

Walter pushes pettishly at the new and horrid typewriter, scrabbles for a notebook, chooses a writing instrument from a jam-jar full.

'The metaphysician, probably German or Scandinavian, conceivably Spanish and certainly Indian, positions himself within his space with careful attention for earth currents, cosmic forces, the harmony of the universe. He seeks freedom from gadgetry, the inessential – doesn't even think about a table. Whereas the technician worries about a good light, measures angles and distances, constructs an elaborate and rigid pattern, binds and entwines himself in matter. Could they ever choose the same spot?'

There's that doorbell again and Sylvie has gone shopping. Walter plods to the observation post (tripping over an electric cable, damning all umbilical cords, mentally sodomising poor Fairy Electricity). Outside is the little yellow van of the Post Office. What does he want?

"Registered letter for you, Monsieur Forestier – bonjour – need your signature."

Contents invariably disagreeable, to be signed for since otherwise the French will swear blind they never saw it. Perplexed frown since there are two and both say 'Palais de Justice'. Much turning of them around (what is on the back? – nothing). Letter-bombs.

Open it and see, Sylvie would say with ostentatious patience if not open sarcasm. True, Walter has a strange reluctance to open letters, even the most innocuous, 'until I'm in a proper state of mind' – this has been known to take up to a month.

This however is officialdom, meaning boredom, tedium, but better confronted – where's our Dunkirk spirit then? It will be that tiresome lawsuit again, wanting him for another day of confusions and delays in the courtroom of the Tribunal d'Instance. But why is it so thick?

Sheets of mannered phrasing, neatly paragraphed. A heading in letters of fire: Au Nom du Peuple Français. By God – a judgment! Whip to the last sentence.

'By these motives the plaintiff's claim is refused and judgment is given to the defendant, the costs of the court and all legal expenses to be borne by the plaintiff' – Walter can't quite recall which is who, makes an effort, has a mortal fear of some legal gloop that has turned things back to front, gets back to the first page carefully defining Thingummy, here represented by Maître Fraudulent-Bullshit, and the Sieur Forestier Gauthier appearing in his own quality – it's a victory per Baccho and for him.

Champagne! Exuberant, the Sieur Gauthier finds this but definitely the right moment for a reconcilly. Sylvie has appeared, hideous, sullen and fatfaced in a raincoat, downtrodden and weighted with shopping baskets.

"Sylvie!" bawls Walter: she looks up startled and absent, a mind fixated drearily upon pork chops. He has suddenly nothing to say. (Dai-and-Shoni went up in a balloon and took two women with them.) There is very little that needs saying (and the balloon started to leak) but he finds no words (so Dai said Jump, quick).

"Sylvie, get some champagne." (And Shoni said What about the women, and Dai said oh, Foock the women, and Shoni said Yes, but have we time?) "And get undressed."

Sylvie has got rid of those frightful pork chops by slamming the refrigerator door on them and says sensibly enough, "Yes, but I need a lot of champagne first." (Yes, but have we Time?)

"Yes, well, au nom du peuple français, hurry up then." Ah, and what then is this other letter from the palaces of justice where time's chariot is sorely devoid of wings – open it then, cretin. No time.

61

"Good," says Sylvie reading, halfway through her second glass, "that'll be a weight off your mind."

"Yes, and a weight on your something-else in about four seconds from now."

"Gently then, and what about the pork chops?" But accepting, and gratefully, an unblockage, and consenting to put in an appearance.

"– but give me time to do something with my hair." And Walter is reminded of the eminent Victorian doctor called to examine an anaemic child and who said, 'Throw physic to the dogs: what the boy needs is a pint of champagne and a mutton chop.' (This last hardly a comparison likely to please Sylvie, so he keeps quiet about it.)

"I can't think what this other missive might be."

"Why not open it and find out?"

"Yes, but do I dare?"

Monsieur Forestier, Gauthier, was with urgency prayed to present himself at the cabinet of the Judge of Instruction. A matter of nocturnal housebreaking and armed robbery, alleged to have occurred.

Not at all good news. Now why has he had the naiveté to suppose one would never hear any more about that? Failure to respond to the present summons is punishable under paragraph Threefigure of the Code of Criminal Procedure.

It would be proper, perhaps praiseworthy, to say Foock the Judge of Instruction. A certain Madame Claudine Rivière, and she might even be young, be pretty. But have we the time?

Very likely it was some snuffy old bag fifteen kilos overweight, in a skirt some months overdue at the cleaners . . .

Thus far the Sieur Forestier, in deep depression upon a bench polished, but only by serge-clad behinds. In a wide corridor, dimly lit and uncongenial, that faced a long row of offices belonging to Judges of Instruction (the word cabinet, generally taken to mean lavatory, in its legal context means a private office).

This animal of a judge was keeping him waiting. The company was not such as to give much stimulus: the usual lady whose nose needed blowing; the usual despondent détenu handcuffed to a black and silver gendarme; the usual businessman, venomous and carefully rehearsed. And how did he look, to these others? He has the feel of greasy steel upon his wrists, and certainly exhales an impression of deserving no better.

At last a clerk popped her head out. A small conniving smile. Walter has a quickly flitting vision of an office unexpectedly gay and decorative.

"I say!" gushing without meaning to, "I like your flowers! Sorry – good morning, Madame le Juge." A small amused turn to the corners of her mouth. And pretty! It is not any invitation towards rape.

"Sit down then, Monsieur."

The clerk, at a side table, is not without merit either: flower-bright with shell-pink horn rims; fair hair in ringlets. Grinning more broadly than her boss.

"We do try, don't we, Geneviève? The flowers help us, from becoming too desiccated? Mm, I'll come straight to the point, Mr. Forestier. I have a report here from your local brigade of gendarmerie, stating that when questioned on this matter you showed yourself a reluctant and evasive witness. What do you have to say about that?"

"True, I suppose."

"That is candid. You understand then that I am not a hostile counsel." Mimicking " 'Oho, so you admit that.' I ask you to explain your attitude."

"I don't have one; I'm simply unwilling to testify."

"I show no surprise at that. But I wish to understand."

"The police seemed to have plenty of evidence. Or they wouldn't have come to me."

"The Sergeant explained that an eyewitness naturally carries weight; with an instructing magistrate – myself; eventually before a court?"

"He put no pressure on me."

"Reluctant witnesses have in general two sorts of motivation. One is shame towards recounting damaging or humiliating episodes. They may feel they don't show up very well. Could that account at all for your standpoint?"

"It's true that I don't much like to talk about the episode."

"There is also fear. Of course many people go in fear of the law. Simply of 'histoires'; of lengthy and tedious procedures. We can eliminate that? Good: fear then of being implicated –

63

of the law's powers of constraint, coercion, even punishment?
I accept your denial. Or lastly, frequent in cases of violence,
a fear of reprisals? Of some vengeance visited upon them for
helping to shop a malefactor?"

"I'm not, I don't – sorry, I only mean that's not my argument."

Smiling – "I'm waiting patiently to hear your argument.
When we've got through your objections or hesitations you
make a statement, my clerk takes it down, and in all probability
the matter's finished with. Is that so hard?"

Things go too fast, and Walter does not 'think'. Later he will
think that lawyers, like doctors, like engineers, are so accustomed to their intellectual superiority over all comers that they
fall the easiest of prey – it's classic – to card-sharps, confidence-
trickers and speculators of even the crudest sort.

"I'm afraid I don't have any statement. Beyond what you
know already. I was visited by a group of youngsters looking for
valuables and who were angry when they didn't find any, and
created some damage. I made no complaint then; I don't now;
and what more is there to say?"

She reached for an ashtray, at leisure for a cigarette; lit it:
weighing something; that was plain.

"People tell the police all sorts of stories. Contradiction and
confusion is a rule, and lying is frequent. That of course is a
misdemeanour and is punishable, but it is human and therefore
tolerated. The relation between the public and the police is far
from perfect. Every magistrate recognises this. It is my rôle to
bring out truth in an atmosphere of calm and of confidence.
And you understand as much.

"One of the risks is that tales told may be prompted by malice.
And the police recognise that: they apply a rough test, based on
knowledge and experience, and it serves pretty well. They may be
placed in difficulty because there are other motives than crude
malice, and it is an examining magistrate's duty to filter these.
One such, which we encounter frequently enough, is domestic dis-
cord in various shapes and forms." Blowing smoke. "This is why
a husband cannot give evidence against a wife – say. We are
wary of cousinages, of brothers-in-law.

"You are placed in no jeopardy. You are not accused. You
feel no need of assistance by counsel, as would be your right

64

during questioning by myself, and you would have the right to consult with your advocate outside my hearing. This is not the case here. But you do feel in some manner compromised. Or so I infer."

"I'll make a statement."

The judge wiggled her finger at the clerk who sat with her fingers on the keyboard of the typewriter.

"Question – 'Would you explain the reasons for your apparent reluctance to testify?' "

"I'm trying to be consistent," slowly, for himself more than for the clerk, who could type as fast as he spoke. "I don't believe in violence: it's with oneself one has to make a start. I got taken by surprise, and from that moment I was a passive onlooker. Now I'm again free, I don't want to prolong the violence. All it ends in is another act of violence, probably condemning them to prison which I don't believe in or approve of. I'm not trying to hinder justice, better said society's present view of justice, but I think it all wrong and I refuse to contribute."

"You have thus as I understand an ethical standpoint and this is an expression of that?"

"Partial, imperfect. I could try to do better."

"An abstract, intellectual expression?"

"What else?" Walter falls into this one. "One doesn't speak like this in the emotional heat of the moment. Unless one's a saint and we're pretty short on saints." The judge has a simple hand code with her clerk, for on or off the record.

"Quite," turning back pages of her dossier. "You didn't react like this when you found pictures that you valued had been wantonly slashed."

"No, I was flaming."

"Or when you found your dog killed?"

"It didn't bring my dog back to life," angrily. "Look, Madame, if I refuse military service as a conscientious objector and they tell me, look, the Russians have just killed your father and raped your mother, I'll go mad, probably, and say give me a bayonet and let me go out and kill Russians. It's human to be stupid. Sure, my argument is easy here in the quiet of your office, and I grant your point and it's still a poor one."

"It is pleasant," smiling – unpleasantly bright young woman –

65

"to discuss an abstract thought, philosophic overtones, socio-logic import. This office however is not my living room: I am – read me back that first paragraph, Geneviève ... now I'm again free, that was the phrase. I am not free, here. I am a paid representative of society, an agent of protection and also inevitably of repression. I am under the constraint of my function and my profession. Freely consented to, thereafter binding upon me. Nor are you free, dear sir. Government, without constraint, does not exist. You are under the constraint of the powers confided to me, responsibility entrusted to me. As binding as the cord, string or whatever they tied you up with."

He must not lose his temper, though, with this woman, who is watching him, reading his weaknesses and vulnerability off his face.

"You are reminding me of a magistrate's powers of coer-cion."

"I should dislike having to do so."

"You could even send me to prison."

"That would be an extreme step."

"They do it to conscientious objectors. I couldn't stop you."

"Quite, you might even welcome it," dryly. "I see that by profession you are a writer."

And now she has given herself away. Walter, now, can afford to smile. She is no more than my intellectual equal: she is – grinning at the notion – my 'social inferior'. A girl from the bourgeoisie, stuck in that mentality.

"A writer of fiction, Madame, and I can see what is in your mind: that I might find it clever to manoeuvre myself into a position of martyr, write a fine piece of polemical journalism and stir up all my friends in Paris into giving me publicity which would be welcome. And to you likewise, which would be less so. All round, a skilful piece of politics. Am I right?"

"It has been known," said the judge, taking another cigarette.

"I'll give you a statement of fact and a profession of faith, and then you can do as you like. One, I've no highly-placed friends. And precious little leverage. Two, writers who publicise themselves earn only my contempt."

"Noted," she said smartly, and crushed the cigarette she had just lit. "I'll give you two remarks in exchange, and note them too. One, the serenity of justice depends to some extent upon knowing when and how to allow time to pass. That's a statement of fact. As a profession of faith I might offer this: your slightly high-flown concepts of personal honour could be said to do you credit, and they could also be thought of as expressions of vanity . . . You are free to go, Monsieur Forestier. We have no more to say to one another at this moment. Naturally, it remains possible that I may send you a further convocation at an unspecified time. The small formality now of asking your signature to Geneviève's record. Just the one page," pleasantly, "concluding in the usual tag that you agree this to be a fair and accurate paraphrase of your wording and sentiments. Many thanks. Good morning to you," standing up, politely, to offer her hand.

She was not, as she might have been, two sizes bigger below the waist. A slim, elegant and attractive young woman. And roughly half his age.

Outside it was full of lawyers, conferring with their clientèle, concocting defences. 'Now we let her have this, see, which we can't contest anyhow, and we take our stand then on this other point and we have her foxed.'

Better at politics than Walter, no doubt. A weaselly crowd for the most part, though looking less well fed – less self-satisfied too perhaps – than their counterparts over in the civil division. There wouldn't be much grand pickings in the criminal court, where once the judge of instruction has done, and the Chamber of Accusation has pronounced your case fit to go to trial, defence lawyering will be pretty hard sledding, and plenty of tough titty at the hands of the Advocate General, prosecuting for the State. Do best perhaps devilling for the tenors, down from Paris.

There was this nasty feeling of 'having been here before' – the same sensation of being bested, and suddenly hung out to dry after being well wrung out, that he had had after that civil hearing a few weeks ago.

But it had ended in a victory, and only a couple of days gone since dancing about in euphoria drinking champagne and acting the fool – and this one may go just the other way.

Walter, boy, do not be a fool. A judge is more than a match for you. Five minutes' hearing, and they have you sewn up. You may think of yourself as a fine fellow; to them you're like all the rest and all small fry. Out on the line, with a clothes peg to hold you.

A shrewd hit, that, to suggest that his honour is no more than vanity? Everything is vanity, and especially to claim that you are free of it.

He feels drained, battered. Tension there, and the need of concentration – and be fair, fear – has taken much nervous energy. Turn into the local pub – 'A l'Ecoute du Palais' – where everybody comes for a bit of bandaging after a punch-up with the Law.

"A quarter of red – anything you like but not Bordeaux."

Reflected again in the red wine is his red vision of anger against Sylvie. To go home now and punch her up, since you can neither punch nor make love to a pretty young Judge of Instruction? A fine display of wounded vanity that would make. She has stabbed him but it is natural. Her dog too, her pictures too, her home too. Despite much tough talk and armour-plated behaviour Sylvie is a vulnerable creature, her apparent insensitivity a blind, her gregarious sociability a – but I'm not a shrink, Walter tells himself crossly, emptying the little carafe. But it's just that . . . oh why must she always . . . look, stop stuttering. You will, when you stop fuming. Simmer down! Have another quarter.

No, don't; getting a bit drunk will lead to something rash: while you still have some prudence make use of it. And he walks instead, along the river bank in the May morning. It is hot but there are chestnut trees: they give shade.

There has been some stability, these ten years. Storms there have been, but of the children's creation; teen-age upheavals. The long succession of generally nasty flat apartments, made necessary by the proximity of schools and concert-halls; the scrabbling and struggling with publishers and agents; above all the relentlessly greedy pursuit of lovers (Sylvie has renounced adultery as often as they have changed flats; a great many times): all this did not come so much to a dramatic stop as peter gently out. It hadn't seemed necessary any more.

One had to suppose that insecurities persisted, despite surface calm. Why else take this matter so tragically, why allow it to become a drama? Was there so much inner violence unresolved in them both? Stopping outside a bank, contemplating the smug dullness of the exterior, so sleekly, greyly proclaiming the huge quantities of discreetly self-contented moneybags within, Walter wishes furiously that masked gangsters would come bursting out (dragging many weighty moneybags) and scatter all the baa-ing sheep including him with noisy gunfire: since violence is what you all want let's have it real. Not just a couple of boys who tied up an old sheep and threw his typewriter on the floor. Let all the howling grimacing folk who huddle together squeaking for security, and protection (more and bigger prisons) gather here to stare (has anybody understood, truly, the amazing power and magnetic attraction exercised by a scene of violence?). And when they are all assembled trembling in sexual bliss then let a mad ayatollah come driving through in a car loaded to the mudguards with explosive.

Feeling better now, dear boy? Then drive home quietly to dear wifey. And don't pick any quarrels with her. She was only sticking up for herself. She never saw the tattle to the gendarmerie as an attack upon yourself. Less still a knife in the back.

It is the tactic of all legal administration, anywhere you go. You forget all about the matter, and conclude that they have done so too. That careful, dignified, so-reasonable explanation you provided, about that small discrepancy of six years back in your income-tax return, has surely satisfied them. And they have so many other, and surely more important, matters to consider.

The reminder that they neither forgive nor forget is disagreeable.

"There's no point, Monsieur Forestier, in making a fuss," said the Judge of Instruction.

"Yes, well, nobody reimburses me for my time or trouble." She just looked at him . . .

"And here," in her unruffled-courtesy voice, "is Maître Cordery." A youngish pleader, placid of expression. Neither face nor name mean anything to Walter.

"I present Monsieur Forestier," went on Madame Rivière. "Our eyewitness," indulgent, "to these goings on." Neither party to this introduction was delighted, but both said they were.

"You might see, Geneviève, what's holding up our détenu."

"It's all that boring handcuffing," said the flowery girl, apologetically.

"Too many instances recently," in the judge's social manner, "of dramatic rescue attempts within the precinct. They're talking now of a security portal between us and the rest of the Palais."

"Lamentable," said Walter, who had realised that he was in for a 'confrontation' and might as well make the best of it.

"Quite so. Weighing us still further down beneath procedural detail. Militating against our tradition of humanity. I don't look forward to having my footsteps dogged by a bodyguard. The Judge Michel you may recall was assassinated. On his motorbike; on his way home. He was a classmate of mine, a comrade and a friend. We've had to do some thinking. I hope that you, as an intellectual, are doing so too." This discussion which might have grown acrid was interrupted by a prisoner-and-escort bustle. Strange, thought Walter, what tricks memory and imagination play. I don't remember him looking in the least like that. I feel no vengeful satisfaction, come to that, at seeing him humiliated, between two cops.

"This," leaning back in her chair, "is Monsieur Domergue, detained by the state upon imputation. Monsieur Forestier, a householder of this region. But I believe you are acquainted."

"You aren't asked to comment," Cordery, quick, smooth, "on anything Madame le Juge says. Only to answer her questions, carefully, seriously. Just reminding you."

"No attempt at entrapment. I don't think the fact is in dispute."

"What's the question?" asked the young man. A low, easy voice.

"Whether you recognise the gentleman."

"Don't know if I do or not. One sees so many people."

"I have here," putting on her glasses, "a number of statements made by yourself and your associates, at different times after your arrest. Together with reports and conclusions by investigating officers. These are full of discrepancy and confusion: that is common form."

"With respect, Madame –"

"I haven't finished, Maître. You are an intelligent man, Monsieur Domergue. I offer you a clean slate. If we agree that much of this is natural prevarication caused by doubt and fear, we can make quicker progress. You can accept, as I can, that the no-I-never, and I-wasn't-even-there, is childish, automatisms, barricades thrown up to cause delay. I'm ready to disregard all this."

"As long as statements made by what are termed associates – clearly inadmissible, Madame. We all know the police tactic; to try and set alleged perpetrators at variance with one another. The pretence that a third person, outside hearing, has made damaging admissions –"

"Let him answer, Maître, for himself alone."

"I'm dead easy," said the young man. "Everybody wants to get into the act. Know him? I don't know. Ask him!"

He doesn't know, thought Walter, whether I've come running in here all full of eager zeal.

"With your permission, then, I will."

"Clearly tendentious," said Cordery. "The witness is asked to identify my client after being told of imputations against him. Was there an identity parade? The police procedure has been shamefully negligent."

"Disingenuous of you," said the judge. "As you are well aware, the police case against your client rests upon the affair of the jewellery shop. No charge has been made, concerning these allegations. It is within my discretion to determine whether or not such an allegation can be upheld, and if so, whether or not the charges could be joined, in court. The question is proper. Does Monsieur Forestier claim to have laid eyes upon the person in question, on a previous occasion? If so, when and where?"

"You have my wife's account of things," said Walter.

"I've been led to believe that she only arrived later."

"That is exact. So that I'm the only one who knows?"

"So it would seem."

"Well, the light was different, for a start."

"Evidently. I have already given my little lecture about prevarication."

"So that it's very hard to say."

"And childish evasions. You may base your interpretation upon feature, movement, characteristics of speech or voice. Upon the quality of your recollections. Which Monsieur Domergue here is free to contest. You are here to speak without

71

fear or favour. And whatever you say, your credibility may be subject to further examination," lighting a cigarette.

"So to be honest," said Walter, "I think it might be possible that it was the gentleman present who dropped in one evening. I wouldn't like to speak with more certainty than that."

"Very well," said the magistrate mildly. "We've plenty of time. We're trying to get it right. A person who may or may not have been Monsieur Domergue dropped in one evening." Without sarcasm. "For a cup of cocoa?"

"I mean whoever it was didn't break in. The door was open. I think he was hungry, yes, and thirsty. I think he'd lost his way, in the hills."

"And is there more?" in a tone of naïve wonder.

"As the Counsellor remarked, I'd like to avoid comment. Put your questions, Madame, and I'll try and answer honestly."

"And whoever dropped in – was he alone?"

"I thought we'd agreed to leave so-called associates aside."

"A yes or no will suffice."

"He had two companions that I saw. I'm not sure I could recognise either."

"Did they, or he, offer you violence?"

"Not very much, seen in proportion. I was tied up. I'm glad you asked because I'm not sure how much violence was involved. People who have often been humiliated will take an opportunity, to humiliate in their turn."

"You aren't asked for psychology; merely for fact. Your dog was killed?"

"Somebody killed my dog, certainly."

"The house was ransacked?"

"That is so."

"Furniture and other property damaged?"

"I've broken things myself in moments of rage."

"In other people's houses?" she enquired politely.

"I haven't found myself in the circumstances we're describing."

"If I understand, you are attempting to avoid an emotional attitude."

"I'm grateful that you do understand."

"You were tied up. A dog was killed. Things were broken, others were stolen. During the – we'll call it occupancy, of your house. The summing up is fair?"

72

"Avoiding sentimentalism, yes."

"At the moment of incursion, you formed an impression of people who came to ask their way and beg something to eat?"

"I'm not sure it's a fair question, Madame, in hindsight."

"Calls for a conclusion of the witness," said Cordery, "He had no means of knowing the states of mind."

"An impression, Maître, not a conclusion as to intent."

"A temptation to steal can arise from an opportunity given," said Walter carefully. "I've known occasions, myself."

"Yes," said the magistrate. "Let me rephrase it. Were you put in fear?"

"Startled. Frightened – yes, I'd have to use the word."

"Casually frightened – of the dark, of solitude, of funny noises – are you telling me that?"

"Imagination readily induces fear."

"I want a clear answer, Monsieur Forestier. You frightened yourself, or you were put in fear?"

"I think I'll have to answer both."

"My last question. While you have been speaking you have kept your eyes fastened upon Monsieur Domergue. Are you now able to feel more definite, on the question of identity?"

"I can't speak with certainty; I'd have to say probable."

"I think you've impressed your hearers by your efforts to be impartial: you'll agree, Maître?"

"I'm not on a jury, Madame."

"Neither am I. I ask whether you find this account of matters biased or prejudicial to your client?"

"I think from hearing him," aware of being close to the wind, "one would say that Monsieur gives the impression of wishing to see justice done."

"And you, Monsieur Domergue, does he impress you as truthful?"

"Plainly improper, Madame!"

"Let me hear it from his mouth and please do not prompt your client. Does the account you have heard given agree with your recollection of events?"

"Can I have a cigarette?" asked Fernand.

"Certainly," said the judge, offering hers.

"One of those I'd prefer," pointing at Walter. "Don't have to say anything, isn't that right?"

"Perfectly correct," said Madame Rivière. "Your refusal to speak may not be held as a presumption of guilt. I am not a trial judge. My function and purpose is not to decide upon guilt or innocence: that is reserved to the Court. Am I clear? Your counsellor has told you this: I repeat it. My job is to collect the information and clarify the evidence that may come before a court, while coming to the decision whether, in fact, you should be called to answer before a court at all. Is there a case to answer?

"In the present state of affairs I find that there is. Your silence is interpreted in law as a reservation of the arguments your counsellors would put before the court.

"You can change your mind, and explain yourself. Your account could alter or modify my opinion. Very well. I am bound to give weight to the evidence I possess. You see? Monsieur Forestier's account goes unchallenged. Prima facie, in light that is of facts as now known, I must conclude that you should be required to answer before a tribunal. The Prosecutor, considering this opinion, may think himself justified in bringing charges against you before the Assize Court.

"You stick to your decision? We'll let you know then, Maître. Geneviève, you'll give Monsieur Forestier his statement to sign and I hardly think we'll need to trouble him further."

Her smile was without malice. How did I ever imagine, thought Walter, that I'd ever stand up against a professional? Effortlessly, she knocked me flat.

A nasty vision of the Assize Court. A President. A prosecutor. Not the same as the little civil tribunal deciding who should pay the rent.

*

Bells of all sorts give Walter trouble. No sound is more unwelcome to him than church bells: in Flanders and in England, carilloning away there or just ding-dong-merrily: tinny clank of a village angelus in France or gloomily tolling a Spanish deathbed.

'I've heard bells tolling.

Old Adrian's mole in (what the hell is that supposed to mean?)

'And cymbals glorious
Swinging uproarious (blimey)

74

In the gorgeous turrets of Notre Dame' (passage suitable to clerics in search of purple preferment)

'Bells of Shandon

That sound so grand on –' – was there ever anybody who found rhyme schemes like those of the Reverend Prout?

It has already been seen that the front door bell, like the knocking in *Macbeth*, is an omen of the blackest disasters. And now this time it's the telephone: we call it a bell, though in some countries it's a bzizz or a brurr, in France it's a Dhzingg of a singularly disruptive nature. With this infernal invention all the choices are bad (close by, the sound turned down? – further off and the sound up?).

"Syl-vi-eeee! Te-le-phoo-ne . . . SYLvie . . . oh fuck."

The thing would now stop ringing, at the moment one arrived. Whereas if one ran, dishevelled and breathless, a cheerful voice was likely to ask whether your preferences went to crispies or crunchies at breakfast time. Chocolate or cyanide? Doubtless both since the invention was both genial and deadly.

"Forestier," says Walter in a discouraging voice.

"Lebreton," says a voice right back, managing in three syllables to sound alert, interesting, and female. "Advocate."

"Oh god, more lawyers." Meaning to sound discouraging.

"Have you had that many?" Laughter in the voice. The French are often godawful bright, but only rarely have any humour at all: he is disarmed.

"No. There are a lot about, though."

"I do see. Could you bear another? For perhaps half an hour in passing? Lucifer bringing light?"

"You want to drop in, you mean?"

"That's the idea. Permission to come aboard? If it's not madly inconvenient?"

"When?"

"Oh, I'm about half an hour away, I should suppose: I can come straight across. If I may." And so disarmed is Walter that instead of a forbidding 'And what is the purport of your visit?' he only mumbles "I suppose so." True, there is a feeling that she wouldn't easily take no for an answer.

"Do I have to ask when I get there? The white house with green shutters?"

"Past the village and keep on up the hill. Red shutters."

"I'll find it." And rang off with no further ado. Walter has not been given time to change his mind. An active spirit. An Ariel. An actress's voice that echoed pleasantly in the ear, cleverly modulated. Well, she'd put him in her pocket. Nothing out of the way for her, at a guess.

Sylvie . . . where is she?

"Oh, there you are." Coming out the bathroom, dressed to go out.

"Sorry, I was just lipsticking: was that call for me? I said I'd go and have a cup of coffee with Janine." Sylvie-the-sociable has quite a few dropping-in points, vaguely called friends: Walter-the-unsociable calls them acquaintances and quite likes seeing them when in the right frame of mind, which is pretty occasional.

"No it was for me," pedantically getting things in order. "Bit of business, nothing interesting. Sure, go ahead. If you aren't back to lunch no worry, I'll just fend. Bonjour to Janine, tell her and Alain to come over for a drink some evening." Not really meaning this, as Sylvie knows well, but it does no harm. If they do come he'll grumble at first and then be illogically glad to see them.

And on his side – of course she'll be late. Alain will be away at work, and time will pass happily. Not very terrible, is it? They'll eat a sardine off the corner of the kitchen table.

Walter's house is unassuming. A bit bigger than most of those in the village. Many such have a wooden balcony or verandah built out on pillars. Most are painted white. The red of the shutters and window frames is an 'indian' brownish red: one sees it used often in the Basque country.

Walter isn't assuming either, in the eyes of the locals. One sees him about, pottering in the village or in his garden, often in overalls, even in sabots when the weather is muddy, and generally in need of a shave. He has to be sure an 'educated' accent but nowise 'foreign' (most of his early childhood was spent in this country), and while he cannot talk the patois, or navarrese, can and does patter 'castillan' – brief, he fits in. Queer chap, and standoffish – so are plenty more. Some airs and graces, but a writer-chap, harmless. Doesn't think himself a cut above everyone.

In all this there is little affectation. He does have one mild snobbery. It does the village no harm when expensive cars, or those with exotic numberplates, are seen parked in front. An exotic air, even slightly magical, sits well. Walter is pleased as well as amused when a scarlet Porsche appears with some dust and even a bit of a boom. Sexy of it. From another planet. The visitor isn't bad either. Jeans, a little jacket. Shapely bottom as she turns to get a largish briefcase off the back seat – the only thing that could be said to spell 'lawyer'.

"Miriam Lebreton." A firm muscular hand. Clear brown skin with blood under it; brown eyes. A fine forehead. Fine hair, brown, black, bronze, and reddish highlights. A southern girl. How ridiculous to be called Le Breton. He says so. She laughs.

"The extraordinary thing is that my father really was Breton. However . . ." Quick eye to the surroundings. Looks to be thirtyish.

When he brings her into the studio she enjoys it, although she says nothing, not even the 'nice room' type of commonplace. When a strong and striking personality comes into a room, the room looks better, as though it too sat up and took notice.

"A drink?"

"Something wet. Like water." She accepts a tiny cigar, turning it in her fingers and examining it attentively: some are quite dreadful and one does well to beware. All of her is worth examining attentively. The hands are far from the pale and effetely tapering appendages one expects, and generally sees; the legs as clean and springy as an antelope's. She would serve for a statue of physical energy. Walter strips her mentally and is not ashamed of himself: he isn't thinking of sex but of javelin-throwing.

She is used to being looked at with appraisal.

"I plead criminal causes. You aren't obliged to have heard of me. But I defend myself too, on the whole."

"So I see," not only thinking of the scarlet Porsche. A vulgar remark but she doesn't mind. Hot fierce eyes. They have a strong leverage upon the object. He thinks of the long-handled pincers with which a steelworker, masked and leather-aproned, grips a glowing ingot.

"So I'm defending this gang. Interested me because they're not simply hooligans: there are one or two unusual features, among them yourself.

77

"So you were naughty? No complaint laid, evasive with the cops, stroppy even towards the judge – she's in two minds about you. The Procureur could take the jewellery thing by itself, a straight smash and grab. He'd like to bring in these dwelling-house cases too and bust them for a big sentence – which is where I come in. They'd like an eye-witness, so when your wife arrived with a juicy tale of tying you up and killing your dog . . .

"We had a little chat, and I learn that you don't want to know. To the examining magistrate, no skin off her nose. As you're aware – I presume – she's dispassionate.

"But the Proc might like to stir you up, convoke you as witness whether you like it or not. Dished up before the assize court since the charge is robbery with violence, towards persons as well as property. Item, jeweller's window, item you.

"If you refuse, the Proc can ask the President of the Court to use coercive powers on you. I don't say that will be so; I'm saying he may take steps to make it so.

"This didn't interest me because frankly I thought you were the usual wet. La mère Rivière tells me I'm wrong, and now I'm here I see I'm wrong.

"If you want to play the martyr with his shirt on fire for reasons or principles – I'm far from saying you have motives of publicity or whatever – it's no affair of mine. Thought I'd come here though, to see. And now I see . . . what is it anyhow? Penal reform, Howard League? Or just Greenpeace or Amnesty – any axe to grind?"

"Just me. And my little notions," said Walter mildly.

"Well, before going into that, I'll put a hypothesis. I can get you off the hook, assuming there is a hook, but it's a possibility, distinct. I can book you as a defence witness, and if the Proc doesn't like that too bad on him."

"That implies what?"

"What you'd expect. Being examined by me in court, open to dentistry from the other side. They'd aim to make a fool of you. They might treat you with a shrug as a harmless maniac and they might act nasty: they don't have to tell me and I've no guarantee. So within the hypothesis, the first question I have is 'Are you afraid of that?' Have you a reluctance to face the court?"

The clear rapid delivery is a fresh wind blowing. Get rid of cobwebs, Walter.

He recalls to himself afresh the civil court: the crowd of sniggering lawyers, the hostility of the opponent, the sharpness of the judge. A three-ha'penny tribunal for trivial affairs. But is there a real difference in the approach? The 'majesty' of the Assize Court is that death sentences were once pronounced there. Three judges. A jury. And then?

"That doesn't worry me at all."

"I must warn you, it can be tough. The Press can take a nasty attitude. So can lawyers for civil damages. Think, that their one idea will be to shake your credibility through your confidence, through innuendo and probably ridicule. To keep your self-command without being provoked into sarcasms or personalities – I'm not saying you can't but I am suggesting it's harder than you might think."

"It isn't that."

"Well, you have to understand yourself."

Walter chooses a characteristic approach.

"Free for me to take you to lunch, are you? Where are you staying – in some hotel?"

She makes her mind up quickly, and no doubt that is characteristic too.

"I don't like talking shop over meals; I get too much of that in Paris. Want it to be an entertainment – on that basis I'll accept with pleasure."

"Twenty minutes then for a shower and a shave? – no shortage of reading matter hereabouts. I'll hitch a ride if I may: I've no car this morning."

A summery day, and not too hot: they are in luck. And only a quarter of an hour down the valley they find a place that looks ideal and where Walter has never been because it's relatively recent. An old mill, and one can eat outside by the water's edge. There is a willow, a few insects, and this early hardly any people, and it is pleasantly offhand. 'Yes of course; sit where you like'. A good terrain for Walter. He is not a particularly greedy person though fond of food. He loves to drink but nobody would call him a drunk. All his life he has loved restaurants. It dates from quite early in childhood when his father took him to Paris and introduced him to favourite haunts:

Larue – now alas long gone – and Lapérouse in those lovely rooms. Moments of happiness, and he snuffs the air now like a battle-charger.

It was a good occasion because bad food in France is worse than anywhere else and this was unspeakable, and they were both in helpless giggles after five minutes.

"Oh no! Shall we just sail out all haughty? I know quite a reliable one a quarter-hour further?"

"Not a bit of it, I'm enjoying myself: what does it matter? Lovely and quiet."

"And now we know why – we'll jump in the water if you feel acute symptoms." And after half a bottle there's no such thing as social shame. He begins to show acute symptoms. To himself; they are not apparent to the company. It's not as though it were colic.

"What d'you have to do, this afternoon?"

"Known as constructing a system of defence. Jails are like convents and interviews with detainees take place in what's called the parlour – and since that stupid girl who smuggled a gun in they long to strip me to the skin before letting me into the precinct. No hurry; one thing about jails is you know they'll still be there when you come. This is likely to be lengthy. Tomorrow, session with the judge on general background, also lengthy. Close upon which, pleading the following day in Poitiers, for a lady who may or may not have killed her husband. Have to make up my mind about that tomorrow evening, because if she did she isn't round the bend: at present she claims she didn't but she is. All that lies in a compartment of the mind at present locked and on the shelf. No drinking tomorrow, although Poitiers – I say, this salad has been in the washing machine and alas, they forgot the spin-drier. Dare one risk a cup of coffee?"

"I'll pick you up in the town and we'll go out to dinner to efface this because it was a good joke but has gone on too long."

"Give me one of your tiny cigars," says Lebreton, and smokes it before saying, "Very well. I'll know more then, about the system of defence."

"Isn't that shop?"

"Shop," dryly, "is the discussion of a plum and how much it can be milked for; 'Fifty you think? – come, I'd say seventy is bottom weight'; and one then devotes lunch to the delicate manoeuvre of splitting that. Talking of which, does your male vanity flinch from the suggestion that the law is a grossly over-paid profession? I think that I can afford to ask you to dinner."

"I have managed to make a living so far without adopting the business principle of Grandfather Smallweed, which was to make sure somebody else paid the lunch." She has never heard of Grandfather Smallweed and he describes with delight Mr. Guppy's lunch in the City. One of my father's favourite characters, thinks Walter, and another debt I owe him.

The symptoms become still more acute while she drives him home in the little scarlet Porsche, very fast on the hill road so that while appearing negligently relaxed Walter's foot is pressing an imaginary brake-pedal the whole way.

"Around seven?" And she is gone, leaving him in a turbulent slipstream. Sylvie is still not back. And he works all afternoon in the garden, getting into a considerable sweat but he is rich; he can afford two showers a day.

*

"So here we are; Mr. Guppy and – what was his name?"

"Bart Smallweed. We were brought up, you see, on the Dickens books. Lessons in socialism. I had them read aloud to me as a child. Could always sleep during the boring bits. It was a very, a . . ." His hands are making a plastic gesture, as though modelling clay.

"Enriching?"

"That's right, and vitalising experience." She had noticed his hands, which are fine, blurred now by middle age and gardening. "Not all of them by any means – four, at the end; when through his enormous success he began to understand – they are about crime, and about suffering. There's one in which a boy, brought up in the house of a village blacksmith, plays cards with a snobbish and arrogant little girl, with whom he is desperately in love. She snubs him cruelly, saying 'He calls the knaves Jacks, this boy', so that he feels unutterably clumsy and boorish, and it changes his whole life – for the worse. For me it was the other way round. I was brought up on the last legs of the old feudal upper class, and taught their vocabulary. A great handicap to me throughout life," laughing, "always to call the

81

Jacks knaves." A waiter came, and in a soft murmur indicated that their table was ready.

With an irritable perfectionism he has brought her to an elegant restaurant in a country town some way from the city 'to eat well for a change', recklessly ordering a most expensive bottle, and damn the consequences. He is as childishly in love with her as Pip with Estella. And perfectly aware that it will do him no good at all. What is he to make of this woman? Love, d'you call it? Making it with her, maybe. That would be a natural expression of something, at present hideously painful: a relief if not release. Love is not the right word. But neither is adultery, which he has looked up in the Concise Oxford Dictionary. Counterfeit, illegal, unlicensed. Adulterated: falsified by admixture of baser elements. That is excellent and accurate, if we are talking about love. It does not describe at all well life as known to him. In all these years, he is slightly astonished to think, never once has he been false to Sylvie. As Jennet says in *The Lady's not for Burning* – 'I am such a creature of habit: I had quite got into the way of living'. As for Sylvie, whose lifelong habit has been so very much the contrary – have her adulteries really cheapened and diminished love? He is not prepared so to maintain. Nor has he ever felt that he had 'to get his own back'. Surely he is not now 'in love'. These sensations that he feels – they are strong, but surely they are ludicrous.

They have had a good, quite small meal. They have drunk a bottle between them (Miriam, he is delighted to see, has hollow bones) of Corton Charlemagne, very grand; another if possible still grander of Bonnes Mares: about nothing, he told her, is he as snobbish as about wine. Thank you, one will leave Bordeaux to the English with pleasure: awful cheek of those greediguts to go drinking the Bourgognes as well. It should be forbidden them. Of the Champagnes there's enough to go round, and one will only interdict them to the Japanese.

"Shall we spend the night here?"

Miriam's laugh is engaging. "My dear boy, you can't seduce me, I'm your lawyer." This is irresistibly identical to a remark made by one of his earliest girls – 'You can't seduce me, I'm your cousin' which when told makes her laugh harder.

"I am further reminded of Madame de Chevreuse. Oh, she's a character in Dumas. She makes a speciality of love affairs."

"Oh dear, I'm stronger on law texts to my shame than on these classic authors of yours – well, I shouldn't go out with a writer, should I? – serves me right: tell me then."

"She's had to make rather a quick getaway because she's been dabbling in a political conspiracy and the cops are after her. So she does a bunk disguised as a man, and the village pub says the only bed they can find her she has to share, and it turns out the sharer is a country curate. 'It came to her what a delightful souvenir it would be in her old age to have damned a curé.' Now I really feel that before reaching old age I should be given the opportunity of damning a lawyer." Miriam's laugh makes two elderly bourgeois at the next table look up disapprovingly from their duck.

"Let's go for a stroll outside: it's a nice night." She takes his arm when offered, and answers him with a slight pressure of her elbow upon her rib cage.

So unaccustomed is Walter to adulteries that though there is nothing that could happen in a restaurant that would faze him for a single instant he much dreads asking a country hotel-keeper for a room, afraid of greasy knowing glances. And instead they hand him a key without even looking. But it isn't adultery. Nothing happens that remotely resembles an admixture of baser elements. Miriam has not in the least the air of the bourgeois female titillated. She is not coy, and she is not blatant. It could be said that she was studious, but there is a bluestocking ring about that. She cannot altogether escape her profession, any more than one would expect Walter wholly to shake off literary attitudes, allusions, and fantasies. It is thus inevitable that the comparison should occur with an advocate asked to replace a colleague with laryngitis at short notice: with half an hour to master the brief. As an extemporaneous effort honourable. She did have a toothbrush in her handbag, which she offered gallantly to share.

As for Walter, he remembers a remark made to a journalist by Jacques Brel: if you haven't given absolutely everything you've got then you haven't made love, that's all. Instancing a child-hood mania; to bicycle through the countryside until he fell off through sheer exhaustion.

"Know anything about bicycles – the competition sort?" he asks.

83

"No," mystified. They are sitting up in bed with the light on.

"By definition something for the poor: not like tennis or Porsche cars."

"Palpable hit, but go on."

"Poverty here is no handicap. The equipment doesn't cost much. A country road is free. A profession open to talent, which can be said of few careers. A parallel here perhaps with crime?"

"I am beginning to follow you closely."

"So a gifted lad decides to turn professional. Little money in that as a rule; bare minimum wage for the most part. If intelligent the talented boy notices that intelligence can make the difference, as much as strength and speed, most pros being strong and fast but not very bright."

"Are you talking about your nocturnal visitor?"

"I don't know, I didn't observe him at all clearly. It's possible. I'm wondering how a young man like that reasons. He didn't have social advantages and not many careers are open to him. He can put his wits to use. It's quite like being a writer, maybe. He has to learn tenacity, and how if need be to suffer. I can think of two examples that may be pertinent. One was a boy from a typical small-bourgeois background, liked to read, tinker with model boats, bicycle as a pastime. Bright, does well at school. Baccalaureat, university reading natural sciences. He has the character at that moment to say 'But this is ridiculous: I get a degree in biochemistry or whatever, I'll get a goodish job – and I have turned myself into pliable conventional cannon-fodder. I've hammered the chains, and they'll hold me for the rest of my days.' This boy noticed he was a good rider, took his bike and turned pro, saying fuck the university. If you're curious to know the suite he hit the jackpot first time and is now a star; the rewards for which are large."

Miriam keeps silent, realising that an over-stimulated Walter is now well away. She is, too, interested.

"Crime's like this, I think. Appeals to boys who would otherwise have a dismal existence. You don't have a very long career but most sports are like that. You might win a few big prizes and be set for life at the age of thirty-five. It's interesting. You travel about. Fresh air, and varied kinds of fun. And meanwhile there are risks, sometimes grave ones. The other boy I mentioned – had a good job. Computer programmer. Fashionable, and good money. Chose to be a professional rider simply because it was more fun; no two days the same. A hard life and a perpetual gamble, but computers are so bloody boring. He did very well. One day he was knocked off his bike going fast on a concrete racetrack. Broke his thigh as well as being bashed up all over. But no regrets – in the ambulance he said that yes, it was a pretty tough trade, but that he still liked it. Prisons, I suppose, would appear as a risk of much the same sort."

It must seem that Walter is being infernally garrulous for a man supposed to be making love to a brilliant and attractive woman. True, he would say sadly (if asked). Writers are all monsters of egomania. But remember too that apart from the dictating ones, probably a smallish minority, writers' work is conducted in utter silence. No chat. Whereas listen to businessmen: a perfect parrot-house all day, and without Ma Bell where would they be?

"Darling girl," he said, and then ran out of words. Roughly a bottle each – it is not excessive. Neither of them had had pudding, or even cheese. Aided by a good digestion they both slept well.

"Tell me about writers," says Miriam, clear-eyed at breakfast.

"Yes, well, the thing to remember about writers is that sitting still all day scribbling their circulation is bad and even in an over-heated room they suffer chronically from cold feet."

"All right then," smiling. 'Tell me about you."

"That would link up," unsmiling, "with all my prating of last night."

"I have no second thoughts about that."

"Are you being a bit professional? 'Systems of defence'?"

"The professional and the personal," gently, "would seem to be going hand in hand to some extent."

"Give me another cup of coffee then because it's something of a sermon . . . We're at different stages of development, you, me, waiter or dishwasher. We depend a good deal on how long it has been since the family got its feet out of the bog. I mean that we are what we make of ourselves, and we are also what a succession of generations made. We were modelled, when we were children and plastic, and long before that too. Heredity and environment.

"If you want to take me I'm an extreme case, and I have to keep aware of it. Because I'm at the end of a long line of what

85

for lack of a better word was called aristocracy. Look at the beginnings of that sort of family, which is often easy enough since incidents and personalities got mentioned in historical memoir, and you'll find a successful gangster.

"Abject, generally. Bit of pandering, a sister or daughter successfully sold to royalty. Risen from well-timed coat-turning, or a skilfully placed assassination. Blackmail. A mercenary band with which you tore up the countryside until bought off with an estate and a title.

"Three generations later you had effaced all this, called yourself nobility, and claimed to be civilised. But what was there at the start? Personal courage, craft, rapacity, intelligence. Rewarded with a coat of arms." Miriam lights a cigarette.

"The failure rate was always high but what was the penalty? Pain – the gallows, your head chopped off. Face it with stoicism. We all learned how to die like a gentleman. You often went to prison too. Pooh, you could always get out again. No need to sentimentalise about prisons. Ordinary people didn't get put much in prisons: there were plenty of other punishments. In fact today, now that we've got rid of the death penalty at last, prison is about the last of the old medieval barbarities that still survives. Still built like fortresses, like monasteries, but we're dishonest today, we behave with a sickly squeamish hypocrisy. We don't want to know what goes on inside. And all the reactionaries scream for more and bigger prisons: themselves thieves virtually every one and murderers frequently. One mustn't say so. But I am well placed to do so."

"It won't do," said Miriam drily, "to have you tell all this to the President of the Assize Court."

"It doesn't do for a writer, either. To be a moralist is a quick way of getting yourself chopped."

"And for getting your client a good stiff dose of penal servitude. Still – I have found elements, here. Forgive? – I'll just go upstairs a moment."

And Walter has to make a phone call. Lies and hypocrisy and that alas is the way of the world. Sorry, but that piece of business went on, and ended in a dinner as often happens and finally I didn't want to risk the road back because I'd had a good deal to drink.

Our ancestors had said much the same. Putting a good face

on turpitudes was one of their skills. Just about the only thing that could be said to Walter's credit was that he didn't feel pleased with himself.

Not much of an excuse, is it, Monsieur le Président?

The phone doesn't answer. Oh, well . . .

Miriam comes down in her jacket and looks at him, in the eye. He knows of course what she is about to say. 'Maître', the title given to legal dignitaries, is not to be confused with 'maitresse'; all the more when the dignitaries are of the feminine gender.

"Nobody is going to say greasily that such things shouldn't happen. Better make it clear though that they won't happen again. That said, can I thank you for a lovely party, as the children say? And for combining enjoyment with instruction? And talking of instruction, the judge is going to wonder where the hell I am – about the Court, I'll get in touch, shall I? Are you going to drive me?"

Which he does, and then he has to go home. You, my dear Sylvie, have done this to me a good many times, and never have you been short of an ingenious tale, which I could not question without adding to my humiliation as well as yours. So I left it at that. I hope you now have the sense to do the same.

'Well you might at least have phoned me. I was alone in the house all night and you know well I don't much like that. And not even the dog, now.' True, and I'll have to buy another dog.

While driving home Walter has rehearsed pretty well everything. Except what happens. The front door is bolted; the side door shutter is still closed. Nothing surprising there. He potters round to the terrace and opens the door there. The studio inside is still dim because the curtains are still drawn. Where's Sylvie?

And while asking himself this question he gets a stunning blow on the back of his head.

*

It is no dream-sequence. He is given to daydreaming, yes; but he would agree: the moment when your skull is ringing from the brisk tap with a hard object is not the moment to indulge. Say that the mind would incline to wander.

A moment when time does funny things. A phenomenon not

very well understood, used in fictional devices. One might instance the Occurrence at Owl Street Bridge: the spy, or was he just a deserter, was pushed off with the rope round his neck; envisions a lengthy and detailed escape sequence in the instant before the noose . . . we have all, perhaps, known something of the sort? A vision of things to come in a leap of the imagination – more often probably a sudden concentration of memory. Some great and unusual happiness, or its contrary. That can be one and the same thing.

Year of adolescence. Year shortly after the war. The dark northern city of Brussels. Winter. It is not Madrid, nor Valladolid, scene of Jesuit-ridden, Joyce-flavoured schooldays: the snow is dirtier, here.

He is beyond adolescence. He lives, still, in that musty flat, dark and decrepit, smelling of rubber galoshes and wet umbrellas, shared with Mama and Aunt Edie – and that, still, is childhood. But he has done Army service; has pottered with undecisive footsteps upon the first notions of what to do with his existence: sadly banal – school of decorative arts, the back doors and backrooms of theatres. A happening, then, such as changes course for one: letter from an old man in Paris, from years back crony and confidant of his father. There has been left in trust, he is told, a small but useful sum of money. It seems a great deal, to Walter. It will buy him liberty. The paper boat, bobbing in shallow, troubled water, can be pushed further out, upon uncharted seas. But first Walter thinks of enjoyment. There seems to have been little, up to now.

It was a fine spring, that year, and a good summer, and produced a splendid harvest: the wines were noble, and had 'charpente', and were long remembered, happily. And Walter too produced a vintage: his first. Sun is needed, and the right soil, and 'holy water' for the vine: and the person to make it.

The nineteenth-century resorts, on the Channel and the North Sea, are all there still, and not even much changed, even the northerly ones where the broad beaches sweep back to low, liquid sand-dunes and Hitler built great ugly blockhouses of concrete – some still there today, if all but obliterated by the kindly sand. And though some were dynamited most of the hotels stood. Shakily it might be, from years of neglect, and occupation by the soldiery, but they were massive structures.

Broken glass and rain coming through the roof, weeds on the terrace and anti-aircraft emplacements on the putting green have been cleared and mended by a busy populace. People wanted holidays, now more than ever. The locals had to earn their year's income in the summer season, now more than ever. There had been damage, and heartbreak, but the sun comes up, the tide flows in. It was the first real postwar season, that year, and spirits were high.

The beach in summer is a frontier boom town of wood, canvas sweat and noise. There must be shelter from wind and rain, from sun and salt, and at all times there must be entertainment. The boardwalk (saving feet from fatigue in the soft sand) stretched two kilometres from the 'bourgeois end' – the casino, flossy hotels, pompously-named 'american bars' – to the old fishing-village where the locals live: along it a hundred fairground structures cater for hunger, thirst and above all boredom. Six years of semi-famine and chronic anxiety left these people mad for gaiety. What they want is a day on the beach, a good stoke-up on shellfish and chips, and a serious evening of booze, and dollymop.

Walter found quarters in a little hotel; basic standards of bathroom and bed, and terms for the season. He was alone, free, and had money. He quickly became bored with the palaces whose food was expensive, pretentious and unimaginative. Gambling bored him too, and dark stuffy bars drinking indifferent alcohol in sullen gloom, in the company of three businessmen and a dejected whore or two. He found other poles of attraction.

A little bistrot called the Bar Mimosa but more often Chez Cri-cri. He was from hereabouts (originally named Christian) but had made money in the palaces of Nice or Cannes, before the war, and acquired the 'cuisse provençale' in the shape of an Antibes girl known as La Maria, now a middle-aged lady with a buxom bos. Cri-cri is short, fat, bald, lazy. Maria is just the first two, and the Bar Mimosa would be trailing bankrupt in the dirt but for her cooking. Instead of the greasy mussels and frites, or the boring sole-in-white-wine, she gives the local fish a southern brio. Too much tomato to be sure, too many olives; Maria is too heavy with lemon juice, but garlic makes the mayonnaise digestible, on the whole her hand is light, and she has learned honest, simple dishes to content her Belgian man; rabbit stew and carbonade, gibelote and matelote and waterzooi. One didn't want fish every day. Not even Walter. And beside good beer there is good Côtes-de-Provence red, white or pink as the fancy takes one. No comparison with the Belgian-Beaujolais of other places, sugared Bordeaux, the dreary muscadet that haunts every estuary from the Scheldt to the Loire. The floor is tiled, it is fresh on the hottest day under the awning, and a big bullied girl known as l'Ostendaise washes the smells away with many buckets of water.

Cri-cri is nocturnal, appears at lunchtime spoiling one's appetite with his sickly aftershave, and the daytime barman is Jan, Flemish oaf, with raw bones, harsh features, metallic hair, but inventive, intelligent. His speciality is to speak all the languages of Europe and mangle every one into a villainous kitchen, like an Antwerp whore at home with anything from Norway to Argentina. He likes Walter, who can parody this art. Together they talk Vlaams, Walter's polite and stilted Dutch in comic contrast to the frightful West-Flanders patois.

It was a hot morning, everyone on the beach and Jan drinking coffee: he consumed enormous quantities, to Maria's disgust. And sure enough the radiogram belting out 'Airmail Special'. This morning the news was that the Big Claus, a waiter at the Bristol, while drunk had ridden his Roller (the Vespa scooter has captivated Europe) down the boardwalk stark naked; and Il Cuocco from the Isola Bella threw a fillet-of-sole knife at a chambermaid.

"Should have been with us, Walter – I tell you, when she saw the Claus running his underpants up the flagpole even la bella iocchi was crying laughing." He has heard of 'la bella iocchi', a waitress with – presumably – lovely eyes, notable for a virtue much assaulted by Big and Little Claus but conspicuously intact.

"Whyn't ch'come out, t'night?"

"I might. Why not?"

"See y'at the Dolphin then. Round nine?"

"Maybe. Look the dollies over." He had never much taken to the pubcrawl. When drunk got sick and hated it. But a Flamand earthiness is needed to disinfect Jesuits, bruxellois fust, Spanish schoolboys' collections of dirty pictures – just occasionally.

The Dolphin was a cheapish hotel at the 'bad end' of the

bourgeois quarter and would be nothing much without its great feature, which is a large courtyard at the back, and in the centre of this a large and beautiful tree – a rarity so close to the sea, it must have grown in the shelter of the buildings. The owner realised that it was a valuable property, built a circular wooden bench around it and hung lights in the branches, showing a greenish dappled light. The trestle tables down the sides are those of any beergarden, but on the hotel side is an area tented over with canvas, and two or three tables served by a waitress from the bar inside, and this waitress is la bella iocchi, whose real name is Manuela, a girl from the village.

It is a privileged area (known as the Midnight Court) for not only can you drink outside even in wet weather but the space between this and the tree is kept clear, to dance: there are loudspeakers on the branches and the barman puts records on the player (this is Glenn Miller country). The tables on the squalid side collect sticky stains, too rarely wiped by a slut with a sour rag, but Manuela is a hard worker who keeps her domain spotless, has flowering plants on the terrace and lays the dust with a sprinkler in dry weather. She works for a pittance, but is well tipped. The table under the tree on that side is the best. You might get twigs or bird-droppings in your beer but you get her service, and her smile. She has no day off, for the season on the North Sea is brief, and like everyone on the beach she must make her earnings carry her the year round. Her apron pocket is heavy with silver and copper, but also with anxiety, for her parents are poor, she must turn over most of her gains, and if the season is bad there will be no new coat or shoes, when winter comes. But you see no anxiety or fatigue, for she is young and healthy.

On her post at the corner of the terrace she looks taller than she is for she is long-legged, and holds her shoulders back. In this light her clothes are seen to be clean, and not seen to be shabby: an old black skirt and a white blouse that comes sensibly up to the neck and down to the elbows. On the hottest evening there will be no sweaty or unbecoming display of breast or armpit. Oh yes; Walter's memory, so hazy and misleading on most occasions, is here intact, exact in the minutest detail. Manuela. Ichabod. There is no going back. But he cannot stop memory from speaking.

She has the healthy complexion of a girl who lives by the sea and is much outside, but is scarcely tanned, for her skin is fair, and she has little time for the beach, during the summer. She has the width across the cheekbones that characterises many girls along this coast: the jaw has a full, shallow curve while the forehead is often narrow, and the eyes fairly small between the strong ridges of bone, giving a piquant, slav look, often very pretty.

Few people, probably, will ever call Manuela very pretty. She is handsome, certainly, and of course she has beautiful eyes. When you sit under the tree, with time to look about you (Walter has come early, about eight, so that if he does not like the look of the dump he can skip, discreetly, before Jan or any of that gang appear) you see her clearly. She has been at work since seven, and has 'done her mise-en-place', but the evening has scarcely begun and she stands loosely unselfconscious, fingers absently turning the small change in the pocket under her apron. She is not thinking of anything at all.

Indeed her eyes are beautiful. They are large, and in larger orbits below a finely modelled forehead, and the brows (un-altered; she wears no make-up) have a natural arch. The lids, creamy as magnolia petals, are deep. There is the beauty of serenity in her look, of balance, of innocence. Her nose is straight, undistinguished, her mouth quite good, the lips well-drawn. The unsentimental observer, which Walter is not, might think that care will pinch that mouth. It is tight at the corners.

In those days only a few bourgeois wore sunglasses. The light upon the North Sea is sharp, the wind is tiger-fierce: the eyes narrow and the more Manuela's. At twenty she has sunray wrinkles etched upon the temples. The eyes are sea-coloured; quite often blue and more often a surprising green, but most often a sea, a North Sea grey. Walter will understand after seeing her parents. Her father has those eyes, in immense orbits, but his are bright blue, the bluer for the reddened face – at the eyes' corner scarlet. And her mother's mouth has vertical folds on either side, like a worn-out purse whose metal armature snap-shutting pokes through the eroded leather. But her grey-green eyes had once lit up and gone blue in joyous sunlight, now for many years trapped in cobwebs, dead butterflies dried.

Colonial wives, when posted to stations in hot climates,

would advise the newcomers that the men had a tendency to get on heat after too much beer and curry but 'if they exaggerate give them a flip with a wet towel' and Manuela – without having thought about it – has a similar attitude. There are in any case few occasions to give anyone the flip with the wet towel, for the simplest reasons: during work one is too busy, after work one is too tired, and at any moment one offers no provocations. Sorry, but the midnight bathing party isn't on. Jan and Claus are neither the hooligans they pretend to be nor the glamorous figures they would like to act – their assignations with bourgeois wives, tales of midnight escalades, concealments in wardrobes and lurkings on balconies exist mostly in their imagination: there are swaggerings and a pretence at cosmopolitan sophistication in the patois of italianised French and talk of the Côte d'Azur, of Antibes and Saint Trop' but they are just the village boys, such as she has known all her life.

Since, as Walter had discovered, one cannot hang about doing nothing in a place where everybody works, where the comradeship is that of shared work, he found work (elementary skills, quickly learned) and enjoyed it. Nor was it only adolescent romanticism that he should fall – a free fall with no parachute – in love with Manuela. At twenty-one he had never before enjoyed the comradeship of a girl. Manuela's quality, worth, were there to see. She was transparent, and shone with a clear light. It does not ever enter Walter's head, and this is not particularly to his credit, for it is simply the way he was brought up, that she is 'working class', a half-educated fisher girl. If he had thought about it – he didn't – he would probably have thought that he had enough education for them both. Gandhi, in a dhoti, was taken to tea with King George V. 'Weren't you embarrassed' he was asked 'at being improperly dressed?'

'His Majesty had enough on for us both'. Which shows that ease of social manner and a sense of real values go together. Some sense of humour will help. Winston Churchill, speaking of the "half-naked fakir", shows his own vulgarity.

There is a party, of course, at the end of the season, and Walter dances with Manuela, and the melody is 'Perfidia' and it isn't Humphrey Bogart and Ingrid Bergman; it's less of a fake, and there is no romantic cliché because romance exists and is never platitude. And they all go for the midnight swim afterwards. Walter the lecherous beast might have entertained notions of skinny-dipping, exhilarated by her unbuttoning her frock, and under it she has a bathing-dress as it was still named, one-piece, of impeccable propriety. She digs her bare feet into the cool sand and says 'That's good' and then says 'Run'.

Walter has told himself that when the season was over he would be going to a theatre and working at it this time because work is something he has begun to understand. And if you want something hard enough, you get it. The first of these good resolutions is defeated by the second. More than to be painter or designer or actor – fatally, he has not made up his mind between them – he wants the girl. Fatally, on a still, misty autumn days, he takes the train.

Of course for old times' sake he went to Maria for a meal, found it dull and squalid, the cooking perfunctory and there's nothing to talk about with Cri-cri. Jan and the Ostendaise have gone home. The tents are shut. The yard of the Dolphin is piled with broken chairs and beer crates (most of the winter work on the beach is carpentering and painting). The professionals have gone south, owners to 'catch a bit of sun' in Mallorca and Madeira, workers to the city hotels for the winter season, or the ski-resorts of the Alps. Locals met with are strangely sour, with no more than a nod or a grunt – Walter does not yet know what a jobless winter is like, on the North Sea coast where there is no industry. Fish? You kill yourself to get it, and when you've got it nobody wants it. Boy, it's cold out there, and stormy. If you have your winter's coal paid for – think yourself lucky. After an hour's slouching about he took his courage in his hands and knocked at the door of the little clapboard house, in the crooked streets of the old village, built of bricks driven into the loose sand.

He was received courteously; was asked to stay to supper. Nobody asked his intentions. Manuela was sewing, in a battered chair too close to a stove that he found much too hot for the small, crowded room. She gave a smile at seeing him but said little: a show of concentration upon the licked thread and the eye of the needle. He was offered coffee in a big flowery cup; strong, sweet, milky. He made her parents laugh with Bruxellois jokes: when her father takes the cigar out of his mouth and the large blue eyes crinkle with amusement he is struck. When

94

he ran out of topics he said "Like to come for a walk?" and she said, "I'll get my coat," and he felt embarrassment at the unexpected loud noise of the lavatory flushing in the thin-walled little house: how bourgeois he has become.

'Walking out' with a village girl!

It was the first of many. He learned too to love the cold wind on the beach, the narrow paths through the dunes. What did they talk about, wonders Walter now. They were happy.

He desired her. Her resistance to any sign of inflammation was gentle, and unyielding. And if they had wanted to make love, where would they go? The North Sea coast in winter is not encouraging. He may kiss her.

One of the big hotels has stayed open. There was little business save at weekends when the casino opened: residential old ladies and retired colonels. Two waiters and one cook; the piano-player in the bar because he is cheap, old, crippled. Not like the one in *Casablanca* but he plays the tune for them. The first time he took her to dinner she was shocked at his spending so much money: shy; poised. Sometimes they took the train to the city: cinema, restaurant, café. A great treat. The childhoods were the same; the thirties, depression. But talk of poverty in Touraine was not the same as poverty, in Belgium. What had he ever gone short of? The bread-and-marge-and-cocoa, clothes turned and returned: these are Walter's first lessons in socialism. A sentimental education.

She likes, in a restaurant, a glass or two of wine; a beer, in a café: in the snobbish bars she takes with enthusiasm to pastis, to a cognac. Once or twice he tries – rather ignobly – to make her drunk: she never becomes drunk. And when he does, through sheer frustration, she remains the same, gentle and patient.

He talks. Probably, thinks Walter, I never stopped. Blithering about art or music. She knows nothing whatever of either. Listened happily to the nonsense he spouted: perhaps it was entertaining. She has never read a book. But with books it is different. He gives her books and she reads them from the first to the last, careful and serious; and gives her opinion naïvely, but it is worth having: thought out with much good sense. She would make a good doctor, or a good magistrate. Her judgments are firm, about things or people.

Coming one day to pick her up he found her father alone

'keeping house' and on impulse asked him out for a drink: the old boy is kept pretty short, and accepts with alacrity, cheering up in the man's world of a little, old fashioned café in the village, and after one gin they were getting on famously, Dad showing off his English in antique phrases. 'Down the hatch', and at any minute he'll say 'It's a long way to Tipperary'. The second gin loosened Walter to the point of saying abruptly "I want to marry Manuela, you know."

"My turn," said her father, signalling with his finger. Glou-glouglou went the bottle softly. The thick little glass brimmed with the oily aromatic scent. Cards shuffled and snapped at another table, with thumps and grunts. "Why not?" The bright blue red-rimmed eyes were steady and shrewd. He licked the gin off the brim. "Need a job though. Right? . . . Can't count on me. Can't count on anybody, this world . . . for the rest – that's a very decided girl. She once makes up her own mind, no budging her off it . . . best be getting home. Or the wife will be marching in. Smelling me breath . . . Get a job," in the street abruptly. "There's enough already here, who are without one."

It was late in the year. A week or so still to go to Christmas – he was feeling guilty, Walter remembered, at not having been 'home' in a long time: poor old Ma; he'd have to make an effort, for Christmas.

They had been at the 'Victoria' – she was used to it by now and not intimidated, making jokes with the old pianoplayer when he teased them – 'I can't get started'. And the barman is used to them too; leaves them in peace. It was late at night and they had drunk a good deal: she was as usual but Walter lurched momentarily upon meeting the fresh air, and she giggled. It was coldish and clear, with a little starshine, but the wind westerly. They did not take the quick way home through the village but as usual, over the beach and through the dunes.

He snuggled, and to warm his hand slipped it inside her coat (she had bought the winter coat, and a good one: it had been a good season.) He kissed her under the ear and she laughed and said, "Don't tickle."

Never had he even got near undoing the frock (dark red wool, little round cloth-covered buttons). Slightly pathetic surely that these should be the details imprinted upon memory, and not the electronic code to a bank account? On the other hand (suggests Walter) the consumption of girls – mm, one must hope that this may be a little less conspicuous and just a little less flavourless than eating a hamburger outside the Museum of Modern Art. The white cotton bra is familiar, hung out to dry. Not, though, in these circumstances.

Since this all was force-of-habit he was taken aback when the policeman's hand did not budge. Much more taken aback when the hand did budge, for then it undid more buttons, reached in and slid the strap off her shoulder.

"That is what you want," said a voice, highly matter-of-fact. And it is time, Walter, to abandon this joky defensive tone. Self-conscious? He is conscious above all of the memory of pain.

The rough wool of the overcoat, chilled, dampened by sea-moisture and unpleasant to the touch, would today still strike an acute contrast to the living silk inside it. Can one come anywhere near suggesting the keenness of torment, the living edge of delight of what has become the banality of every beach? How lucky for us males of whatever age to have this crude biological constitution, that a barebreasted girl never quite induces boredom.

Walter lies upon cold dry sand, slippery and unstable. He tastes the inside of Manuela's mouth. Her teeth bump against his. It is an exquisite agony.

He twists, trying to be less wooden: she often tells him to be less wooden. She is supple, and humble, and thinking of nothing but of giving. It must be an odd discovery, that the adult male, large of bone and muscle, hard of jaw and raspy, dark of smell and fierce of breath, should thus come again to be baby and wish to lie at her breast. To equate Manuela's innocence with ignorance would be ludicrous: apart from bulls and billygoats she is acquainted with homosexual boys and girls and the most she would say was that she hadn't taken to either with enthusiasm. To underestimate Manuela's purity would be obscene.

"There," she said gently. Tit is for babies. She is unselfconscious about her own. They are decorative. They are occasionally an annoyance. It is tiresome that the boys should be obsessed with same. Her nipples are small, fine, and erectile. This is now a matter of some small pride.

As for Walter, he is twenty-one. He has been to bed with

97

maybe a dozen women. He has not learned how painful a state is peace. The pain was acute: he gripped her waist angrily and made her gasp. Taking hold of the hem of her frock inspired a sort of terror. Assent is more to be feared than denial. Forgotten now too – forgotten? – is the complicated geometry: the horizontals of stocking top, the verticals of suspenderbelt, that ridiculous metal clasp and rubber button. Flower petals still do exist, and the texture of a girl's inner thigh.

Manuela's abrupt movement was for her unnaturally awkward. She pushed him violently away, in the same muscular effort struggled to her feet and stood flatfooted, ashamed, not knowing what to do. Walter in a turmoil crouched. She stood bewildered, dishevelled, her breast bare in the pale light on the silver beach and a dark unknown sea. Her face white and strained. Perhaps he mumbled something. He raised his arms in despair, put his hands on her hips, on her bottom, made a monstrous effort and dragged at all that stupid elastic. She put her hands on his, but it was to tidy. The housewife's instinct is the strongest: it was her only good pair of stockings. She did stand a moment to be admired, but lay down at once again. Stupid thing. Idiot triangle. "You'll be more comfortable now," she said idiotically (not very comfortable about the satin lining of the new overcoat).

This curve the hand fits to perfection. Hand-polished, silk-perfect – axehandle, rifle-stock, bow. First line seen, first ever drawn. Magic, and sacred curve.

But, and that is the horrible part, for Manuela cannot, she does not know how, the wretched fumble with buttons; absurd, and humiliating fact that the girls' pants are easier dealt with than his own: an enormity.

Too much for him. (Walter, on the hillside, feels the tenderness in his temples, beneath his fingertips.) He is trying to be gentle; he cannot bear the thought of forcing her. He was too tense, he lost it. A hoarse, harsh shriek and he clenched himself against her but too late. Fury and burning shame scorched him. Is one never then free of pain?

Manuela stayed still; solid, anchored. "My love," she said softly. She put her hands to the back of his neck, on the nerves: her fingers press and release, on his spine. "I am here." He lies shivering, uncontrollably.

In every man's life there will be . . . but there is no telling: each man must judge himself. The slope of grass and weed and field flower (tiny, exquisite) is unchanged: the smoke from chimneys rises as tranquilly. In his own life Walter can find three, four such moments of hideous self-disgust. There is no stopping the mind once it starts. One must go on, the whole way.

But this is not such a moment, at which the soul shudders. Here is nothing ignoble. A boy and girl commonplace of inexperienced overtension. The 'fiasco': we have all known it.

To him a moment bitter to recall because the turning was missed. A path that could have been followed, and was not: an opening wasted, and a great prize thrown away. The scar is painful still, pain reaching in to the bone after all these years of adulthood. One must grip oneself still, breathe slowly, wait in resignation for the pain to ebb.

Manuela pushed him gently off her. He lay in the sand clenched double (a body scorched by fire that causes the tendons to contract: the pathologist's term is 'fencing position'). She climbed to her feet slowly. "I mustn't have a baby," she says. Her pelvis sticky, assoiled, with the mess that is him.

The pain is lessening and he recalls the many women he has seen washing: moment of great beauty, subject beloved of every painter. This is still a moment of vividness beyond most, when the pupil has swallowed the iris and it is no longer dark but smoke of pearl and opal. Aphrodite coming out of waves is called anadyomene; what d'you call her entering them? There are not really waves: a stilled and gentled North Sea around Manuela's bare ankles: she has tucked her skirt up in a housewifely dread of salt water on the wool. A slim bottom, long shapely thighs parted the easier to stoop and cup water in her hands. A biblical stance and a biblical act. Spilled seed. A Rembrandt drawing.

The pain is gone and there is nothing left now but the shrill acridity of regret. Ichabod. No going back. So easily he could have gone back. In convalescence, the pain of the childish humiliation was so trivial. A bee-sting, a pique at an imaginary loss of self-respect. Manuela would have thought nothing of it. To him he had stolen her honour, his own. Such foolishness. A tiny step, and he had brought her happiness; and himself.

A year or two from then Jacques Brel wrote a poem, of the same bitter regret, addressed to another Vlaams girl.

'Ay, Marieke, Marieke – le ciel flamand . . .'

Six weeks have passed. Boy-like he had drowned his pain, throwing himself headlong into a new fascination, a new passion, to still that small, simple, innocent voice. The name of it is Sylvie. She is a girl of the bourgeoisie. So much easier to recognise, and predict. She has honesty; and honour. But she knows how to handle men.

He is madly, foolishly in love, and his mind is in a frenzy of irritable excitability. He would be capable of anything; however idiotic. He does things that are worse than idiotic. Among them, a vile crime.

He is in the Central Station of Bruxelles. Where do they propose to go, and what to do? – he has no longer the slightest idea. And what can it matter? Sylvie was late again. She always is. She is to this day, and being late will cost her dear one day. But not yet.

He is pacing up and down in nervous tension. There is a passage there between platforms, and a squalid little coffee-shop, with a smell of stale dregs and sour dishcloths, of unwiped tables and slogans written on walls. For lack of anything better to do he looks through the swing doors.

Manuela is sitting there, straight upon the mean chair, nobly profiled against a shit-coloured wall. There is a half-empty cup of coffee before her. She is quite still, her hands folded in her lap: she looks out in front of her, but what is in her eyes and in her face? – one cannot tell. One can see only the free, pure profile.

Walter stands outside the door. How easy it would be to walk in, to sit down opposite, to hold out the hands. Nothing need be said. No drama, no sentimentalities are at all asked for. I have no job. But marry me.

He who hesitates. He who plays the coward plays the whore. A lot Sylvie cares about his having a job! A bourgeois family. Tja, one takes risks. One goes up and down. One is rich, one is poor. Work? – hell, one can always get a job: that is nothing!

A tap of high-heeled shoes, contriving to sound indignant.

"Oh, *there* you are!" said Sylvie's voice; amazed at his stupidity; and as if he has been keeping her waiting . . .

Ay, Marieke. And where are you?

As with Touraine, so with the north coast. There is no going back. Too many bills left unpaid. From Zoppot or Norderney on the German sea, to Deauville or Cabourg on the French side of the channel there are too many young girls, in flower.

*

The coming round – as from an anaesthetic: moment of unreality, unfocused: the enormous blurred shape hanging menacingly above one, resolving into a face at first monstrous, then fleetingly recognisable as Sylvie before again dissolving: the normal speaking tone that is a great booming shout and instantly a faraway thready whisper. Why on earth am I on the floor? To be unconscious is a toxic state, and dangerous. Do not shake me; please let me sleep.

A dream of Amsterdam. A city Walter enjoys, as one does a place known for nigh on forty years, tasting the changes and the unchanging and relishing both: canaille city still and cattiva.

But is it still as it was then. Has he not disinfected all that? – as with a North Sea beach. Surely he would no longer shiver, at certain times of day looking uneasily about, lest a turn of the screw show him something he would rather not see. Something had gone wrong with time: had he been, a moment ago, transported somewhere else belonging to these far-off days? Le Touquet, had it been?

There is noise all around him: the voices of Amsterdammers. An obstreperous crowd, defiant of law and contemptuous of regulation, violent and talkative and for ever noisy. Noise was judged by different standards. True, the narrow streets echo to a racket of trams and dustbins, a perpetual clatter of crosstalk and backchat but there was neither the widebodied Boeing above nor the widebodied Diesel below. There were hardly any cars at all, funny little potato-shaped trundle-autos of the time before the flood. Grey-suited, sober-hatted collar-and-tie Ministers of the Crown arrived at their offices, unstrapped their briefcases from the crossbar and bent to take the clips off their trousers. In the courtyard of a big city hotel there were three cars parked. One was the manager's, and he lived outside the city, and was Swiss into the bargain. One was the lounge headwaiter's Beetle, and everyone knew they got rich through bribes. And one was Walter's Citroën deux-chevaux, conferring some prestige but less than his known eccentricities, of which this was only one. He could easily have bicycled and frequently did, for Sylvie liked to drive about (a woman driving attracted stares, but Sylvie attracted them anyhow). He didn't have far to go. They lived like everyone else in the warren of the old city, in one of the tall narrow houses like storks that had steeper narrower staircases than anywhere in Europe: if one had any furniture it was hauled up with a rope outside and heaved through the window.

Sylvie and Walter lived in a third-floor front; plenty of light (the deux-chevaux lived on the pavement amid bicycles and handcarts). They had a big living room, with rush-matting and rattan cane furniture – like most of Holland – warmed by a cast-iron tortoise stove: likewise. Commercial travellers had cars but even the wealthy bourgeoisie had no central heating. They had a tiny kitchen, a tinier bathroom and that was a rarity, and two small bedrooms heated by leaving the doors open. It was quite a long way up, though nowise sous-les-toits, but one was used to that. Outside the window was a 'spionnetje', like a rear-view driving-mirror, fixed to the frame and angled to oversee the street. Everybody had one. You could see who rang at the door, catch the baker and the milkman on their pedal tricycles – and everything else that went on.

Walter's hours, like everyone's in that damned business, were punishingly long, ten in the morning to ten at night with a three-hour break in the afternoon, and Sylvie was much alone, but two tiny children kept her busy. She disliked too much neighbourliness, the dropping-in and gossip over coffee cups that was such a feature of Dutch life, but there was anyhow the barrier of their both being 'strangers': the outsider might think a Dutch-speaking Flamande would not be much of a stranger in Holland, but you'd be surprised. A 'funny accent', but also her individual personality and style: her exotic clothes, her odd way of doing her hair, her striking blonde looks; almost vulgar if redeemed by ladylike ways in public.

Amsterdam, however, cosmopolitan city, was tolerant of foreigners and indulgent towards artists, and Sylvie combated solitude and boredom by having many friends of both sorts. Walter was not gregarious save at work, and his wide acquaintanceship among French cooks, Italian waiters, souteneurs and

102

undesirables, was not seen at home, but Sylvie swam happily among intellectual fringes, and since the children kept her largely pinned to the house, she was hospitable to a gang which drank tea and brought beer, lent and borrowed books and gramophone records, played with the children and paid for the odd meal by doing the washing-up. Walter liked a bit of quiet, of an afternoon, to put his feet up and potter about, and by an unspoken agreement they were then not much seen, but on his free evening, by something of a tradition, there were generally three or four of the gang, often with their wives or the girl-of-the-moment, and the most intimate might stay to supper, and if in funds they might all go out to the pub for an hour while somebody stayed with the children and a book and the radio turned low.

They didn't have to chat. Some were compulsive talkers – like Walter – and would argue endlessly on all the usual subjects: some liked quiet and would write up a journalistic effort, fiddle at some contrivance in silence while Sylvie knitted and drank endless cups of tea – they liked the warmth (chilly-Sylvie keeps the stove humming) the peace, the domestic scene, children on the floor with a toy. And she was happy, with the company.

One or two, for they had both a soft spot for a painter, would often take a piece of paper and begin to draw – a child absorbed, a woman counting stitches, or the cat. Most were torn up as worthless but many sheets of cartridge- letter-, even wrapping-paper survived with pencil, crayon or sanguine chalk, and some are there to this day in odd corners of Walter's house: a charcoal of handsome mop-haired children, a skilled if rather mannered Indian ink of Barbara elegant and hieratic (she bore a slight resemblance to Queen Nefertiti here breast-feeding a baby), an overworked but pleasantly Bonnardesque interior on a sunny afternoon and Sylvie in numerous poses of thought or work.

An assiduous member of the gang was Jan, Polish-Jan because there were so many Dutch-Jans; handsome, tall, perpetually smiling so that it looked insincere until you noticed that his lip was scarred with a slight sardonic twist. He was not a very good painter, though he had undoubted talent, and a most undeniable skill at selling his work – and as usual the easiest-selling the most meretricious. He talked well, in much funnier-accented Dutch than either Sylvie or Walter, but he was funny 'sowieso' with a sense of the ludicrous that made him an Amsterdammer by adoption, as it were by right. He was better still at not talking, at doing nothing, but his hands, craftsmanly shaped, were skilled with mechanisms and he was always to be seen mending an alarm-clock, freeing a rusted lock. Mechanisms melted apart, were carefully examined, if small through a jeweller's loupe he carried in his pocket and stuck in his eye: bits were worked on with one of the small tools that lived in his jacket: oil, and tiny metal shavings and filings got under his fingernails and Sylvie said, 'you have to buy me a new nailbrush'. It became a game, for Walter has a thing himself, drilled into him from early childhood by his father, about hairs-on-the-collar and unpolished shoes: one is one's own valet, had been one of that old gentleman's precepts. Sacred allegiance is thus owed to clothes-brush and shoe-brush, and Jan is forever borrowing both, and one doesn't know whether to be glad or sorry. If it were to stop there . . . but Sylvie, not being Dutch, is no lover of housework and is slovenly about cigarette ash. Jan never needs prompting – quite the contrary – to get the dustpan from the kitchen and brush-around-the-stove. And when they penetrate the sacred studio (it is nothing of the sort; Jan lives in a prim little apartment in a distinctly bourgeois neighbour-hood: in the hallway are three doormats and a smell of floor-polish) – yes, all the paintbrushes have been meticulously scrubbed and stand in clean jamjars.

He loves to drink, and tiny glasses of gin stand about ready to be sipped at. He loves the children, and from small round logs of ash has constructed a train: splendid locomotive with a big boiler and three lovely trucks all handrubbed and given three coats of pale varnish. Trains are a thing, indeed, and he paints many pictures of crossing, intertwining tracks and spidery patterns of the power lines overhead. Deserted stations with empty platforms – why are there no people, where are these trains going and where do they come from? Strange, obsessive and secretive creature. He has a girl, rather nice, funny great mop of black curls, always known as 'Gypsy' but seldom seen – 'on her knees polishing the floor all day', says Walter.

The year before Walter married Sylvie he had looked at the bank account, a thing he did as little as possible, and found the nugget dwindling unpleasantly fast. And one had to have a job.

He had been on the Coast, at Cannes. A sentimental memory had come up of another Jan? – big Claus or the cuocco from the Bella Vista? Vaguer than that. Countryside of the tourist business, and much of it too on a flossy scale. Why not have a shot? – Sylvie encouraged him in this – 'I like you in formal clothes'. He looked all right, he supposed, and he'd had some education even if he couldn't add up. Presented well, and he spoke the languages – and he felt at home in that world; it suited him. Why not? What does one need for hotel management anyhow; what does it take? You need only put on the good suit, polish your shoes, see that your fingernails are clean, and go and ask. Palaces all over – the Ruhl one way and the Negresco, the Hôtel de Paris the other, the Carlton and the Martinez right across the road. And the same answer everywhere.

'No difficulty. You can do it two ways. The hotel school at Lausanne . . . can't manage that? – too expensive? – well, you can do it direct. I can take you on as stagiaire, unpaid of course, but you get your food, lodging if you want it, an allowance for clothes eventually. It would be hard work, you know. A year in the kitchen, a year in the salle, then housekeeper, control, front office, conciergerie, reception, bar, the last year in the back office. Not much point in asking whether you've the talent for that. Five years' hard. Costs me nothing to try you out for a month: start you tomorrow if you like. All right,' scribbling two lines on a piece of memo paper, initialling, 'take that to the chef, page'll show you – get him a page' to a silent underling, pale in formal clothes – would that be him, in four years' time?

And Walter was lucky in his first chef: not of course 'the chef' of the kitchen, who was not just grand and unapproachable but by universal consent a proper bastard – but his 'chef de partie' or department head, a man in love with his work, and who loved to teach it. And brutal though the kitchen was, Walter found that he liked it. Even if the first two months were simply army drill over again, do it fifty times and do it on the double, and it wouldn't have surprised him in the least to be told to scrub the square with a toothbrush . . . (Jan will be borrowing a toothbrush any day now – isn't he getting to be too much, just a little too much of a housefly?) . . .

But finding a quick pupil, quick as little Johnny the apprentice, a lot quicker than slowcoach Danny the piccolo, brighter than either, better all round than that Gerald (on a 'stage' from Lausanne . . .) he began to take Walter seriously. And he was a good man: among the best I ever had, thinks Walter now, and I've seen plenty . . .

Waiters he disliked, the arrogance less than the servility. He had not yet learned Ludwig Bemelmans' classic summing up – 'all cooks hate all waiters' (and the converse) – but he quickly decided that he could only take the restaurant from the customer's end. Rougher, harsher, hotter, fiercer the kitchen might be, but not more painful. And after his year he decided to go on. In a way he had to. He was married by then. There was a living to earn. Sylvie would have worked – but with a baby . . . sloppy, that. Milord, she would say in after years, and she wouldn't be joking, was too high and mighty to bother about little details like giving a woman a baby.

He had been well trained, and those first four years in good houses had given the small boat a push into deeper water; and when a good-sounding job came on offer in the city of Amsterdam (a nice town, and both spoke Dutch) he had gone after it, got it.

Not as good as it sounded, not by a longish chalk. Too much politics, too many little jealousies: he had too little experience of the world's ways. Walter was a good technician, having discovered (to his own surprise) that he had the tour de main, the 'natural hand'. He was a highly, perhaps over-conscientious worker, taut and unrelaxed. Rather too anxious. This new, added anxiety was one he could well do without.

A phenomenon applied then, and it still applies today, that the ambitious young man who is anxious to climb in his profession does not take into account. The troops when ill – and even when simply lazy – stay away from work: the officer, who is responsible for that work, must supply the deficiency and discovers that he himself has not the right to be ill. The management will view his little chills or pains with no favour.

The hotel, or restaurant, is a Victorian invention. Before the nineteenth century there were only inns, some good and some bad, and all easy-going. The business to this day is imbued with the moral beliefs (in hard work, devotion to the cause) and puritanical standards (work is its own reward) of the time. An evangelical mentality. The young man today, entering this delicate and interesting business after five somewhat wearisome years at the hotel school in Lausanne, during which he is buoyed up by the religious belief that this is a Camino Real, royal road to the top of his profession, discovers to his consternation that the top of the profession is a rarefied air in which – for another twenty years – he will be expected to work without stopping and especially when everyone else is on holiday or 'en fête' and that seventy hours a week are the norm. Walter who was just a cook has never in his life worked less than sixty. It is a sly irony that now, when he is a distinguished elderly gentleman of liberal persuasion and left-wing as a matter of course, union talk of thirty-five hour work weeks gives rise to sarcastic snorts. For every state functionary, tranquilly awaiting his pension, can look forward with placidity to thirty more years of an untroubled conscience. One need not feel surprise at the commercial chappy, who lives in fear of the morrow, taking to extreme right-wing views: when the company computer sneezes he catches pneumonia. Walter who had private reasons for badly wanting just one day's diplomatic indisposition found it hideously difficult. A slight case of anal prurit wouldn't do. While taking pains to get ahead with work; one must not arouse suspicion.

An acute go of lumbago would do the trick. Walter knew exactly how it takes one. He stayed for most of the afternoon in the quiet kitchen making chicken stock into chicken velouté and that into sauce suprême, and hoping fervently that he was making a fool of himself. And at half past five of a foggy evening, after telling a cook that now there was nothing to do but watch the customers eat the stuff he made a dignified exit at an angle of seventy degrees from the ground. The back door man was sympathetic about the difficulties of getting in to the driving seat of a deux-chevaux under such circumstances. It is a strange sensation for a cook, being headed homeward amid the throng of office workers on their way home. The classic spectacle of streets flooded with Dutch bicycles whose peculiar high and dignified build made the spectacle comic and impressive:

energetic pedalling in this position brought a bobbing, swaying movement of the body: a field of wheat rippled by the eternal westerly wind. But Walter did not have far to go – to that salient of the antique city where the Brouwersgracht meets the Lijnbaangracht. And parked what is called a stone's throw away: far enough for the noisy unmistakable sound of the two-horse to be inaudible in the street racket. He went upstairs quietly, not expecting anybody to be at home, but taking precautions, like a prudent householder.

No, there wasn't. He had left a phone message with the corner greengrocer. As one did, thoughtfully, when kept at work. The question now was to work out how long it would take before anybody was at home. It wouldn't be all that long. Because of the children.

It hasn't changed all that much hereabouts. More cars, and traffic lights on corners. But the problem is the same. Live up here and you're in the old city still, and in one of its most awkward corners. To cross the centre you can do one of two things that to this day have almost equal disadvantages. You can go around the ring, by the dreary Marnixstraat and the wide but congested boulevard of the Stadthouderskade. Or you can tell yourself that a straight line is a shorter distance than the circumference of three-quarters of a circle. Then there are thirty humpy little bridges and as many narrow alleys where a bicycle propped up carelessly will block your progress. And you must cross all the main roads that open like fingers from the palm-grip in front of the Central Station where all the trams stop, nuclear point of the traffic. For Jan – doing rather well for himself – lived over the other side of the Amstel, beyond the Waterlooplein, in the comfortable district that surrounds the Artis gardens. By either route it will take a longish time. Walter was in a fever the whole way. A foolish fever. Wouldn't he have done better to stay at home? But the moment when one wishes most to know; isn't it the moment when one knows already? On a vague principle of 'middle way is safest' he chose the Prinsengracht, and had so often his eye on the other side of the canal where the traffic went in the reverse direction that he had three extremely narrow squeaks from knocking over an old lady, a foolish typist and a man carrying planks – what were these imbeciles doing on the roadway?

108

And parked comfortable and tranquil, arrogant and shameless, is the green Volkswagen. Rather rusty round the lower edges. But Jan is going to see to that, just as soon as he has time left over. From adulteries.

Walter did not want to lie in wait in this street of a thousand eyes behind lace curtains. But he had, with each moment that passed, fewer choices left him.

And he knew the wait could not be long. Sylvie had always her mind clear, the clock of her day well organised. Say or think what you like, an excellent mother, whose sense of responsibility towards her children was at all times sharp; by day or by night always alert to leap out of bed. And there was a sense of hustle now as she came half-running out on to the pavement, supple and light and with a heaviness too – was that imagined, that movement at once loose and weighty like a cat walking away from a saucer lapped empty?

The traffic now had quietened. Instead of the Thin Bridge, home by the Blue Bridge across the Amstel and along the Singel. And Walter glued behind, the whole way. The two accusing eyes of the deux-chevaux could not be held menacingly upon the Volkswagen's rattly rear end. The road was too uneven for that. But he had the satisfaction – a dicey word: satis means enough; is it thereby to be equated with content? – of seeing Sylvie turn quite often, to stare in puzzlement at first and very soon in fear at the hound dog, her eyes dazzled by the headlamps glaring in the wet misty air, the uncertainty turning a vice upon fear, so that she spoke urgently to the placid figure of the driver beside her. Which shrugged: why fuss? It's the same problem as the police have all the time. They may know. But can they prove anything? So shut up, and keep your nerves quiet.

Walter did not, does not forget this journey. There was a numbness first. And then anger. He put his hand up to rub his mouth; a feeling like pins-and-needles, traced to a rictus of vengeance anticipated, cruelty whetted. But before they even reached the Muntplein it had leaked away. He was not talented – he was not skilful enough for the cunning trade of cruelty and vengeance. He could have taken a knife quick enough, there on the pavement had he been out of the car and standing ready – why had he not thought of that? He has always been too quick to imagine consequences, and this holds back an already leaden

109

arm. He didn't like knives: used them too much at work. A cook does not fear a knife, but he has learned to respect it, having learned that through pain.

This was not a pain, long before reaching the Brouwersgracht he knew it, at all like the sting of a knifeblade. A crippling, laden ache. A lumbago that is not lumbar. A paralysis as though by curare or some such drug, of the solar plexus, of the nerve-centres. A great labour in breathing; venomous pains lancing through the gut. And time to feel a deadness mounting towards the heart, the mouth drying out. Like Socrates after drinking the hemlock? But that was said to be painless. This is not.

Walter collected himself before getting out of the car, slowly. Whatever – he was by now frightened – this was, one did not let it be seen. The flow of adrenalin enabled one, even, to behave quite normally.

Sylvie was turning her flutter into a great show of talkative concern.

"But darling, how hideous – you must be ill – I see it, you're overworked – and you came looking for me – oh dear and I'd no idea – I'd offered to help painting the flat – such a mess – turpentine – can you get up the stairs – let me help you . . ." It trailed off. There must certainly have been a very odd look about Walter's face.

"I need no help." Voice coming out dry, but quite controlled. "Yes, I am ill. Yes, I am about to go to bed. No, I need no doctors. I wish to be left alone." He did not glance at the man, who was busied with earnest study of the rust spots on the Volkswagen, but the message was not lost. An intelligent animal. And, moreover, a highly self-protective as well as self-seeking creature. Not at all inclined towards worrisome encounters with nasty-minded husbands.

Irony was coming to Walter's help. A nicely legal phrase had occurred to him – shall cognisance be taken of the said occurrence? The Marquis de Montespan created an alarming scandal at Versailles by driving about with an enormous pair of horns affixed to the front of his carriage (that, between the headlights of the deux-chevaux would look rather fine) – and the laugh was definitely not on him.

But one said nothing. He looked from one to the other of the shuffling pair. They'd taken cognisance, all right. He took out his latchkey and began slowly to mount the steep, narrow Amsterdam stairs. The pain was an immense, dragging weight.

He got into bed and lay cramped until warmth gathered round him and bit by bit he could stretch and come to terms with the hurt. It was no longer on top of him, crushing him: after all he could hold his own. And then it ebbed slowly downward, away from the heart, until only lumbago remained.

He could hear through the thin wall the comfortable small domestic sounds of Sylvie giving the children supper, washing them and putting them to bed, cleaning up and tidying; the quick light footsteps of the excellent mother and conscientious housekeeper. He took cognisance of that in the little room. The street sounds came floating up, familiar and kind.

Heartache. A heart attack. Why not? The notion is physiologically as exact as any valvular dysfunction. The word heartbreak attaches but only in cheap fiction; a foolish phrase. We are not discussing, hereabout, anything in the nature of a rupture: certainly not of the strongest muscle in my body. Somewhere over in the old quarter there was or had been a pub called The Broken Heart. Good name for a pub. But not for me, nor my house. We will sleep now, quietly. Peacefully? Is that a word which could be admitted? – mm. Well, I dare say.

He woke, a little, two or three hours later, to a small glimmer of light, the small rustle of Sylvie slipping on her nightdress, the tiny jolt of her sliding into the narrow bed, making herself small, trying not to move, trying to keep her breathing noiseless. He grinned a little, and there was only a moment's recurrence of pain, small and easily controllable. Why should not whores sleep as peacefully as anyone else?

Sleep. Tomorrow you must work.

The episode is chiefly to be remembered now, thinks Walter, for a conclusion of genuine dramatic irony. For something like ten days later he got a real attack of lumbago, and most unpleasant it was, hitting him at work and at a busy moment when in perfect innocence he bent to pick a pot off the floor. Leaving him absolutely helpless. And next morning there was the Director making a long face and saying that one made every possible allowance but this was a bit much, you know. The sack. Bleak. It hit him quite hard, at the time. But there were other jobs.

111

Other cities. Other countries. One had a lot of heart, in those days.

Sylvie made no murmur, never hesitated, was always and would always be resolute. Was he not her man? And wherever he went, whatever he did, she would not complain but would follow. A moment of mourning for her green plants. A little like Walter's complaint about how damned heavy books were when considered by the shelf-full, and what a pity to throw them out.

PART TWO

Day One

To Walter, swimming up out of sleep, there came the dis-
orientation which attends a morning after; a strange bed; a
nightmarish conclusion to a day of strain and effort and movement: a distancing in time as well as in space.

His eyes took in dawn, broadening to daylight: where the hell
is this? He had been in Amsterdam, in bed with Sylvie. He sat
up, to look at a sleeping figure wound in bedclothes. Right
woman: wrong bed.

Rain trickled on the panes of a half-opened window: through
the gap came a strong, pleasant smell of wet foliage. He had
slept too heavily; he had been dreaming. The King had been
drunk and flung a gold cup out of the window. He had gone
down to search for it among rain-soaked bushes. Night: the
Princess is reading in bed, a sad story which brings tears to her
eyes. And the Knave sidles along the passage, slips the key to
her room into the lock.

It is not a dream but a memory: it is the poet Conrad Aiken.
It has got muddled with another memory, of rain sounding on
the windows in childhood: his father teaching him an antique
Spanish cardgame. The Master is the Knave of Hearts –
Quinola.

Quinola had tapped him on the head! Nothing much, he had
been stunned, unconscious for probably no more than a
moment. He remembered feeling sick and Sylvie's face, sharpened with anxiety, bending over his, looming large . . . and
then the pale, clever face of the Knave, thinned and bleached
by a few weeks of prison.

Walter lay down again more quietly for he was beginning to
understand the telescoping that had brought these events
together in a muddle into his sleepy half-consciousness.

This was not Day One at all. This was the dawn of Day Two!

113

Day One had been full of startling happenings, and he had better collect his wits.

It had started outrageously, in bed with Miriam Lebreton. Perhaps that had brought forward a memory he now pushed resolutely away into the back attic of his mind; the cutting, burning memory of trying to make love to Manuela, on the beach . . . A night in a country hotel, and here he was in another, a couple of hundred miles away. They were in the Landes! And the day, properly speaking, had begun with the Knave. What had the Knave been up to? He had told them. He thought it a pretty good joke!

For the Knave, it was unlike other days with a change in the routine of the local House of Arrest. 'Right, let's be having you. Smarten up a bit today; you're for the Palais. Clean shirt, clean socks: here's yer razorblade, get a move on.' And after all the elaborate byplay of locks and keys and body-search the three of them – the girl produced from the 'women's side' – found themselves in the yard, being hustled into the back of the blue gendarmerie van.

A shortish drive to the Place of Justice, and as they were dismounted in the forecourt and the rigmarole of handcuffing began before bringing them up the steps, he was aware – not sleepy, not apathetic, not him – that there were three of them, and only two escort gendarmes. The other two were cuffed to the one – one to each wrist, while he had the other to himself. As they were pushed and bumped about one dropped the key and swore mildly, and he was swung with his mouth on the girl's ear and whispered quickly 'I ask to go piss, say you gotto take a crap, right?'

"Not so much chat there," shaking the chain in reproof.

"Just saying hallo to my mate," humbly.

"Okay," she said, blinking her eyes in understanding as she was bustled up the steps, under a pompous portico, through the stony echoing hall and up the stairs, round and down the corridor of the offices of Judges of Instruction, and plonk down on the wooden bench to await the judge's pleasure and their lawyer's arrival. Lebreton was away for a couple of days, she'd said, had to plead some place but the devilling local black-gown would fill in. They knew the routine by now, though it was the first time they'd been taken together. Endless stretches of waiting and yawning but anything was preferable to the boredom of 'home', in the early hours.

"Ey mister. Mister, sorry I got to take a piss, I'm bursting."

"Whyn't you do it before starting?"

"Didn't have time with all the hustle hustle."

"Me too," whined Jo at once. "My bowels are all loose from those goddam beans every day."

"Yah ya," irritably. "You take them both, Max." Fumble with keys, rearrangement of – and he kept the key in his hand! Jo for decency had to be let free to rush into the cubicle while he got stood up against the urinal, yawning gendarme boredly looking at graffiti above the level of the greyish old tiles – and they were alone, alone. He had a big thing of shaking himself down and struggling with a stuck zipper, and got the gendarme with his knee in mid-yawn and mid-crutch, and as he went limp got his hands up and thumbs on the carotid arteries squeezing. 'Jo – Jo' in a frantic whisper, and between them dragging the semiconscious guard into the cubicle, bolting the door, dumping him on the seat, getting his shoes and socks off, tying him, gagging him with his socks – good, the shoes were a bit loose but fitted, that's better than his sandals. No pistol, damn it, in his holster.

"Sshh – I'll watch – you finish tying him, get the belt round his neck," and slipped quickly out. But he didn't watch – he bolted. Let Jo look after herself. He didn't need her any more. And she was unreliable – too violent and brutal; couldn't keep her head. Walking quietly, gazing at doorways, as though hunting for the right number he turned the corner: interminable passage past the tribunal of Grand Instance, judges' rooms, clerks' room, witness rooms; at last another corner, back stairs down, no one and he could run, and the door out to the back parking lot and in moments he had melted into the crowd shuffling along city streets, just another anonymous shabby young man with nothing on his mind, in grubby jeans and a faded pullover and the gendarme's wallet in his pocket but hell, precious little money. He had to get out of this city quick, wanted no trams or suburban buses. Don't know this town much but – an arrow on a lamp-post said 'Gare SNCF' – the railway station. There was not much time. Discovery would be in seconds. The alarm, cumbered by a prisoner and a groggy guard and a right panic, would take five minutes, and another ten before getting relayed; he had a quarter of an hour. Christ, this boulevard was interminable. He broke into a run, slowed it to a deliberate walk, could not stop himself breaking again into a jerky movement of run-three-steps-walk-four – but there at the end he could see the station. Always cops there in front; take it easy. What was the first train on the indicator? Foix: where the hell was Foix? But take a ticket, matey, won't do to be caught without, getting yourself noticed, remembered. "Foix single," praying he had the money but he thought it was quite close – somewhere there down towards the Pyrenees.

Not even a proper train – suburban 'micheline' but he'd made it, he was out of this stinking town and he had time, now, to think. Pyrenees – could he make it over the frontier? If he had a map. And then suddenly he had an idea.

"Stupid git!" yelled the gendarmerie sergeant. "Mugged in the shithouse like a greeny, standing there sleeping with the key in one hand 'n' yer dick in the other, what's the matter with you then, oldest trick in the fucking book. I'm delighted he strangled you, I wish he'd put yer head down the pot 'n' pulled the plug on it that I do. Oh well – it's only a tearaway."

"One tearaway more or less or even two," said the lieutenant gloomily. "Nix general alert, fuck that, looking even more charley than we do now, dear-dear we got rushed in the palace bog and will you please help us find this naughty man we've lost somehow. Good bloody riddance, put our usual to the brigades and the autoroute detail, country patrols and watch trucks for hitch-hikers but it's a dead loss. Comes from Paris no? – that's where he'll head for, natch, slip them a telex, three weeks more or less and who the hell cares?"

"What's all the noise?" asked Madame Claudine Rivière irritably. Her clerk went to see, came back sniggering slightly.

"Prisoner managed to do a bunk from the lavatory – one of ours too, the boy and girl from the jewellery snatch and the country house series –"

"Well, we've plenty of work and be grateful it's lessened, a tiresome affair, that – go straight on to the next and we gain time."

116

Still, something at the back of her mind stuck there all day; but it was evening before she caught it – something to do with Miriam Lebreton, a woman whom . . . tricky customer into the bargain – "Geneviève, get me the gendarmerie barracks would you, Captain Cardenal – thank you – Captain? Rivière at the Palais: this boy who got away, it so happens I'm instructing that – yes, outside my door. You know your own business and I'm not about to teach it you. A grain of information for what it's worth and if you think it likely – I'll leave it to your judgment to evaluate that. One of their exploits was a house up in the hills – yes, that's right, owned by the man who took up an amusing attitude – you've probably forgotten . . ."

Captain Cardenal was cross. They'd picked up that girl quite quickly in the town, arsing about not knowing what to do, and she'd been considerably vexed at being diddled by her ex-boy friend there, but it hadn't been a help, in fact it had been nothing but a red herring, the boy was the bright one, likely enough a dangerous one, and he was the one they wanted. He listened to Madame Rivière.

Walter feeling the tender place on the top of his head with a delicate fingertip decided that no great damage had been done. Physical damage. That is. He went and sat on a chair as though he had just come in from a long walk and wanted nothing better than to get his boots off. Your head hurts or your feet hurt – what odds? He felt no anger, and no fear. It was the arrival of something long known, long expected. Earlier, one got frightened, as usual by one's own imagination. That pain, of disquietingly long standing, can that be a cancer by any hazard? – and when sufficiently worked up by alarm to go see the physician the reassurance one has of course been seeking comes at once in a gust of laughter. My dear man, we're all like that: a touch of indigestion and we all think we're dying, hohoho. Run a couple of lab tests shall we, just being super meticulous?

By the time the silly fellow rings up to say there's a little anomaly in the tests there which he's not quite sure of, and it might be clever to have a second opinion – aha . . . Understand one another, shall we?

117

There is something that has come to an end, and that is this existence proper to a retired bank manager. Going for a nice walk every afternoon with my dog. Walter had often been aware of cutting a comic figure: it was a thing the children made jokes about. The entertaining contrast between Mr. Stiltstalking, dignified but wooden, not to say pompous; and his dog's loose easy trot. When I lost my dog I should have understood quicker.

His massaging finger came away with a tiny smear of blood. Something heavy of metal, with rounded angles – but angles. Like a spanner. He looked to see what had hit him. And there again . . . he'd known already. That it was worse than a mistake he had always known, and why he hadn't thrown the thing away long ago he had always wondered. You'd almost say he'd kept it just for this moment. All these years. Bought long ago; when young and silly; possibly when a bit drunk. The idiotic convention of it's-as-well-to-be-secure, living in an isolated country house. Covering one's idiocy by telling oneself that it was for Sylvie really; a reassurance if she should be alone upon occasion and feel nervous. Sylvie had never touched the thing, being a sensible woman refused to lay hand on it. 'What earthly use is that?' Slightly snubbed he'd put it away in-a-safe-place, and being Walter forgot where the safe place was. It turned up around once a year, generally when one of the boys was rummaging around, when they took it to play with, alarming him; so that as soon as they got bored he put it away in another safe place.

The police had been pretty easy-going about such things in those days, where respectable householders were concerned. And he'd yielded to a caprice the way men do, seeing a toy and fancying it.

'Self-defence?' asked the armourer indifferently, barely pretending he didn't know why people buy arms. 'Let's see your hand.' Expert thumb and finger felt his forearm through the sleeve. 'You're built light – you'd be around seventy-five kilos?'

'Just about,' mumbled Walter, ashamed of being so light, ashamed of the five pounds too much around the belly. The man with his priestly air opened a drawer, considered the contents.

'Mistake all amateurs make is looking for too much gun,'

118

enjoying his own expertise. 'Nobody'll look at a vest-pocket model now. Even a woman wants something to look impressive – well, it's her handbag, sez I. Truth to tell anything under a seven sixty-five, American thirty-two, isn't serious, but if you're serious, what I say is being overgunned is as useless as something itsybitsy. Tell you straight, sir' – a skilful salesman – 'some fat-boy walks in looking for a big magnum I'll tell him straight out, at the risk of losing the sale, but that's my professional conscience.'

At least I'm not calibred as being fat-boy, thought Walter.

'Revolver or automatic? – you'll leave that to me, good – the non-professional . . . now this will suit you very well. Good German weapon, simple, well-made, nothing elaborate or cumbersome, nothing to give trouble. End for end, fifteen centimetres including hammer, height eleven. Nice and flat, three wide at the butt and two at the barrel. But a satisfactory weapon, good stopper. Eight millimetre calibre, eight in the magazine, weight with that aboard, six hundred gramme. Nice grip, good spur below the hammer. Take ahold, sir, fits nicely – ah, you're left-handed but no real odds.'

'Uh?' understanding nothing.

'Ejection chamber's to the right,' patient with imbecility, 'safety to the left under the right thumb. No harm. Semi-automatic, single or double action, pull a bit stiffish deliberately. Right, sir, take a good look in the mirror – come come, that's the man in the moon in jeopardy there; you've been watching American television, relax your wrist, point it like your finger, firm but not clenched – that's more like it.'

'Here to learn,' humbly. And Walter wondered now whether this young man shouldn't have a lesson from the armourer. It hadn't been loaded – certainly was now . . .

'Quite right, sir, only cowboys think they know it all. Now there's a couple of dummies. To arm – hook your fingers on the knurled grips there on the breech, safety off, snap the action back – that cocks the hammer as you'll notice, let the action return normally. You've a cartridge in the breech of a cocked pistol, that's death. Be so kind, sir, don't point it at anyone, even me, ha ha, dummy or not.

'Very good, sir, I'm satisfied if you are. Work the action again, cartridge will eject; go on till you're sure your magazine's empty. Here's a box of blanks, to get you accustomed. And this is the real thing. Take that down to the range sir and fire it in, get it well in hand. Lethal weapon there,' paternally. 'Barrel of eighty millimetres, accurate to say twenty paces, quite normal for a non-professional civilian weapon, all the more reason not to forget that a bullet finds a billet. Right now, certificate, guarantee, tampon, my signature on your licence – that's thirty, fifty, hundred, many thanks and good morning to you, sir.'

Walter was out in the street with a smallish cardboard box. Eight millimetre Commander, six hundred grammes, blued steel, saw-check walnut grip. He wouldn't call it a pretty object. But harmonious; well-proportioned and balanced. Simple, efficient. Useful too, we'd call that.

Useful for what use?

Lethal weapon. We speak of a lethal dose, a lethal impact, and now anyone who jumps upon fat harmless Walter will have made a lethal error.

He remembered: he stopped dead in the street; a man bumped into him; there was an irritable look, an irritated word; does your mother know you're out? Careful Jack, or I'll drill you.

For two pins he'd have gone straight back, slapped it on the counter and asked for his money: he'd been chatted up . . . Too late now. Never ask a man to look foolish in cold blood.

And now I look a lot more foolish. And it's by a very much longer way too late.

He threw a rueful look at Sylvie; she opened her hands in despairing impotence. The boy caught the look and grinned.

"She had it hidden away. But she told me when I asked her nicely."

I'd rather not know, thought Walter. And you were there comfortable in bed with Miriam Lebreton. Serve you right . . .

"Stop waving the thing about, then." It was an altogether new voice, petulant and unpleasant, with a shrill saw-like note in it, familiar to Sylvie and to the children but not often heard outside; a voice of complaint to the servants that the puppy has done it again in a corner of the room, and it brought the boy up short.

120

"Put it away, in your pocket since you insist on having it, but I'm not having guns waved at me in my own house, least of all."

"Forgotten have you? – I do the ordering about."

"You do no such thing," said Walter testily. "You're a total dead duck, at best a lame duck sitting there waiting for the dog to pick it up. You break jug or so I presume, and the cops are after you; and all you can think of is to pop up in this hole where there's nowhere to go, imbecile that you are, which is one of the first places they'll check." And had the satisfaction of seeing the boy look taken aback. The morning-Walter was a very different cup of tea from the jaded harried shadow of last thing at night. There are moreover mornings such as everyone knows, when everything is cross-threaded. You get soap in your eye, drop the towel in a puddle and spill the coffee, which tastes revolting anyhow: if unhappy enough to catch sight of your face in the glass you will be still further put out. This was not one of those days. He had slept well, felt comfortable within his skin and was on excellent terms with himself. Now that the worst, long expected, had occurred, he knew where he stood; there was nowhere to go but up.

"Alone, are you? Where's the other great lummox, and that fearful slut you trail about after you? Whatever idea you have it's stupid. Standing there with that potty pistol waiting for fifty cops with carbines and tear-gas? This house is approachable from all sides – has about five doors – and there's cover at the back. How did you get here anyhow? You were probably noticed by half the village."

"Took the train and hitch-hiked," sulkily.

"Fellow's down at the gendarmerie telling them all about it this minute."

"He isn't then," nettled, "because he's from the village back of the hill and thought I was one of your sons, he said."

"Heaven forfend," conveniently forgetting that he had thought the same thing himself, once upon a time.

"And I took care not to be seen getting up here – I came through the woods and did it real quiet: your wife got quite a surprise," maliciously, "you think I'm thick in the head and you've a shock coming. You have anyhow," tapping his forehead, "capito?"

"Yes, that's almost exactly what I think," said Walter conversationally, sitting down, making himself comfortable, crossing his legs, feeling for a cigarette, patting his pockets for a lighter, adrenalin at full gallop. "You've just as much liberty as a fly in a cobweb; you can jig about and that's all. You've exactly two choices. You can shoot me, and then you're worse off all round: a homicide charge against you on top of the rest, and you haven't even got me to help you. My wife is myself you understand? – I'm solid with her. Or you can trust me, meaning her too. And then it is barely possible I could do something to pry you loose. Highly problematic but conceivable, maybe: depends how much time we have."

"To shop me, yes."

"Listen to me, I don't want to call you lad or junior or anything to diminish you, what's your name?"

"Fernand," sulkily, anew taken aback, telling the truth.

"Fernand! That is the first tiny clue to this personality. That old-fashioned honest peasant name. He's ashamed of it, would rather be called something he thinks snappy, like pop-singers. Johnny Rotten and Sid Vicious. Our Gang! Typhoid Mary and the Head Knockers.

"Listen, Fernand," quiet, "and don't let your mouth rob your ears. To shop you would be the last thing to come into my head. You tied me up, yes, and came on with the heavy menace, pretended to burn me with a lighter. You stole some stuff of mine and bust up a lot more. And you know what made me sorest? An old clock that belonged to my grandmother and an old typewriter I'd used for better than twenty years. I got over that fairly fast. My wife stayed embittered a lot longer because this is her home and that's part of a woman's being. And you killed my dog, and that was hardest of all. Follow me when I say it's because of all this, as well as in spite of it, that I, good, I won't be so arrogant as to say I'll help you. I don't know that I can; I'm inclined to doubt it. The hardest part may be persuading you against the odds that you can trust me.

"Keep the gun; I make you a present of it: I hope you'll come to see that the best thing you can do is chuck it away, but keep it for as long as you think it's of use." The animal sitting there with what is known as a knitted brow: try again.

"Have you or have we any chance of getting out of here?

What's in your mind? – let's try that for a start. Anybody want some coffee? You hungry? Anything you want to eat? Maybe the best thing you could do for a start is have a shower. You look pretty grotty. I've nothing to fit you but we might find some gear of the boys that would come closer; it's worth trying."

"You're going about it quite a clever way, trying to put me in your pocket, and you better make your mind up I'm no lump of sugar that melts in a cup of coffee, when I want to eat I'll eat and don't need no kind lady coming with a sandwich, and make up your mind to this, mate, when I decide to move out it'll be in my time, on my terms, and you'll walk in front and do as I say, and the gun behind you. You've a big mouth now but with one in your kneecap or up your arsehole you'll sing a very different song. And the coffee I could do with so the two of you move into the kitchen and hump it. Drink some yourselves, I've no objection. Just so's you know, chatting me up's a waste of breath so keep the lid on, and when I want info I'll ask for it. Nicely like I always do, recalling I might go nasty if you let off too much wind."

"It's midday now and we're wasting time and we've none too much of it and you sit there chatting about kneecaps like you think you're the IRA, there's plenty of them and there's only one of you, mate. Know where I was yesterday? Had a talk with your advocate. She's got some head on her shoulders and saw what you apparently can't, that I would do what I could to get you out of this hole you're in. We might not get you the whole way, but any port in a storm. Didn't you listen to her? I suppose not, you listen only to yourself and that's not clever you know – digging your own hole deeper: I ask you again, what d'you think you can do?"

"Out and into Spain and with the two of you on each side they can't stop me, and after that maybe I'll ditch you in the mountains and maybe I won't, and making yourself small will be the best guarantee you've got of your own skin, and now shut up and make that coffee: I don't drink so you can't get me pissed."

"Fernand, do understand simple facts of life. We aren't at all far from the frontier but anywhere in this province it's such an obvious move that it's exactly what they'll expect, indeed the

123

first thing they'll think of and you haven't a prayer. Second you're French and if I'm not they'll still see me that way and I'm talking now about the Spanish. Do you know that seventy-five per cent of them hate our guts? You'd last about half an hour.

"And a Spanish jail would have you thinking kindly of the one here, as the place where they bring you breakfast in bed of a morning."

Sylvie had still not said a word: reached out and took one of Walter's cigarettes; made a face of it before sticking it in her mouth. He looked as though seeing her for the first time. Her pullover, in a loose knit of an irregular, perhaps hand-spun wool, had a high wide collar that flattered her figure, taking the emphasis off a heaviness around the hips and jaw. When dressing that morning she had brushed out the long hair that was still the original ash-blonde, and pinned it up into an Edwardian sweep which tumbled down before long but looked very nice while it lasted. The pullover was a greenish-brown, much the colour of a Havana cigar and almost exactly that of her eyes.

The young man played with the gun, snapping the action and deftly catching the copper-jacketed cartridges as they were ejected, in mid-air. He slid the magazine out and packed them afresh, in a finger movement recalling that of a man tamping a pipe. Big hands, strong and good-looking, artisanal. The silence became heavy and seemed to irritate him. There was a rough snap as he jerked the magazine home in the breech.

"All right, mate – since you find it hard to learn – maybe we'll tie you up again. You look good that way. And give missus here some physical exercise. She might like it, and how about showing you?" She punched her cigarette out slowly, chin down in her collar, watching her own hand. Walter felt himself fortified in his new-found placidity.

"It needs no underlining." Since he was expected to say something. "Me you could kill. Her you could rape: it's obvious. At this age there aren't many surprises left, good or bad. It would make you more nervous. Like drinking. Get you killed quicker, since you'd get more and more reckless.

"We have three boys. They're around your age. I feel respon-sible – answerable – towards them, plenty of ways. I've had to learn to keep my mouth shut. One finds it difficult to accept:

124

they paddle their own canoe. Mustn't go preaching them a lot of good advice they don't want. I've been making the same mistake with you. Do as you please. Do whatever you like. Learn your own way. Your pigeon – fly it."

Sylvie had had three children. All boys, which was somehow typical of her. A pity not to have had a daughter, 'though it might have turned out like me' as she had once remarked with irony matching any of his own efforts. One at least was his – strongly observable hereditary traces of grandparents – and two equally markedly hers, though one said, one had to admit with relief, that he had not known her parents at all well and would gladly take her word for it if she detected resemblances, and two other sets of grandparents one hadn't known at all, and one would remain unperturbed about this particular gap in knowledge.

For this biological stuff about 'one's children' could be overdone. They weren't 'one's children', like so many brown-paper parcels. This business of the possessive pronoun was hideously bourgeois. My nailbrush, and our packet of soapflakes, and everything getting treated as though it were portable property. The strong family feeling that led simple people to speak of 'our Jack' and 'our Lucy' as they did of 'our mum' – now that was quite proper. But children aren't 'mine': one didn't have any title in them. Nor does any piddling government. No Ministre de la Guerre, the jelly-bellied flag-flapper, is ever going to point any finger at ours and say come die for your Fatherland. And one had never had any kids. Nor even kiddies.

He missed them, nowadays. All grown up and taken wing. He had been, he supposed, as tyrannical, insensitive and heavy-handed a father as anybody around. And a delight had come his way, drifting on the wind as light as a dandelion seed, that had been as sharp and painful a pleasure as any he had ever known. Perhaps the loveliest present he had ever been given. Just the other day . . .

A telephone call. The youngest (by a long way the most violent and difficult, and utterly hateful, of the three). A great rawboned chap with the build of a rugby forward – second row, a jumper – big square head, four-square Flemish looks: Sylvie's father had been an urbane, polished, silver-haired and business-suited version of the same physique, with rather over-much liking for gold jewellery and immense American cars. Sylvie's lover of considerably more than the moment was an entertaining personage, a good drinking companion if an undoubted hooligan, so that one imagined him as the entrepreneur in shady business deals, sitting in bars with a strict eye to the girls working the pavement, with a calculating machine behind the humorous eyes notching up every trick. Under this influence Sylvie was filled with expertise in getting things at cost, paying no income tax, and – but no, that all gave far too simplistic and superficial a picture. There was a whole side to him that made the flesh creep, of snobberies and social climbing and vulgar luxuries and unmentionable rogueries (he owned a little metallurgy workshop that turned out phony antique coins and bogus medals, swastika badges and SS daggers) but he was too sensitive to let it show, and too tactful ever to be a house fly. And all his good stories were those told against himself. He had much simplicity, admired and envied Walter's inherited ease with head waiters, and would say earnestly 'Look, d'you take the band off your cigar, or leave it on?'; or appear with knotty problems, about the right address to use to a viscount, with a candour both real and assumed; so that like all complex persons he was interesting and not merely a hypocrite.

And the child was complex: heavens what a bundle of uncontrollable violence, hypersensitivity, outrageous meanness over tiny details (hating to strike a match or lick an envelope) while of a generosity still more outrageous in everything of moment. Walter hated, loved, and valued this cuckoo's child. What was one to make of a monster that loved flowers and tiny birds but that would kill you a pig without turning a hair and ran a secondhand car business amid shady associates – with a medieval sense of honour.

"Pa?"

"Meself. That's a nice surprise." Nothing had been seen or heard of this boy for months. "How's life then?"

"Oh – okay," evasively – what a boring subject! "You all right? Health good? Mama all right? Oh that's fine, fine. No-o, nothing special, just thought I'd ring. Taking the temperature, don't you know?"

"Tja, nothing ever happens here," with almost perfect truth. "Work, you know, and the garden, and a quiet cigar now and then at sunset." This was the only one of his sons who would suddenly say, 'May I have a cigar?', generally at the oddest times.

"It just occurred to me, I've heard you speak of that pianist you like who was in prison a number of years?"

"Ah yes, because the generals took a dim view of his preaching Bach to the natives."

"Happened to see that he was giving a concert in the town and wondered whether you might like that."

"Many thanks; I'll look out for it."

"Well, it's tonight as it happens."

"Oh dear."

"So uh, bought a coupla tickets 'n' thought praps you'd let me invite you. If you haven't anything better to do that is; flog them again easy enough I dare say."

"Nono, good god, I mean yes, of course, shit, I mean I'd be thrilled, what a lovely idea, whereabouts, in the big palace, can I meet you outside?"

"Why don't you pick me up at the flat, say eight, no, a quarter to, we could have a drink, 'n' afterwards maybe we'll eat something – if you felt like that?"

"Enchanted," said Walter, cursing himself at once for using a word that never sounds sincere. "Look out for me then. Tot ziens," for talking Dutch with this one was a sort of code. "Did you want a word with Ma?"

"No no, give her my love. Tonight then." Ting . . . Children! How old was that one now – twenty? Twenty-two already, after some laborious arithmetic. Now that was not expected.

Children, his or anybody's, were a lesson, the best and maybe the only good lesson to peoples in how to deal with a minority in their midst, of Arabs or Turks or whatever it happens to be. Since a child is always a minority.

They had been his, all of them, from the moment of their birth and he meant moment, since with them all he had been there with one couldn't say help so one had to say anyhow moral support while Sylvie managed the giving birth, a thing she did well and without affectation.

'Bit of head there, appearing upon the scene.'

'Oh good. Ouh. Enormous head. Jesus.'

'No, not Jesus, or not yet, anyway.' Wiping her face, with a hanky soaked in eau de cologne.

'Don't let me push too hard or I'll split my kipper. There – is that better?'

'Good seat in the saddle there.'

'Good Flemish mare you mean, good Flamenca cow. The wrong everything else but the right hips. O what hard work, travail is the word.'

'Boy again – here, have a look.'

'Oh god, what a horrible huge beast, darling, listen to that frightful voice, give it to Nurse and push my tummy, there's all the nonsense still to come.' The hard worker, and the good craftsman.

Perhaps he was a complaisant husband. But not, one hoped, complacent. This child you have given me. I take responsibility. It comes from outside – another horsain, another forestiero.

"I'd like this one called Manuel," he told Sylvie.

At a quarter to eight on the dot he was ringing the doorbell. Always punctual, Walter. This boy was the same.

"Like a beer or something?" Touchingly, he had a half bottle of champagne on the table.

"This is going to be good," meaning the evening, too.

Simply the name of this pianist tells you he is going to be good. His name is Estrella. Look that up in the dictionary and you will find it says star, lot, or fate; and he is all three. His given names are Miguel, Angel. It is extremely agreeable, thinks Walter, to go to a concert given by Michaelangelo Star. He is a little man, with a most gentle and beautiful face and a comic, ducklike walk so that sensibly he wears a dinner-jacket. When he sits, and concentrates be becomes illumined: he is at all times a star and when he plays the light becomes transparent.

Lovely programme: Mozart and Bartok, Beethoven and Liszt; with Mozart he is perhaps not quite totally right but one is not knowledgeable enough to know why, and the others are right on, and he is generous with encores and there is a Chopin impromptu that enrapts and a Schubert fragment that goes straight to heaven; and at last for fun and because they shriek he breaks into his saint's smile, and does the tiny Argentine tango that becomes bigger and bigger and bigger.

"Hungry at all?" growled Manuel.

"Very. Was that nice?"

"Yes, yes," not saying. Walter to whom a concert was plain

intoxication and who was apt to become maudlin, had forgotten that one would drop dead rather than show emotion, at twenty. And had hastily to cover up with chatterbox nonsense about other pianists with a comic walk, and where shall we eat-I-leave-it-to-you.

"Know of a place that's fair. Mean I know more that's lots worse." And drove the car, a dilapidated Alfa-Romeo, terrifyingly through the narrow streets of the old town, so that Walter was at once much afeared and quite relaxed: it would be quite a good moment to get killed if such were the Lot. They did not get killed.

Manuel's suspect associates were Italian, and Walter found himself eating pizza that was very good, getting a great deal of service from a pretty waitress and seeing pretty quick that it wasn't on his account, and drinking the Rioja that Manuel ordered, knowing that he liked it.

Nothing is more difficult, in life as in fiction, than to express simple emotions in unselfconscious simplicity. The writer trying to convey physical love, and finding himself making daisy-chains laboriously to be wreathed around Constance Chatterley's quivering cunt, throws his pen down in disgust like Byron's angel, and blood and dust upon the page is a great deal easier to handle than sex: in the classic phrase, it is easier to put it in the lawyer's hand than to make it stand up in court. And that's only sex. Try doing a father–son scene some time – it crossed Walter's mind that despite a lifetime spent in reading fiction (he had been a tediously precocious child) he would be hard put to it to find a good one.

To succeed in being completely unselfconscious he would have given free reign to eccentricity – since reins strictly are only given to horses – thought by everybody else to be exhibitionism though it is no more than self-indulgence. Most to be found where most expected, in the haunts of the English frequented by the more arrogant among that singularly boastful people. Such behaviour, characterised by the ringing voice, the appalling loud laugh, and a peculiar lack of coordination in the limbs, may be all very well in Club Land but won't do at all in the pizzeria. Sylvie, accustomed to behaviour of this sort, would have treated it with easy-humoured tolerance. Walter's London publisher, a well-known exhibitionist, would have encouraged

129

it quite shamelessly under the stimulus of competition. Anybody else will be bored, save the age group between twelve and twenty-four which will be paralysed by extreme shame. With his two elder children, whom he knew quite well and with whom he enjoyed sufficiently easy relations of mutual respect and ironic regard, he would use laughter as a cloak for his affection. Manuel was not lacking in humour, but a serious young man, at a serious age, must so be met. However, Manuel had the gift, invaluable on boring social occasions like dinner parties, of easy conversation with the most wearisome partner. Manuel would never be a wearisome person – not named a gift of God for nothing – but didn't find the tête à tête the easiest of the evening's entertainments.

"No, nothing more to eat – very good pizza, that – can drink some more though. And you'd like a cigar." Says Walter.

"You aren't bored?"

"Stop being ridiculous. Look, this is a nice place but apart from that I'm being perfectly sincere and you know me well enough to catch me if I were lying, when I say I've never been in better company."

"Yes, well, I get nervous."

"You get nervous because I'm a perpetually dissatisfied person forever complaining. I've become a sour old sod because I'm dissatisfied with myself."

"What a stupid thing to say."

"Sounds like self-pity, right, but at my age one starts drawing up the balance and it's not very encouraging. I'd hoped for something better."

"I get a bit narked when I hear you talk like that. I know nothing about your books since I can't read them."

"Of course not; don't be absurd."

"But mumbling on like you were some kind of nut case irritates me. You get depressed when it doesn't come as good as you want it, so do I. Everybody tells me I'm a maniac, I don't care. You're a colossal bloody egoist, well we all are, and you're worst when you think you aren't."

"Am I now?"

"No. I like being with you very much. You're a bore when you start about being a failure."

"Wounded vanity."

"Probably," paying the bill. "Tell you this, whatever you haven't done you've made a damn good job of your children."

*

"Forget about Spain altogether," said Walter reasonably, "that's a wasps' nest if ever I saw one. Look at it from a cop viewpoint; you've got to try and get inside their head. On the grounds they were holding you before – you know it as well as I do, they don't even take a great deal of interest, you got away with it for I don't know how long, and could have gone on I don't know how long again if it weren't for that jewellers' shop. A hold-up but how many are there – ? – if they've got the knife out now it's on account of mugging the guard and tying him up in the jacks, that's saucy they think, so they're bloodthirsty. But for how long? Three-four days, while you're fresh meat here, and a telex at the top of the spike in another province. So get out of this department, in fact get out of France until it's gone stale. Italy maybe, but you stand out too much and all along the south coast – too risky. I'd say Belgium. You speak the language, you look right – and across France in that direction is not what they'll expect. Plenty of tourists from up there still around and will be heading north: looking natural, and the moment you're acting in a natural fashion no cop gives you a glance." At last he had the boy listening. You've got to give him confidence. Guns and rapes and beatings-up and smashing the place . . . a moment of calm even gave Walter amusement: I'm getting quite warm. It's the technical aspect of the job that interests one. Women don't see things that way.

"A Dutch tourist," said Walter, seeing himself as a Dutch tourist. A part he could play . . . and that would give Sylvie no trouble either. And – as long as he doesn't crouch there rigid, waving guns about (a thing Dutch tourists would not normally think of . . .) – but of course he could pass as my son. Why not? The others always have.

"A small Dutch car, of some commonplace type. Hell, my own would do, if it had Dutch plates." The chap was looking at him now. "That's the trouble. Changing French plates, I dare say you know all about that. But Dutch plates are yellow, and the letters–numbers system is different – no, can't quite see how we'd go about that. French car it'll have to be, and mine

131

would be too easily traced. So – now I wonder . . . Accounting for being away; that's no strain. I quite often do go away, and spend a few days frigging about in some corner, when I feel the battery is a bit flat." The remark, understood or not, aroused no comment. Fernand – surely an appropriately ridiculous name for a ridiculous personage – wasn't bothering about writers and their little ways: he had a new perspective.

"You're real strong on imagination, aren't you? Just don't let it run away with you."

"Yes, sorry," said Walter. "Professional deformation. But it's not stupid to plan, you know. I set up a hypothesis, a project call it, oh, call it what you like – if you don't like it knock it down. There's always the unforeseen. But on that account, foresee what you can. That way you get your temperature down. Less feverish."

"Shut your yap then." True. Gabble: explanations: repetition. Too much. All his life long too much talk, hesitating between no action and the wrong one.

Time to observe Fernand, who has put away the gun, possessed himself of Walter's pocketknife, and is playing with that, instead.

There is nothing abnormal about Fernand.

I'm probably more of a psychopath than he is.

The commonplace cliché of the police-court? 'Father unknown. Mother prostitute'. It isn't good enough. It never is, even when it's true.

Got bored with school. Not on account of being backward. Of being forward, more likely. His mistake, before, was to associate with the backward. Now that he's shaken them off he's more himself.

You can't fit these people into slots. The most you can say is that they're talented.

Yes. But what at?

They come from the wood outside. Like me.

Fernand is thinking too.

The countryside is full of cars. Hardly a villager who has not a couple of rusty old bangers for the odd jobs: himself and his wife. Hardly a French boy above voice-breaking age, out of the moped stage, who has not three or four; to be played with, cannibalised. They're to be picked up for nothing. (Nobody, in

France, dreams of roadworthiness certificates. They can't be imposed because they couldn't be enforced.)

A number plate is no problem. Off any junk tip. Faked up in half an hour. Car though, don't want an old wreck. Walter's is no good. Too easy – the moment the cops get here – and they will. Be signalled straight off, and the same applies, to anything I could lift around here. Change it three times and you're still only one step in front. Job like that can't be improvised. And you have to improvise.

The car unfaked, and bluff it through? Taking them with you. True what the fellow says: you're tourists, nobody looks at you. But what reliance can you place on him? Less still, on the woman. Across France, and awake the whole time? True though about Spain – the blue-arse fly will be thickly clustered on those crossings. You've won yourself a couple of hours' respite here. But that's maybe all it is.

This sympathy act. Pretending to be all cooperative. Well, I can do that too. Gain a few more hours, that way.

"I don't think it need be a problem," says Walter. It is always aggravating to have someone follow your unspoken train of thought. Holmes was in the habit of doing this to poor old Watson, who took it well. Fernand's sharp glance of annoyance and suspicion should have alerted Walter.

"I've a son in the business. One could always give him a phone call."

"What son?" trying the knifepoint on the wood of the table. "What business?"

Keep your temper, Walter tells himself: hold your brains together. If you're a forester look at the wood: don't just see trees.

"The son whose jacket you're wearing. Car business."

"No phone calls," underlining that with the knifeblade.

The train of thought is again clear. The second-hand car salesman is the prototype of crooked dealing. Stolen or smuggled, or simply totalled. Front end? – saw that off, glue the rest onto another one that took it in the rear! Everyone has their pet horror story, making Manuel laugh. He's the one who's honest – somebody was bound to think of it sooner or later . . . Walter hunts about, finds one of the little folders they leave around, saying 'Arturo and Manuel – Used Cars'. Arturo is the financial end. Had need to be, says Walter, since he has an immense Italian family of grannies and nieces and uncles (skilled mechanics). Fernand looks at it and says "Police spies." It is his natural logic.

"You please yourself," said Walter, beginning to be bored. "If you learn to trust me I can get you out of here. Trust my son, it's the same thing. What choice have you got?"

Sylvie made the difference. She had been in the kitchen making minestrone, like the good housewife she is, and came out now with her hands in her pockets and her obstinate expression, to say "Come and eat." Her eye fell on the business card.

"What are you doing with that? You want a car? To get Bogart here out of this? Dragging Manuel into the mess? As though we didn't have troubles enough? Let's keep them to ourselves then. Without bringing the children into it.

"You," aggresively at Fernand, "think yourself smart? Stuck up here in this neck of the woods? You've nothing to do but wait for cops to get here. Which they will. Between sooner and later. What do you do then? Use us as hostages to try and wriggle out.

"It won't work, it never does. They hold back, but they hang on your heels, they wear you down. You can't do without sleep indefinitely. So you'll be crazy by then, if you aren't already. Big drama then. You kill us, and they kill you, and that makes you feel better? Taking a few with you, isn't that what it's called? The vanity of it! The sheer stupidity of it! And so the senseless violence goes on and on and on. I do care for my children though," angrily at Walter. "Oh well, why should I bother? Woman-go-and-make-the-soup. So I have. Now it's getting cold. Eat it or not. It might put some sense into the two of you."

"Your nineteen-thirty gangster scenario," said Walter, eating soup, "– is there some parmesan? – is based on the self-pitying notion that he's all alone. Against the world. Exactly the mentality I'm trying to avoid. I ought to know, I've had it all my life. One has to try and break the vicious circle somewhere. He isn't alone. I'm in it along with him. So are you, if you were to stop and think for a moment."

Fernand said nothing. Filled his mouth with bread. Put soup in on top of that. It was good soup. He'd had nothing since

134

bread and margarine for breakfast. Jail coffee isn't always hot, but the thing it always is is weak. She makes good soup anyhow. Did he know it was a thought Walter had often had.

He looked at the parmesan and said, "What's that?"

What is he? wondered Walter. Where does he come from? What has he done, and where has he been, in these twenty-three or four years? The other two gave at least the impression of being straightforward dead end kids he had met with in some reformatory, on some street corner, in some slot-machine gallery – but it's of no real consequence since he has shaken them off.

Stupid questions, Walter tells himself. If they were put to me, what answer would I give? What are you? Where do you come from? What have you done? And I am over fifty years of age, and at that moment they're quite good questions. What purpose has he, what use is he? Or as a child would put it – 'What's he for?'

What kind of mind has he got?

One that functions only from the minute to the next and needs instant gratification? Or one that knows how to wait?

Suddenly Sylvie knows the causes of her unease and dislike of sitting at table with this beast in her kitchen as though invited – in her kitchen . . .

"Why did you kill my dog?" with a brutal abruptness that is both feminine and Dutch and takes the wind out of Fernand.

"I never – it was – no I –"

"Yes you did, you were the leader, you were responsible."

"Look I l –" his tongue trips on the word love, "like animals . . ."

"Better than human beings," interjects Walter.

"You said it. Less treacherous."

"They don't talk," said Sylvie, dry.

"You said it. Shut up. S'you talking about killing all the time, shut up then."

"Everybody finished?" collecting plates.

"Just be careful you don't say the wrong thing." He has still got Walter's knife, holds it loose in his right hand: with his left holds the spare ear-piece of the telephone. Like a bad schoolmaster with a ruler, ready to rap the child's knuckles.

"Manuel," says Walter into the microphone. "Pa. Listen, explain when I see you, cutting it short, you got a car I could borrow? As a favour. Something dead ordinary, Volkswagen or whatever. Just a bit bigger than ours. Little trip. A few days."

"No problem; when d'you want it? Won't mind a bit shitty," knowing Walter's unconcern with the exterior of things.

"This is it, two important details. Both are important, I know I can rely on you. First, can you bring it up, as far as the super-market parking, outside Saint Gaudens? Meet me there and ride back in ours? Soon as you can and when would that be?"

"In an hour and no strain."

"Great, and wait for us out there on the lot. And listen - second point. The most important thing of all – say nothing to anybody. Nothing seen, till I get back, around a week. I've my reasons for not wanting anything known, I'm just shutting the house and pissing off – with Ma – okay? – I'm counting on you. Total quiet. Just an eccentricity of mine." He feels the knifeblade, prodding him lightly, saying don't explain so much. A weakness of his. But Manuel is unperturbed at his caprices – as had been explained . . .

"And man – nothing conspicuous – not a Porsche. See you."

"Bags are packed," says Sylvie woodenly, obstinate disap-proval in every line but as always 'where you say, I'll follow'. It is her basic loyalty. Since always.

"Just this last detail, then."

"I don't like it." Fernand has already said this. "I don't like this at all."

"It's indispensable," says Walter, also repeating himself. "The essential thing with cops is to give them a story they can believe. In this, there's nothing out of the way. And what the old boy will tell cops – Christ, I should have a gold napoleon for every word. I slip him the key, he doesn't have to know you exist. You get down on the floor so's the neighbours don't get inquisitive, he doesn't even see you."

*

"Send the patrol up there then," grumbled Captain Cardenal. and somewhere near nightfall the blue station-wagon steamed up the hill with two cautious gendarmes ready to call upon reinforcements even if it was only the old man making a fuss.

One never knows. They were a scrap disconcerted at finding a house shuttered and still.

"Neighbours then." Knockings on doors, salutings.

"How the hell should I know? Often goes away. Come to think of it saw the wife carrying a case out to the car. He's funny, right? Tells Jesus to look after the house when he's gone. Think of it – set bloody house on fire likely as not. Could ask any of us but no – Jesus!" Ambiguous appeal, perhaps addressed to the one up there in the sky.

"What can I do for your worshipfulnesses?" spoke Jesus with great courtesy. "His Eminence? He is so kind as to repose confidence in my humble self. The key's in my pocket. Great as is my esteem for your Honour, your servant could by no means be unfaithful to this trust. Nay nay, not even by orders from his Holiness. I beg of you to accept the expression of my most distinguished considerations."

"Can the bullshit. D'you know which way he went?"

"I was by no means informed. Curiosity is a villainous vice, my brothers. One step drags in the whole body. No doubt my own dear and never again to be beheld motherland. Vera Cruz, your gracious excellencies."

"Let's piss off quick or the old man will snatch our balls."

"Frontier's on alert anyhow. Pass it along for what it's worth," picking up the radiophone. "Car seven, calling into you. Calling home, car seven. Is this sodding thing on the blink again?"

Day Two

We are in a country hotel, outside Mont de Marsan, a smallish, pleasant, fairly undistinguished town more or less on the border between the forest country of the Landes that stretches for hundreds of miles south of Bordeaux, and the valleyed, well-watered, agricultural country of the Agen-Périgord. A wind had got up, and branches were tapping against a pane. A pleasantly cool sweet air from the pine-woods swirled from the open window. He breathed quietly, listened to other quiet breathing.

He recognised that he was keyed-up. Well, there was no sense in that. He stretched out and loosened himself, breathed deeply, waited for a lighter, sweeter sleep to enfold him.

Up to now there had been little disagreement. It was evident that they should shun the whole Toulouse area, above all the major east-west traffic axis that follows the Garonne valley. They took unimportant side roads through the thinly populated Gers; roads that – avoiding Auch – lead nowhere much and made for tedious driving in the dark, but in the tourist character, of a family interested in large meals at low prices, it was important to be going nowhere in particular and in no hurry. In fact they met with no road blocks, and the occasional glimpse of a country gendarme showed him interested in nothing but his supper.

One had better stay vigilant, for all that. It was hard to tell just how seriously the authorities were going to take the escape of a mere break-and-enter boy, even if he had left a cop half-strangled in the jakes.

"It depends," said Walter sensibly, "how busy they are. If they have other fish to fry, say a bomb scare or any rumour of terrorist activity, this gets forgotten. There's another side to that: one might get stopped by a road block looking for something else altogether, like discontented farmers sabotaging truckloads of Spanish tomatoes. Keep the radio going, alert for any sign of unrest."

There'd been nothing at all, and reaching Mont de Marsan, a good two hundred and fifty kilometres by country roads, was surely a sign that the heat was low. An unexpected direction to take and part of a zigzag pattern that Walter pointed out would allay any suspicion aroused by some incident at a stop, the sort of thing that gossip would comment upon and might remember.

Manuel had done all that was asked of him. He had been waiting as agreed on the supermarket's parking-lot, with a biggish, oldish, dark blue Alfa. With, also, his obstinate expression meaning disapproval; few words and those tight-lipped: making quite a thing of being in a hurry, not wanting to know, and looking ostentatiously in other directions. But nothing of this was noticeable in a crowd of shoppers, intent only on transferring piles of junk from trolley to wagon amid domestic scenes of the type 'Where are the car keys, Bonjour?'; or badly-brought-up children bawling for chewing-gum, and now shut up unless you want a clip across the ear. Fill up the tank while we're here because there's two cents' discount on a litre of petrol. That Fernand was again twitchy and edgy and fingering that pistol in his pocket, passed unperceived. Walter, fidgety fusspot, had of course to say again and unnecessarily 'This interview is with Deep Throat' – Manuel snatched the keys in a huff and slammed the car door before accelerating noisily, so that Walter had to give further needless reassurances to the fidgeting Fernand.

Why? Why? Whoever put the questions, and to whom, none of the answers would have made much sense at the time. With hindsight, the threads of 'psychology' would be easily enough untangled. Even at that moment, knowing nothing of the cir-cumstances but with a wide experience of Pa, Manuel could have come pretty close to an explanation, driving home in the VW and a sullen glower and biting his nails at traffic lights, but he had other things on his mind too and didn't bother. Pa is a whatdyoucallem, neurotic and quixotic individual with two manias: one for complicating simple situations to his own un-doing; the other for running up the down-escalator, however many people are standing on it with bulky shopping-bags.

He could do better, and did, subconsciously, by the day following. Better still, and consciously, by the day after that, when he knew a lot more of what went on, and had pieced things together. It was not that complicated; not even all that quixotic. But people would still ask 'But why on earth?' All that Walter should have done was sit tight. The police would turn up, probably by that evening – as indeed they did. There were innumerable small signals whereby he or Sylvie could have conveyed, without putting themselves at great risk, that they were held hostage by an armed and violently unpredictable criminal. The police would have known what to do.

Instead he races off, completely harebrained, on this idiotic adventure and helping this infernal boy, who is simply an anti-social menace, to confuse pursuit and evade recapture, in every way he can imagine and dragging Ma along with him into this lunatic chase that can only end badly, in whatever way. Pa is known and generally tolerated (either for the sake of quiet or because there's nothing much one can do to stop him) as a catalogued loony, but this is a bit much.

If pushed, Manuel would give answers.

'My father had a rough time, you know, over many years, sorting out his marriage. Ma is a woman with a great many qualities, much strength of character. They are both right and wrong for one another. For some years the wrong went wronger. The personality clash compounded fundamental awkwardnesses in them both. Dependence, interdependence, look, I'm no shrink, and if you want psychoanalysis apply elsewhere, I've not much use for it; you can start things, and finishing them will give you more trouble: look out you don't bite off more than you can chew, okay? I know whose son I am. It doesn't bother me five cents worth. But it sure's hell worried my father. You think it's easy, being the complaisant husband? Not that he was, but that's the impression he gave, deliberately. It's so much easier, and the cretins will call it acting-like-a-man, to say "You adulterous cow, I've caught you, shit, I'll divorce you." He didn't, and it wasn't selfish, and it wasn't laziness. It was for his wife, and his children – you hear me, *his* children, okay?

'He hasn't any real hang-up on this class thing, leaves it to people a lot more unstable than he is, and less sure of themselves, to worry about their standing, and the kind of accent they talk with. You want proof? – he's let all three of us choose any life he likes in any surroundings: never put the slightest obstacle in our way. But it wasn't always easy, being half-English, half-German. Brought up in France – of all goddam places – and schooled by Franquist Jesuits in Spain. And that damned anachronism, the land-owning aristocracy that no longer owns anything and has no other rôle to play. You think it easy? Being cosmopolitan – you're at home everywhere. You're also at home nowhere. There isn't anywhere on earth a piece of ground where you can bury your feet and say "Here I belong".

'Nor is it, I can tell you, such a slice of cake as it looks, being a writer. Da is no genius, I agree. Just a talent; that's already sufficiently rare. Doesn't fit into categories along that branch of enquiry, neither: he's an original. Nobody likes that. What the commercials like in this business is exactly what they look for in any other. The big public is extremely conventional, and the ready sale is for the recognisable category that follows predict-able paths. My father never did, and didn't get much thanks for that.'

This would be said in the private room of an instructing judge. Not Madame Claudine Rivière – a long way away – but an elderly and experienced man. And who moreover had been unconventional too often himself; as a polite means of letting him know it he has been left for his whole career in an obscure corner of the French countryside.

He would be amused by Manuel. This big, ruffianly-looking young man with the hard scarred hands; six foot four and a size in boots to match, lecturing him on sensitivity.

'Artistic temperament – the nonsense there is talked about that! I've lived with it: you can take my word on the subject. My father doesn't look strong – well, you've had as yet no very good opportunity of judging that. Stronger than he looks; however, the energy there is nervous. Works like speed-pill 'f y' follow me. People like that, they want a high level of effort or concentration, they can summon it up, from within themselves. Need no pill. But the effect's the same: it has to be paid for. The higher level you call for the longer time you need to re-cuperate from that. They flake out, take to their bed. I've seen him after a major effort, on his hands 'n' knees. And he bounces, or used to, back fast. Twenty-four hours later, as good as new. Put everything he had into this, and towards the end, like a boxer running on speed, he didn't know what he was doing.'

And the judge would smile a little, and Manuel seeing that and misinterpreting it would lose his temper.

'You're a judge, you're doing your job, okay! I respect that. You're an officer of the law, appointed by the state, and I've got to respect that. But about life, about the world, sorry for saying it if it offends you, you know fuck all. University, law degree, Magistrates School in Bordeaux, big deal, but from where I stand you're still sucking Mummy's titty.'

And, understanding, the judge would apologise for the smile, saying gently that even country-mouse has known painters, writers, musicianly people. One doesn't have to live in Paris, you know, to meet them.

Manuel would apologise at once for his outburst.

'Paris! I suppose you read a lot of books. Mean to say, one lives in the country, there aren't a lot of people as a rule one finds all that interesting; I mean, one has a little circle of friends and they're sort of permanent but there isn't the flow, current of casual acquaintance like in a city. Books take the place of that. Characters who tell their adventures, people discussing their problems and troubles – and at another level rather higher people who think. You can talk to them; you can hold a dialogue with a good book. You know, my father used to say he wouldn't have wanted to know Talleyrand in politics, and still less when playing for money, but he'd sure as hell give five years to have known Talleyrand in a library because there'd be no better company on earth.

'Right, I'm a country yob, and never went to any university, and I spend quite a lot of my time in Paris, I like to go to the Louvre and such, and I like bookshops and I buy quite a bit. Sorry, seems now I'm gassing about myself but this has a point. All those writers – all in love with their own navel, sorry to be crude, I'm a crude fellow but they'd be sucking their own dick if they could get to it. For a book to be any good the writer's got to turn himself outward, accept the world. Very few of them do because they don't like it, and that's the trouble with most what they call literature.

'My father knew this. Lived buried down there in the Pyrenees, saw very few people, lived almost entirely in his own interior, found that a bad thing. You gotto understand, when this gangster fellow came crashing in, all guns and big mouth, Da didn't see him just as a stupid nit. Saw him as a piece of life, interesting and worth taking trouble over. Shouldn't let that get wasted, shouldn't just let that go to prison – my father has a horror of prisons, they cause immense damage. Send someone to prison only if you're convinced the whole way down the line you've done everything – everything – in your power to avoid it. He couldn't do much about that jewellers' shop but he was damn well determined not to let that stupid caper up at his house get blown up into a big public-enemy thing on account of property. Property is theft? – well, anyhow, too much property is the result of theft, and too many people who ought to be in prison never got sent there.'

And the judge would go on listening; nowise thinking that

142

this was a waste of time. There are bad judges in France: there are good ones. Nobody knows what the percentage of either may be: these are not statistics verifiable by any computer.

A country hotel, outside Mont de Marsan. Eight or ten rooms; as many more in an annexe. An old place, much 'modernised' in the usual restaurant bad taste, with beams and refectory tables and chintz-upholstered windsor-chairs and phony coach lamps to light the steps up from the drive. But comfortable, glowing with warm light, friendly and welcoming. A good restaurant trade; big tarty menu with lots of folklore, specialities (between the Gers and the Landes, foie gras in every damn thing, lots of duck: the great locomotive for the whole area is the famous Monsieur Daguin in Auch . . .). A big salle for parties, weddings and anniversaries and get-togethers of the Class of Forty-five: any excuse for a good blow-out. The boss is a big smooth smiling man like Long John Silver in cooks' clothes. His wife is no parrot, though she does mention the pieces-of-eight fairly frequently.

There was a discussion, with raised voices, in the dusty dark blue Alfa out on the parking lot. Fernand has been persuaded, at last, to put that damn gun away. To take its place he has brought out a quarrelsome bullying manner which Walter does not take to at all kindly. Sylvie might be tempted to think (she is still keeping the obstinate silence, a good deal) that the only bullying tolerated by Walter is his own. But – since they've got into this – hereabouts she is on his side, decidedly: there are limits to these invasions of privacy. In her own house she couldn't go to the lavatory without written application in triplicate?

As was to be expected, the discussion is about bedrooms. Fernand – proximity leads to familiarity – had caught the habit, irritating Walter to frenzy, of using first names (Walter's own fault, for asking his?). He intends to keep them well under his eye.

"And how often do I have to tell you – be natural. What d'you want these people to think; that we're some kind of dotty crew? Incestuous or have we some extraordinary disease that we want to keep hidden; that somebody has nightmares or pisses in the bed? The indispensable thing is that one should not be remarked

143

or remembered. We're a family: anybody who asks to prove identity, to verify a cheque or whatever, gets my passport. All above board and no problem. You want people getting suspicious and writing down the number of your driving licence? Adjoining rooms, okay, no problem. Further than that, you try to force it, you're asking for them to call cops, the way they would for a troublesome late night drunk. Be a tourist. Eat the foie gras! Without a proper meal, a proper bed, a good night's rest" – it might have been Nanny telling them now eat up your nice rice pudding. Sylvie, accustomed as she is to this booming English voice, the District Commissioner, firm with tedious natives ('Now run along,' said Mr. Baldwin to the Trades Union leaders) is amused at Fernand's being sufficiently impressed to keep his mouth shut.

There is likewise the Viceregal Eye at dinner. Sylvie has seen it all often, and has sense of humour enough left to avoid the obvious remark; that if Walter really wants to pass unperceived he should not speak to waiters in quite such ringing tones (the children have so often been mortified by Walter's behaviour at meal times in public that for many years they refused point blank to be associated with him and have even insisted on eating by themselves at the Buffet de la Gare rather than squirm at Pa's loud comments in the Hôtel de France. In fact, after reading, some few years ago, *The Forsyte Saga* she had devised a slogan for such occasions: 'That's no way to serve port: take that away and bring the bottle').

To do him justice he no longer gives a damn. In his younger days, made insecure by poverty, he used, it was true, to fuss about the children's table manners. And in restaurants those prevailing at other tables would be pointed out as fearful object lessons. 'Petty bourgeoisie, quite typical, holding their knife and fork like knitting needles,' 'Just look at that, ducking his head almost into his plate with every mouthful, snatching and gobbling like the dog at a dish.' It has no longer any importance – he was entertained to notice Manuel looking so like himself; very upright, sitting slightly sideways and crossing his legs.

An observer of any acuteness would have seen immediately that whatever Fernand was he did not belong with this couple. At table the complete peasant, sitting sprawled over the plate ('Sit up straight and do not hunch your shoulders') gripping knife and fork in two fists and holding them at an angle above the plate as though about to fight a duel with them: in fact alternately sucking fork and knife while the mouth was full, while staring around with restless unquiet eyes.

We cannot get away from childhood upbringing, thought Walter. These little things sink in, and leave a stamp, becoming moral, religious. One would like to have seen D.H. and Frieda Lawrence at table together, the son of the Nottingham miner and the daughter of high German bourgeoisie. Did she make a thing of wiping her mouth with the napkin before drinking? Did he insist upon wiping his plate in circles with a piece of bread to economise on the washing-up?

'I bullied Sylvie, when we were young together. I ridiculed her bourgeois ways, lost no opportunity of making stinging remarks about her respectable Flemish upbringing. She has turned the tables on me, since. It has been right that I should pay for my insensitive intolerance. She had to assert her individuality, as well as her womanness.

'And it is again now a protest against interference by the past that leads me to bind myself in this absurb way to this young man's fate.'

Walter was reminded of a joke Christmas present he had once had from one of the boys. Carefully framed and glassed, it was a large piece of poster paper, on which a small German child had printed in big careful letters, using a brush and gouache, the ultimate slogan: WIR BrotesTIEREN. The joke had been successful and Walter had hung it in the studio. It had escaped damage, during the raid.

What have we in common? It has nothing to do with idiotic political labels like socialism – the only difference between left- and right-wing governments was that the left did slightly sillier things, but with slightly better intentions. And a pox upon you both, milords. (Come! – a Popular Front government had the courage to grasp the nettle of law reform . . .)

The trouble with country hotels is that there is nothing to do in the interval between dinner and bed except go for a walk or look at the television: the first is less of a yawn but Mont de Marsan of a rainy September night isn't very exciting either. Is 'going for a walk' a very English pastime? Somebody said once that the English climate was the only one under which it was possible to go for a walk every day of the year: the speaker, presumably, was English.

Fernand, it was to be expected, saw no merit in the notion: what is the use of that? True – it's a class distinction. He saw a chance to reassert himself.

"On se tape une belote à trois." The phrase is pretty well untranslatable but it is the universal card game of French cafés. It is complicated, subtle and ruthless. The card values vary, and Walter has much ado to remember these – you can alter the trump, or elect no-trump– and he hates cards anyhow, is useless at them.

Humiliation thus; almost utter disgrace. Sylvie holds cards cleverly, plays astutely: in the game 'à trois' the declarer is matched against a partnership of the other two, and with Fernand she forms an unbeatable pair. Paired with Walter she complains openly of forgetfulness or inattention. Paired with Fernand against her he is but a lamebrain. The two sharpen their wits upon one another while he is perpetually adrift, regresses further into childhood, begins to forget the French vocabulary and use German card terms. As though he were back in the gun room, with his grandfather. 'What's trump now – kreuz oder eckstein?'

'What, what?' mutters Fernand sarcastically.

(He recalls his father, in facetious frame of mind, disguising the knave of clubs, that unlikeable card, with a forelock and a moustache to look like Hitler . . .)

Probably it did Fernand good. Becoming increasingly uneasy throughout the evening in the gratingly fake atmosphere of a country hotel giving itself the airs of a grand restaurant while struggling to maintain the illusion of ye-olde-coaching-inn, he might have become frustrated enough to do something violent, irretrievable. Walter must have got on his nerves a great deal. Without the card game to show his manifest mastery in an area where it was safe to do so – Christ, he could make this whole crowd skip if he so wished, shit theirself with fright, a notion to toy with – it might have been fatal, that first evening. As it was he relaxed. All right, let them feel cosy together. He had them in the hollow of his hand.

*

Miriam Lebreton had been forgotten by all concerned, and had forgotten them herself: a lawyer knows how to concentrate

146

upon the matter in hand. She had – it was true – thought a good deal about odd aspects of existence – odd in the sense of bizarre – after Walter had left her. But she had work to do, promises to keep, like the man in the poem miles to go before sleep. From Toulouse all the way on a main road, to Agen, Bordeaux, Angoulême, and Poitiers: even in the scarlet Porsche a goodish step. Not to be done by lunchtime, and the client was a difficult one: pleading irresponsibility on account of mental derangement was not by any means always a skilful tactic. And had a dangerous facility that did not satisfy her. And it was a confused, sloppy dossier. She was a professional, and knew how to put her own – call them bizarreries – resolutely out of mind.

'*Une brave fille*,' Miriam; as elderly members of the Bar were accustomed to saying with indulgent paternalism. Ever so slightly tinged with both envy and lechery, for she was a pretty woman, and her rise had been rapid. 'Brave' – the translation holds good only slightly, and that in an old fashioned sense of tenacity and hard work. On bourgeois lips it is decidedly condescending, and '*le brave homme*' is likely to be the reliable janitor, willing in small services and who keeps a civil tongue in his head.

Miriam Lebreton, driving up to Poitiers, was rehearsing bits of special pleading in her car.

'Promiscuous? – may I ask what this word means? You cannot expect a lawyer, sharpened daily in criminal pleading, to let pass so loaded, so blatantly polarised an expression. In law it means nothing whatever. Technically – used of any matter that mingles readily with others. But in morals: oho, members of the jury, you are told over and over, everyone repeating till they turn blue, that our court of law is not a court of morals. And you still don't believe it – quite right. The two are hopelessly muddled.'

Lebreton being rhetorical! In court she never was: rhetoric no longer impresses juries much. A self-indulgence, the 'stately antithesis'; even interior monologue during a long boring drive should avoid it. It's when a cause is lost in advance, when one just has nothing to say, that one resorts to rhetoric.

But look at that stinking word, would you. Promiscuous! Women are, and men aren't: the word smells of black, celibate trousers. Criminal law is still soaked with it, the ecclesiastical canon.

You'll find a natural law though, in the traffic code. I'm privileged; rich; drive a Porsche (not the nine-eleven though; not that rich!): must obey the same rule as the student there in the tatty old Beetle. Wealth which gives me speed, comfort and glamour, gives me increased responsibility.

Society constrains me (Christ, people still think freedom means absence of constraint: the truth is the exact contrary). The rule is that I must not put others at risk; their lives, their vital space. That's right: vita means life.

Most of it is left to my appreciation – judgment. We mustn't multiply pettifogging regulations. Traffic must be fluid. Fluidity implies precaution: to look ahead of caution. I'm obliged to use my loaf. Taking into account: slow reactions, fear, fatigue, timidity, inexperience, recklessness. In brief, all the others. Before launching this dangerous weapon upon the public highway, and before climbing into bed with people.

It's a reasonable code; works fairly well. People being both unreasonable and irresponsible there are a lot of accidents. Even if I don't have them I cause them. Can anyone – even the most accomplished prig – lay hand on heart and say, 'No, no, members of the jury, Nevah has lack of prudence or foresight, or consideration for others been lacking'? There has been no accident? Irrelevant: there can be one, the next second.

That Sunday driver, that trog there in the middle of the road doing seventy, he thinks he's being prudent.

You're one of the biggest dangers out, said Miriam aloud; slamming past in second gear.

Rhetoric, pleading the lost cause. When we pass, members of the jury, the mass of twisted metal: the ambulance at the verge and the gendarmerie taking notes; and we hang out of the window, excited . . . We are giving way to an ignoble perverted instinct, the sadistic glee of the voyeur. It's pretty bad, that. I don't call it superstition if we shudder and cross ourselves: it's a threshold of awareness. 'There but for the grace-of-god? We're trying, at least, not to be vain and complacent. What's grace? A lucky star, shining on you or me? Don't count on it. God takes no responsibility for you. Take your own, recalling that others do not take theirs.'

148

Adultery – it's another of these clerical collar words. Under the Third Republic, Mister, you could have your wife taken-in-adultery by a commissaire of police and condemned on that count to fifteen days in prison. Monsieur Clemenceau (national hero) did just that.

Miriam can't even remember whether that particular statute has ever been officially repealed!

Still a naïve girl, Lebreton. Still relying overmuch upon her intelligence. The lights and brakes of the Porsche are in good condition. Safe little car.

*

She drove to Poitiers, settled the affairs of her client. In a way satisfactory to neither, but as well as could be expected; with hardly any rhetoric at all. A brief affair, briefly pleaded – Miriam knows when a judge wants his dinner. Client got three years; could well have been given seven.

She was having dinner alone in the hotel when called to the phone. It was her dogsbody, the young lawyer devilling for her in Toulouse. He had news. He had talked to the judge of instruction, and to the Procureur. Conscientious, he had rung the colonel of gendarmerie, who had told him as much 'as was good for him to know'.

"Oh dear," said Miriam, fairly placid. "All right. Tiresome, yes, but don't let's get in an uproar. I'll be back tomorrow. Yes, I'll drive down . . . Look, I'm in the middle of dinner. I didn't put the idea in the boy's head, you know."

Walter's name had not been mentioned, and she didn't mention it either. Her thoughts were her own and so was her life.

That, in any case, was the way she read the state of affairs.

*

Walter had had a bellyful of byways the night before but buckled himself stolidly into the driving seat. He was tired of his mind going round and round. To keep his attention fixed upon a necessary chore would help shut off the interior dialogue. To pilot on an unknown road through the heavy morning traffic was welcome.

It had been discussed, at breakfast.

"Why should one stay glued to these frightful little side roads? Now that we're out of the area . . . why not a main road? As long as we don't keep too long in the same direction."

149

Fernand let fall the one word, "Cops."

"They'll only look for a car known to be stolen. This is Manuel's and he lends it to me. No catch in that. Even assuming the worst, that they tracked you up to my house, found me gone, and now they're looking for me, they'd be looking for my car; not this one."

"Computer."

"How could they tie me in? I suppose I'd better not write cheques. But what do I have to buy? – petrol, food, and a night's lodging. Do it with the credit card. That takes a time to clear. I don't think they've the right anyhow to snoop on those accounts. Even if they got permission – we'll stay away from banks, and big shops, who might have a terminal. These little places only pay in a day later. And we change direction: we don't stay like hens on a chalk line. They can't lay in wait because they can't foresee our passage at any given point."

"Photo."

"I suppose they've one of you and could circulate that. What does it amount to? Some constabulary lurching about showing it, and 'You seen this man?' and everybody says 'don't know'.

"So look at the map. We're here. So I'd say Périgueux, and then head over, towards the coast. Angoulême and then La Rochelle. Nice town. Why not, come to that? Good place to spend the night."

Fernand suspicious, but allowing himself to be convinced.

"And then tomorrow – I don't know. Back inland. Poitiers, that direction. If we're going up towards Belgium we don't want to spend too long at it."

Poitiers – where had Walter heard that town mentioned recently? Miriam Lebreton mumbled something about having to plead there. What one called ships passing in the night. She'll be back in Paris, I suppose, by now. She'll make a face when she hears her client walked out of the Palace of Justice after clonking a cop . . .

Sylvie says nothing throughout the whole discussion. Sylvie has said very little, since the start. The flow of sprightly chat, she leaves that to Walter; it's his speciality.

Sylvie is maintaining a tactic? That sounds altogether too conscious, too deliberate. Her silence, just this side of sullen, is not thought out.

She is not sure of her ground. But she has made up her mind that she's going to see this through. Her famous Flemish obstinacy.

Fernand put her in the front, and got into the back seat. He felt fairly contented, and even safe. Let them sulk, or let them gab, as they pleased: whatever they did it was overdone. Yesterday – all his energy, his inventiveness had gone into bopping that clown. He'd had to make it all up as he went along. He hated that; it wore one down. No planning, no margin. You couldn't see anything coming; never a chance to catch your breath, like.

But today he's had a good sleep and feels in form. And whoever is in which front seat doesn't bother him for a second: he is doing the driving.

Yesterday he couldn't make it out. This complicated act of theirs puzzled him. As a means of getting out of the hole he was in, well and good, but was this Forestier as dingaling as he seemed? In Fernand's experience people didn't try to chat you up into some project unless they saw a payoff for themselves, and where was it? He'd had the car keys, and he had the gun. He'd made sure there were no handy telephones around, he'd locked them in the next-door room, and he'd been alert to any clever gags; they weren't going to go knotting sheets and climbing out of windows. When he dropped off himself it had been comfortable, confident that his senses were sharp enough to wake him fast as light, at any funny noises. And the moment he woke up he felt fine, because he'd understood.

Face-saving! That's the bourgeois for you, all over. They've always got to make out they're in command, and when they aren't they've got to seem it, and when they can't even do that they'll invent an elaborate tale. They've got to have a pretext for deceiving themselves, see? And once he'd understood that he had a ring through their nose. She can play the haughty madam: much good may it do her. He is in charge.

He is bright! He's been told so, often enough, and has put it to the proof more than once: he thinks quicker than others, and he doesn't lose his head.

Fernand has learned that he can manipulate people. If need be, force them, but don't waste force. That was the mistake of all the dimwit bandits: force all the time, and they had nothing in

151

reserve. With the bourgeois, the threat is enough, because there's nothing they care for more than their precious skins and their precious property. You tickled the one to get the other. The gun is there if needed, but it is much better that it should not be needed.

So now let's have a quiet day, and time to think things out. There's this much sense in ol' Gauthier's scheme of zigzagging, that if anybody did pick up a trail they'd be kept guessing: nobody could know what he would do next. And nor does this pair, for all they think they're smart.

Hostages! Everybody took them and they got you into trouble. The trick was in getting rid of them. He'd already made up his mind about that. Any quiet place would do in the middle of the countryside where they wouldn't be found too soon, and all you needed was a ball of string. Wrist to ankle and a loop round the neck that tightens if they pull: that'll keep anybody quiet.

But once they'd kidded themselves they were friendly, willing, one could bring them a long way. Belgium? He quite liked the idea. An easy place both to get in and out of. Choice of three different countries. I know it already, and they don't realise that.

You'll have to get rid of them before then. And leave the impression that you're going to double back.

The only really annoying thing is the lack of cash. They had hardly the price of a beer between them: they go by the cheque book and the credit card. That's all right as long as it's Forestier who pays. He would go along with it, right up to Belgium. And then they'd see.

You can sit back. But keep y'r eye peeled. Funny things can happen, and when they do they mostly happen suddenly.

*

Walter is only talking to himself a little. And not, at all, about the ethics of helping a known criminal evade justice. France is a country he hates and loves, and here is where he belongs. He only wishes he were riding a bicycle: rather slowly. Countryside; towns. What you see from the road is filling-stations and fast food, and you might just as well be in Bakersfield, California. You could be on one of the pilgrimage roads – there are

152

three, if memory serves – that lead south and west to Santiago de Compostela. But you're not giving yourself the chance to stop, to look.

A town now: is it Angoulême? He has been too dulled to notice. Driving a car, the approach to any French town is the same. There is inevitably a long and dismal boulevard, with many traffic lights and the arrowed signs saying 'Toutes Directions'. The day was warm, the pace slow, the faubourg stuffy. And if Walter is thinking at all, it is of a good stop for lunch. He has his window down, his elbow out. Frankly, he is dozing.

These dreams of lunch, of a drink, of two or three drinks, of subsequent peaceful digestion and of letting Sylvie drive, are interrupted. The light was red and traffic both ways halted for it: why should there be a sudden loud honk? French cars are in general equipped with a muted klaxon, to discourage the illegal but ever-ready tooter who has neither patience nor forebearance. The German car has still an old-fashioned blare on occasion. Walter woke up, and recognised a red Porsche. Familiar, as well as conspicuous. He had not realised that Miriam Lebreton might be going back to Toulouse. She has a surprised look. She is just saying 'Hallo there'.

Fernand is awake because hungry, and was going to tell the man to stop. The red car means nothing to him. But his recognition of the driver gets an immediate echo. A dead giveaway and he loses no time. That Lebreton there should know Walter, without noticing himself at all, does not occur to him: why should it? She'll raise an alarm!

"Stop the car. Stop, I tell you!" And startled, Walter braked abruptly. So that three cars behind him honked with indignation. Fernand was out and across the road before Miriam – startled – had put the car in gear.

"Turn. Turn I tell you!" She'd been told the fellow was loose. She hadn't been told he had a gun.

Sylvie had not been asleep.

"Drive on," she shouted. "Quick!"

"Can't." There was another red light. Fatality.

Walter followed the little scene. A fellow jumped out slamming the door and bolting across the road to another car. Nothing untoward in that – so he suddenly saw a friend. Nobody

153

paid any heed. The Porsche made a U-turn against traffic. In a car like that you get away with it. Fernand leaned out of the window and made a hand signal saying stop further up. Walter got the message.

French towns have large desolate squares. Tourists stop, to sort their direction out.

Fernand had lost no time sorting out his direction. He couldn't let her go: she'd have a hue and cry afoot in no time. It was an extra hostage – and could be a valuable one. He'd think about that later. Her car was conspicuous, and had to be ditched.

Miriam had regained her composure. She saw now, how things fitted. It was important to show calm.

"Naturally – you know one another."

"How do you know him?" asked Fernand suspiciously.

"I thought of calling him as a witness." Sylvie was asking the same question back to front: getting the same answer.

"We look for a car park," said Fernand, cool. "We leave your car there. Come to no harm. You're coming with us."

"I'm beginning to get the general drift of your argument," said Miriam.

"You keep saying I can trust you," he told Walter ."Now's your chance. If I can't – she pays." It didn't take above five minutes.

"Do a bunk. Find a cop. Do anything," shouted Sylvie. "Her bad luck!"

"No," said Walter. "It won't do. I wouldn't even consider it." She controlled herself, staring at him.

Away over in the Catalan country there is a traditional folk dance. The steps are simple, the rhythm slow. One picks it up in no time and tourists join in. The sardana. Everyone links arms, in a ring around the musicians. Walter is linked, a woman on each arm. Fernand, Manuel – a partner further. The feet point, the bodies bend, unbrokenly together. The traditional melody, doubtless very old, stays in the mind.

Miriam appeared, looking elegant, and fairly unflustered. Fernand politely carrying her suitcase. There is room for her in the back of the car.

"We'll eat something," says Fernand pleasantly. "And then we'll drive on. Just the way we were going, before."

"People will be looking for me," she offered.

"Maybe they will. But they'll just think you changed your mind. Found something better to do, like. And that's right. Isn't it?"

"I did think that defending you might have unexpected angles."

'And I can do with a drink," said Walter.

Day Three

Night in La Rochelle. Bad time. It would have been bad anywhere, no doubt. So one can tell oneself, thinking soberly upon it, putting reason and experience at the service of judgment arrived at late: too late. My bad judgment led to this, says Walter, alone, at three in the morning. He has nobody to tell it to, and would it serve any purpose if he had?

Nice hotel! A roomy comfortable place of solid build and generous proportion; neither large enough nor grand enough to be classed as palace – the nicer for that, perhaps. Quite a massive castellated affair, not far from the harbour. Walter's memories were vivid but vague. When he caught sight of it he jumped as the iron to the lodestone. Everyone was tired, hungry, grubby, and no one objected.

Large horseshoe shaped windows and Art Déco incrustations. Tiled floor and a solid mahogany counter flanked by palms in brass pots and looped velours curtains – to Walter, irresistible. Here one would be comfortable.

"Two doubles?" the reception-lady taking them in with a practised eye. "We're still quite full but we can manage you nicely. Are the cars outside? – you wouldn't mind bringing them down to the garage – free of course for residents." And first an embarrassed explanation (Walter's fatal habit of explaining too much and unnecessarily) about a car left for repair nearby (sounding unconvincing even to him) and the question that everyone had dodged: who was sleeping with whom? Trapped by his own reiterated insistence on 'behaving normally'. Even Miriam, bewildered and probably in slight

155

shock, did not react. But the overwhelming flavour of bourgeois respectability – a smell, a taste – in places like this helped to inhibit her. In her simple, expensive black trouser suit she looks younger – and Fernand, drawn and hollowed by strain, looks older. They could well be taken for a couple. What can one say in a public place like this? Walter is drawn and hollowed too, but by fatigue and hunger as much as strain.

"A wash, a drink, and dinner," he says sensibly. "Then we'll feel better. We can talk things over then, quietly." And Fernand, at first intimated by this place which is so different from anything he is accustomed to (the Edwardian style in buildings is indeed so overpoweringly immovable that no amount of modernisation changes its nature) is reacting, in his interior, with some violence. He has an idea: a surprise for these people.

But he's keeping that in reserve. Right now, another new sensation – dinner: in the restaurant: with the rich . . . Old Gauthier has plenty of money, and the lawyer. Look at those diamond earrings. Real!

They get a nice big table, by a window overlooking the terrace. And beyond, the harbour. The chairs are heavy, comfortable. Enormous menus bound in heavy leather; people dining in heavy silence. A rich, heavy smell.

Fish; Walter loves (Pisces is his sign) fish. Mouclade, local dish, of mussels with a little curry in the sauce: lotte in white shiny steaks, américaine sauce made of lobster débris. The local muscadet, companionable Loire white wine. Walter becomes expansive, and drinks too much of it.

"Water for me," says Miriam chillingly. Fernand looks suspicious, ejects the monosyllable "beer".

There is a slight initial stiffness, between the two women.

"I don't quite understand," says Sylvie, "how you came to meet." Miriam is ready for that.

"Simple enough. They were thinking for a moment of pegging him for complicity, since he'd been a bit bloodyminded. Article one-oh-four of the Code of Procedure. I thought if I could persuade him into being a defence witness . . ."

Delicious town of La Rochelle, where he always feels well. A strange quartet they make, around this table. Platitudinous idea, but he feels this to be a dream. He has been here before, with Sylvie. They sat at that table over there. Bourgeois on holiday.

He is drinking too much. He is having dinner with Miriam Lebreton. The last dinner, so vivid in his mind, so recent – the night before last! – has faded too, become unreal. Or is this the unreal occasion?

He makes social conversation, the bottle aiding, but it languishes. The last of the twilight has turned to night, outside. It is not late but the scene has gone cold and bleak. Fatigue and anxiety come up like a spring tide with the wind behind it: nobody has any wish but to go to bed. And Fernand who hasn't uttered for the last hour springs his mine.

"There's going to be a change of partners." Just to show them who's in charge, here. And they look at each other. What can they find to say, in this ponderous, over-upholstered dining room? But what would they find to say, anywhere?

A silent corridor, a carpet smelling of dust, leads to bedrooms.

Miriam, polite and unhappy, stood looking at Walter across grey concrete stretches of counterpane.

"I prefer that you don't share my bed."

"I wasn't proposing to press myself upon you."

"Well . . . would you like the bathroom first or shall I?" And Sylvie, along the passage, is facing Fernand across another desert.

"You want to sleep with me. Even though I'm old? You'd better understand. If you behave brutally towards me I don't care if you've twenty guns. Whether you hurt me, whether you even kill me, I'll fight you. I'll scream the place down right now." She has hardly drunk anything but her colour is high.

Fernand says nothing, does nothing. They look at each other.

"I don't ask much. Just elementary consideration. Let me pretend that I have self-respect, still. That's not complicated, surely? May I go to the bathroom, please? And you'll wait here, then."

*

Miriam coming out with her hair brushed, in black cotton pyjamas, has a vaguely Vietnamese look. As though she should be wearing a straw hat. Young, and vulnerable. Walter was still in shirt and trousers, lying on the bed, smoking a cigar. She dropped the hairbrush and bent to pick it up.

"I suppose," she said, "that we ought really to be giving the alarm?"

157

"I've been thinking about that too. Even if it wasn't for Sylvie – I don't think, you know, that it would be likely to do any good."

"I didn't anticipate this. That's a stupid remark; I didn't anticipate anything. Deliberately. In a way I felt confident. I wasn't afraid, whatever might happen. I mean – I'm sorry – his taking Sylvie . . ."

"Don't try to explain."

"No. The one thing I didn't anticipate was meeting you."

"I think perhaps you'd better come into bed with me. If I may ask."

"Will you forgive me if I don't?"

"Not only that. I'll understand."

"Good scout," said Walter, trying painfully to laugh.

*

Walter, on his back, was snoring. Miriam sat bolt upright in bed. One wasn't having this.

"Stop it!" Quiet voice, that would not carry further than the bathroom, but a tone of command. The practised pleader has an ear for pitch. A phrase that however short will have impact upon a brain dulled by many things: unwillingness, fatigue, hostility, confusions and distractions of all sorts. It is useless to shout. An interjection conveying only indignant protest, 'Monsieur le Procureur, I must interrupt you,' is of little weight in a courtroom and better ploys are called for. Condescending amusement can be double-edged: one must watch the President carefully for a sign of boredom, irritation, a suppressed yawn or digestive rumble. A note of faintly ironic surprise? Man – you're snoring!

Certainly Miriam is good at it. Walter rolled over good as gold, his breathing instantly quieted.

She leaned back on her elbows. She worked a cigarette out of the packet on the night-table and smoked it about halfway through before squashing. Punched the pillow, a time or two. Sat up again. Slipped out of bed. Dressed.

The old boards under layers of worn carpeting in the passages creaked noisily as though designed to entrap the slinking adulterer, but the marble squares of the vestibule were silent under her feet. There was the unaltered smell of dusty curtain and stale food. The night porter – a patience-player? a Russian-grammar-learner? – raised an unsurprised eye.

"I'm not sleeping; I'll slip out for half an hour." Nod. "Door unbolted?" Nod. Nothing untoward. Too much lobster. "Be back soon. A quarter of mineral water. An alkaseltzer if you have one," tipping him. Provide people with a reasonable explanation and they will see no cause for mistrust.

The streets of La Rochelle, at three in the morning. Peaceful. It is too late for revellers, whores or muggers, too early for the shift, railwaymen or cleaners. The odd bicyclist or pedestrian minding his business, the odd car with a quiet purr, an untroubled conscience on the way home from a card game or sitting up over the accounts. Traffic lights set to amber winked placidly. The hour when the police and the firebrigade have written up their log and fancy a cup of coffee: ambulance men stroll across to out-patients for a chat, and the night nurses open the fridge for a sandwich and a pot of yoghurt.

It's not an enormous place, and whatever you're looking for is quite easily found. And they rather pride themselves, here-about, on their common sense. The local folk are on good terms with their administration: it is a rarity in a country where tammany-style politics are still distressingly frequent. Miriam stood on the pavement looking at the Commissariat of Police, where a bit of yellowish light had a peaceful and a reassuring look, and told herself that there need – there should – be no trouble. There would be a telex message somewhere: there was the necessary legal authority. A couple of phonecalls would have to be made, and somebody competent got out of bed. Technically it should be easy enough. A garage was a good place for a pinch. Breakfast time: it was a simple matter surely to seal that off discreetly, with no great brandish of boots and guns. One young man, and relying more upon moral suasion than the pistol in his pocket. Four or five plain-clothes cops, sober and experienced: no need for any scandal. Her own rôle in the matter need not be explained nor even mentioned. What was stopping her? Why were both feet in the gluepot of a sudden?

'I am a modern young woman and my equilibrium is excellent.'

Lebreton has good marks for the lucidity of her analyses and the clarity of her syntheses, and her physical reactions are swift: she fences, she plays tennis. We've been over it all. There is Sylvie, to whom she has taken rather a liking, and who has a certain emotional involvement. There is Walter, whose involvement is that much greater: hm, on two or three levels and that must be contained. There is her own; should we smile? A commissaire of urban police, perhaps an inspector of Police Judiciaire, would be people with a level of some sophistication besides experience. 'Female frailties' – a small smile, a stroke of the pen through that. Counsellor Lebreton feels, as a member of the opposite sex, an increased sensitivity towards the problems of her client, but nobody would call her 'involved'.

Well, what are we standing here rooted for?

This is really funny. 'Hysterically funny' and she is not quite sure of either this adjective or this adverb. Qualifying plain verbs is to be avoided, where possible, in pleading.

Avoid them then. Are you frightened to cross the road? That is neurotic. (She recalls a colleague telling that his awareness of an incipient nervous depression began with inability to cross the road.) There is something here that goes beyond the physical dimensions of a simple business.

A metaphysical element? It is hardly a notion that has ever much touched this modern young woman, who has not the philosophical mind. She has indeed given little thought to such concepts since classroom days; oh the boredom of Bergson. Michel Foucault's book about prisons. A certain impatience with abstractions.

She does grant that going to bed with Walter could in a certain light be seen as frivolous or irresponsible: how was she to know? It isn't possible that as unimportant a thing as sex should ... If purely on account of sleeping with people one should ... Walter had made a comic, ironic, breakfast-time remark. 'My wife is rather a believer in sleeping with her friends. Oddly, I never have. Rather like saying I would never wear suède shoes or eat pudding with a fork. Social attitudes to which one is brought up. Now that I have, I wonder whether I give it too much importance.'

And I, thought Miriam, I wonder whether I give it enough. Part of his honour. Did he lose it, or give it me? Or lend it me, in trust. To me it was little; to him it was much. He was not 'my client'. An absurd piece of 'deontology' to say that one doesn't sleep with one's client. What would I have done if, instead of casually announcing that he intended to sleep with Sylvie (and what was his motive there?), this young man (what is impressive about him may one ask?) had pointed his finger at me? I would have shrugged and told myself that it had no importance, that nothing which happens has any importance?

Are you being honest with yourself? Did you feel some slight indignation there? Lebreton may sleep with Forestier, because really nobody could care less. She's just a loose end, to keep tidy.

You are paralysed. Did you get out of bed and dress and walk here, tap-tap, with it all clear in your mind; no hesitation at all, a simple, commonsense, material decision? You like the shoes or you don't. You do? Then buy them. Life has always been like that.

Walter lying on his bed, drawing on his cigar.

"I'm sorry, Miriam. This is my fault. I have no explanation. It's no use saying that I wasn't to know. To me it wasn't something to think out. I had a sort of contract, with this man. Boy – whatever. I have to see it through, to the end. I wanted to get him out of the country: I thought of this means. I owed it to myself. And now you. The whole equation goes haywire. Mine always do." And mine never have. They do, now.

Miriam turned on her heels and went back to the hotel.

She nodded to the night porter, who said 'Sleep well' with indifferent, formal courtesy. She went up the creaky stairs, let herself noiselessly into the room where Walter was sleeping as though he'd never wake up, like a man with a clear conscience. She undressed. Naked, she stood between the two beds before putting her pyjamas on. It would be agreeable if self-indulgent to get into bed with the man; waking him gently, putting her arms round him, saying, 'I need to be loved: I'm short on love. Like calcium. I haven't enough. I don't want it metaphysical. I'm not any good at that. I want to be screwed as though my life depended on it, and maybe it does. Do you mind?' In the diffused light through the opened curtains she stood looking at him for some time before shivering and feeling thoroughly physical goose-bumps. She put on her pyjamas then and got into bed in a hurry: on her own.

*   *   *

Walter lies in bed, decidedly bleak, trying not to fidget, aware of a long and lengthening row of nasty occasions in his life; toads to chew and snakes to swallow: like a general reviewing lost battles, except that generals will always succeed in finding some one else to blame.

I am not wise in the ways of the world. The garage-man's remark that became a classic. 'But Monsieur Forestier – you're living in the Middle Ages!'

Indeed, I have taken too often the easy way out, abdicating. The practical details of existence – even answering the telephone – have been left to Sylvie. No wonder that she feels deep resentments that go far back. Women forget nothing. My disloyalties . . . the one for which I feel most shame, now, was a remark that seemed at the time sheer exasperation, even afterwards hardly more than a loose-tongued indiscretion – 'As she gets older her lovers get younger.' The friend to whom I spoke went and looked out of the window, in an unhappy silence.

Try not to fidget. Because if Miriam is lying awake she'll be wondering sardonically how long it will take before I come creeping across the floor to shuffle into her bed. And Sylvie, wondering where I was the night before last, is sure now that she knows. The wheel spins: Hitchcock (cheap fellow) called that *The Lady Vanishes*.

Why in god's name do I do these things? That I pose the question at all sums up my futility. Virtually everybody found lengthy explanations of why General Lee lost the battle of Gettysburg. Except, probably, General Lee.

Did Napoleon ever come up with an honest answer as to why he behaved in so peculiar a fashion at Waterloo? That sleepiness, and apathy. That he couldn't sit a horse because of trouble with his fundament (the excuse of every rider who has lost a Tour de France when by all logic he should have won it has always been 'saddle trouble') – no, it isn't good enough. Why leave Davoust, a winning general if ever there was one, behind in Paris? Why rely upon a notoriously lazy incompetent known to all as 'the miserable Grouchy'? Why, biggest question of all, leave the entire conduct of the battle to Ney, who had completely lost his sense of judgment? In the first world war it was called 'shell-shocked', and in the second 'bomb-happy', but recognisable a century before, no?

After a futile question, a futile digression.

Fernand – there's nothing complicated about him. Did Miriam say that, or had I worked it out already? – she said only that it was idiotic to plead all those snivelling sentimentalities in front of a tribunal, going on about his childhood like a social worker. When our ruling passion is no longer survival it becomes comfort. To someone whose passion *is* survival our preoccupation with comforts is ignoble and trivial, utterly selfish; there's no way it can be justified. It can't even be understood.

There are millions of them out there, any colour but mostly brown or black, without food, home, job or shelter, and with no hope of getting any, so get hold of a gun at all cost and take a couple of the screws with you. Out there, at least numbers are on your side, and you can call yourself something-or-other's liberation-army. Back here you're just a public enemy, something to be stamped upon. You interfere with our comfort. The two words aren't east and west, or Cap and Com: they're just have and have-not. And the haves don't like the have-nots. Get picked for that side, and we'll make your pips squeak, mate.

And the tribunal, the court, is picked from the haves.

I ought to know something of this. My ancestors, simply, were bandits. Exactly like Fernand, able and intelligent: the only really stupid thing about Fernand is that like me he's living in the Middle Ages, when you could still get away with being a bandit . . . Successful bandits built a castle on a hilltop and set up as robber barons. There was no way but a flight into the future. We worried about survival too. Afraid of a bigger baron, stronger than ourselves, afraid of losing what we had, we went ahead and thought up ways of making it legal.

We had, already, the qualities that were to congeal into a code for the upper classes. Personal courage, indifference to pain, hardship or suffering. Stoicism, when one lost. Physical self-control: it was said of Talleyrand that you could kick his arse without its showing in his face: an ancestral skill presented as hypocrisy. On the contrary: there was an absence of cant. A spade always stayed a spade.

And gradually they got better. With the notion that everything belonged to them by ancestral right they developed the idea that something was owed in return. Right up until recently they kept their 'knightly' code: never to hold envy or rancour, never to allow pettiness.

At his best a gentleman became gentlemanly! being, indeed, gentle . . .

Never to be self-seeking: from being brutal, vulgar and greedy they learned self-mastery over bestial appetites. Frugality, the hatred of show. Scruple: the habit of examining their conscience. But by then of course they were decadent and fatally weakened. Easily swept away, witness my grandfather who could do nothing when it came to Hitler but hide in the gun-room. Not come out.

And through 'public schools' they passed on some of these notions to the bourgeois who sought to copy them. We reached perhaps a high point around nineteen hundred. But the bourgeois never really understood. Scott and his companions died in the Antarctic like gentlemen but stupidly; unable to grasp their own incompetence, never realising that being 'officer class' froze them into selfconscious attitudes – they died of being cut off from the lower deck. They swam in sentimental fantasy, dying in Ruritania for Princess Flavia or the no less sentimental but much more repulsive fantasy of being Bulldog Drummond. They are always sentimental, the bourgeois, because they are never honest: forever vulgar and odious because forever out for what they can grab. Like 'Lord Milner's young men' in South Africa; greed naked in a sauce of sententious pieties. No member of any genuine upper class anywhere ever gave a fart about the Empire.

The wheel has spun. Sport. Invented as an exercise in mastering the self, and in conquering pain. Now the most blatantly self-seeking of get-rich-quick showbiz. The bicyclists were among the last to survive, since you had, in order to conquer the mountain, to conquer everything else. They have been speaking of 'starting the Tour in Japan'. At least a journalist made a sarcastic note on that bright thought. 'If we get really poor, we can always sell them the Alps.' The wheel spins. I defended myself hitherto, with varying but moderate success. And then I grew fat, comfortable, bourgeois. And in a moment of fatuous sentimentality I identified myself with this young, tough and unsentimental bandit who is raping my wife in the next room. I put my fingers in the vice, and twisted it myself.

Like my grandfather, I have come to the last turn of the vice. I am in the gunroom. I have locked the door. Have I thrown away the key?

I am the last decayed, wormeaten fragment of a segment of society that was never worth much but did contribute something: Frederick of Hohenstaufen and Roger of Sicily and Richard the Third: some poets – Surrey, Wyatt, Sidney: even La Rochefoucauld. No, it is not contemptible. Even if only La Mole or Cinq-Mars, beautiful and brilliant young men who loved the wrong person and died well. Worth having.

Walter has slept, and woken again, and has sense enough left to know that it is the bad hour 'when the cattle wake for a little': probably a myth, that. But the hour when black ideas sit on one's bed like the black beast, grinning at one. There is a lot of light, showing Miriam Lebreton's form in the other bed; straight and neat, calmly disposed like that of a mummy. She sleeps sound: what it is to have a well-ordered mind – lucid, legal, balanced – factual. Rue the day, girl, that you took up with writers. Kittlecattle.

It is warm, and no need to slip a jacket over his pyjamas. The moon is high in a bright sky, subduing the loom and blink of the lighthouse save where dark ragged scraps of cloud scud before a big booming south-west wind that surges like the sea against the buildings – sea which Walter loves and no narrow piddling sea but the big beautiful Atlantic. How would I not love it, fish that I am, man of Europa, the peninsula, the presqu'île, last of the western lands before the sea. Europa – there's a Hebrew etymology there somewhere: Abendland, the evening country, you are mine. It isn't England or Belgium, France or Spain. All are dear to him but none are more than a part. It is all here, in the old harbour of La Rochelle, enclosed in the towered gateway to the West, here upon the old huguenot shore of refuge.

And to Walter along come friends, and first the old master who wrote that the south-west wind before the dawn had ever been of good omen to him. Writers – rarely, in general, are they friends, for their little egoisms, born of terror and vanity, create obstacles to understanding. And what does that matter? It is by their work one judges them, and it is with their work that friendship is born. Walter does not have to summon these

165

spirits. They come by themselves, when least expected but when most wanted.

The child Theseus, in the Isle of Pelops. Familiar to Walter through the fine words of Mary Renault. 'The ruin of beauty, the ebb of valour, the fall of strength' – the child is watching the sacrifice of the King Horse. 'The grief, the burning pity as he sank upon his knees and laid his bright head in the dust.' And immediately comes the lesson in royalty from the child's grandfather who is king.

'It is not the sacrifice or the bloodletting that calls down power, but the consenting. Readiness is all. It is when we stretch out our hands to our moira, that we receive the sign of the god.'

Bereitsein: the readiness. We don't have to leave honour to the likes of Theseus or King Lear, do we? They understood that force and craft could make of you a bandit chief, but that only honour could confer nobility. Few people had it: no wonder that everyday folk thought of it as a sign of being god-descended. A scrap of blood so precious that sixteen generations afterwards your 'quarterings' were your chief source of pride, and mostly the only one you had. Honour might be met with anywhere. Attributed to the wrong side of a god's blanket. Walter went back to bed in good humour, slept well and woke clear-headed.

*

Others had a night of disquiet. Manuel, who was accustomed to sleeping well because it would not occur to him to sleep badly, even if his imagination was playing him tricks. Disquiet was a hair lodged between the shirt and the skin: all you had to do was to find it. Tall, strong, filled with energy: one saw a highly physical person in rude health. It wouldn't occur to one to suspect a metaphysical habit of thought.

If he had read the local paper he would have been quick to add things up; but if he looked at it at all it was at the small ads. Something to follow up professionally. The rest was self-advertisement.

He doesn't like complications. Look at Pa, whose existence is a misery because he can never leave well alone and complicates everything. Life is simple. Obey the rules. There is more to it than getting up early and working hard: plenty of people do that. He doesn't think of it much. Certainly he doesn't think of it as a key to success!

It's as simple as it is rare: he is candid, he is unselfish, and he is honest. People like him at once and trust him within moments. He is good at other people, and his business runs well in consequence. He is always quick-tempered and often peppery, but as patient as a donkey underneath, with other people's shortcomings.

He lives alone in a small flat. Not that small – he likes space around him. It is bare, and oldmaidishly neat – but like most pejorative adjectives that one is meaningless.

Walter reads the local paper while crumpling it to light the fire; Manuel hasn't a fire, and reads pieces of grease-stained paper that have wrapped tools, or fried fish. It was on the repair-bench in the workshop that his eye fell on the small item about a highway bandit who had pulled the gag of jumping a guard in the tribunal jacks. And made-good-his-escape (the accomplice had been apprehended) and had so far succeeded in setting-at-defiance the zealous forces of order and protection. Manuel would have given this no thought at all but for the hair that had been tickling his back. He was absent-minded for an hour, with what the Italians called his obstinate face on.

Manuel was well accustomed to Pa's eccentricities. Walter wanted to borrow a bigger car, had been mysterious about it; even secretive, but there was nothing in that. He was for ever cooking up lunatic schemes, and refused to run the gauntlet of curiosity about them, or sarcastic comment. So wait in patience: Dad would tell the comic story in his own time. These theatrical effects were due to the streak of exhibitionism in any artist. Sure, as teenagers they had all writhed with the embarrassment of being covered-in-shame by Dad in public.

The lesson has served Manuel. He has learned that just about anybody did extraordinary, unheard-of things: and were very much more tortuous about them than Pa ever was.

Thus, Walter's peculiar behaviour on a parking lot had not bothered him (finding the car in a hurry was a nuisance, and he'd been peppery about that). The chap in the back of the car? Pa's talent for incidental acquaintance – a writer's thing, that; picking people up and making much of them for an hour. If the fellow had not been wearing that old pullover – it wasn't that he grudged lending it! But the detail had struck him. It struck him again now. Now he was asking himself questions about it.

*

Walter made rather a fuss about having a good breakfast. Needed fortifying, he said, to restore nervous energy. Was cross about a boiled egg being hard. Miriam was if anything amused. Nervous energy got wasted by this display of temperament, and then working hard to make it up in a further display of rather obvious charm towards the chambermaid. The lavish tip, she thought, was as unnecessary as the lavish todo. But it was one of the things about Walter that had first entertained her and then (in both senses) seduced her. Elaboration of being courtly with the middle-aged Portuguese biddy, who had been sullen at having to make a second trip for more coffee, and apologising now about that goddammed egg!

They were having breakfast like a settled married couple! She had been to the bathroom first, was showered, combed, dressed. Looking and behaving 'normal' – and why not? Walter was still plootering about half-dressed, shaving between cups of coffee, wondering what shirt to put on; and that was normal behaviour too.

"Why didn't you skip out?" he asked suddenly, "You could have, easily enough. While we were all asleep. You could have gone to the police, had the place quietly invested. You've a legal mind. You're an 'officer of the court' – your duty to see the law is respected."

"I'd a lot of reasons. I thought about it, yes. Yes, that's what I should have done. Yes, it would have been easy. Yes, I decided against it. I don't want to go into all my states of mind."

"I'd still be interested in your reasons."

"Just let it lie, would you!"

"You didn't want to put Sylvie at risk. And I'd like to thank you for that. And you shied off, I think, from a situation that would have been painful and humiliating to her, and why not admit it to myself as well. And thank you for that, too."

"Walter, shut up, will you. For a supposedly intelligent and occasionally sensitive person you can be remarkably stupid, tactless and boorish."

"So my own dear wife has never ceased to tell me. Shit – this infernal jam on my trousers."

168

"Stay still," said Miriam, wifely, holding the corner of a towel under the tap.

'There was some other motive too," standing lamblike to be scrubbed.

"Look out, mate, you're vulnerable to a swift punch in the whoosit," acidly. "That's better. If a little damp." Dry . . . "Yes," straightening up, "I do have another motive. It's part of my code to see things through when I've started . . . I went shooting once. I shot at a deer and only wounded it. The hunter who was teaching me – another lawyer – told me there was no worse crime than to let an animal get away, to die very often in pain. He made me go after it though it might take hours. There are too many so-called hunters who don't. It's too much trouble. A lesson that I took to heart. And now fucking well belt up."

"I was seven years old when my grandfather told me the exact same thing."

"Then you ought to realise," said Miriam softly, "that I don't want to . . . oh, stop hammering at me. While your – while Sylvie is being – look I may have a legal mind but I'm not pleading in front of a court and I'm trying to get into your thick head that in these circumstances I'm not able to express myself in clinical terms."

"You haven't any coffee left in that pot, by any hazard?"

*

The subject of this conversation? Sylvie (also 'first in the bathroom') while taking a shower had put it in terms which while not clinical were brief; and without stammering.

I've been to bed with a few men in my life. That was a time when I said yes. And when the children were growing up – what with one thing and another I changed my mind. My mind got changed for me, would be an honester way of putting it. I started saying no. I am a free woman? Freer than I have sometimes been. The freedom to say no is more important, and better worth having.

I did not think that a moment would come when I did not have this freedom. It has taught me something.

I can be grateful. I may be out of practice, but I have experience. Men while in bed: to borrow a favourite expression of Walter's, a lot of clichés apply.

I suppose I've seen most attitudes. Not – mercifully – all. I

169

have never known sadism in any direct physical sense. But most. Since my somewhat melodramatic introduction – la la la, in the snow at St. Anton, but that is an episode that stays between me and St. Anton – simply, I discovered that I'm one of those women that like it though I had every reason to believe the contrary – tja, I'm what's called a daughter of the game.

Which stands me in good stead now. And stands someone else in good stead too. Walter was quite right. Once given confidence: once he understands that a woman . . . the boy has known nothing but sluts who give it like opening a tin of sardines. Or wretches who use it as leverage and generally mercenary. Girls who are not women at all. Who know not even the first thing about being a woman.

You'll have to forgive me, Walter: you have forgiven much: I have too often been crude and stupid. I go on learning. You are a bastard in a varied and sophisticated number of ways, and some were wished on you by me. Since the children were small you have not cheated on me: it is irrelevant (another of your words) that I have done no worse. You spent the night there with that woman. I can see it in your face! But you didn't do that in any vicious spirit. You are trying to do better as a human being, and you're confused about that. I've given you hard knocks: I've just given you another. Sorry, I'm not very good at this either.

Miss Leguen or whats your name, you seem to me a sensible woman. I'm sorry, that this puts you in an unhappy and a false position. If I'm right you'll know how to steer.

Walter – I suppose you aren't bad at your trade, but you know? I'm never very impressed by writers. They can tell a good tale, but in general, even the good ones – they know so pitifully little about human beings! I see books praised to the skies, given prizes – not just unreadable but downright silly. I feel ashamed for them, these trivial, futile people. Be a musician! You aren't given the chance to cheat, there. You think yourself an intellectual, my poor man, and you upbraid me for being a dumb cow. And you know nothing! I wish I had some kind of telepathy to convey all this.

Dried. Dressed. Brushed. Made up. Tja, Mum, the Belgian cow looks better than I had expected you to, by daylight. The face is inevitably green cheese; always was, even at twenty I looked good really only by electric light. Known worse days, though. Haven't we!

"Good, there's the bathroom free. Tell you what, while you wash I'll order breakfast, and we can have it here in peace."

"Can one do that? I never knew."

"Can and will. Coffee?"

"I like chocolate best. Is that . . .?"

"No strain. You go shave or whatever. Room service? . . ."

"Good, you look nice. And here – while it's hot. Eat my croissant – I don't like them. Raining again out, a pity. Funny, being in La Rochelle, thinking that tomorrow we can be in Belgium."

"Will you come with me?"

"I'll come all the way. That's agreed. With you – after that? No. You wouldn't want me. You might think so now, but starting from scratch will be easier in the long run. And a woman, you know – one man at a time. I tell the truth; you know that by now. You and me – no, too much like incest."

"It's the trouble, right? Nobody ever tells one the truth."

"I do. Walter has, as far as he knows it. As he sees it, that's what one has to understand, with him. You ought to; you're much the same. As you see it. Not always the reality. That's my job, to know reality. The real under the illusion. Trust me for that."

The telephone burred irritably and Sylvie made a complicated face: eyes expressing serenity, wishing and trying to reassure while the mouth did something between a pout and a grimace that said 'Reassure me', while Fernand who had been sprawling relaxed – nobody had seen him like that – tightened up and sprang taut as to a fire alarm.

"Yes?" said Sylvie drawling it.

"What are you all doing?" came a scratchy quack. "Breakfast is now over, no? – we ought to be on the way. There's a lot of road out there."

"Time to pack my toothbrush."

They found Walter fuming and fidgeting in the garage. Miriam with her hands in her pockets, taking a deep interest in the arrangement of fog lamps on the bumper of a rather ostentatious sleigh near by. She did not think it would be easy to find the right tone of voice – the correct social expressions – with

171

which to say good morning to the man who has spent the night with one's wife. Rather like (had she known about it) Walter on a foggy evening in Amsterdam long ago, she was wondering whether in place of all these show-off lamps on the fender a massive pair of elk horns might not be more to the point. Did Sylvie also remember that nightmarish slow drive in the twisting narrow streets with the two yellowish eyes of the deux-chevaux just behind, saying 'I saw you'?

Fernand – tight as a violin string, thinking – what? Does the young bull think about to lock horns with the old bull? Does it stop and think of a tactic, telling itself perhaps that the young bull is stronger but that the old bull is experienced, perhaps craftier? Making a plan – to edge out, say, to a flank and take the initiative with a sudden feint to the vulnerable side? Whose horns are the longer, and have the wider spread? Nobody quite knows how a bull thinks. Rudyard Kipling once made a good tale of one that did, but nobody present has read it save Walter, and his mind is not on English Literature.

"I've paid the bill," in a harsh jolting tone. "No comments, no queries, no reference to little lists: let's get on with it."

Miriam is not going to say anything. It isn't the moment for review of the legal aspect.

Fernand is not going to say, 'Look, I'll leave you here, enjoy your holiday, since it's enough that Sylvie comes with me.' His mind is full of bull-things. Kipling's bull assassinated rivals from behind, by twilight, disembowelling them by an oblique charge. He says nothing because he knows nothing about a situation where the gun in his pocket is meaningless.

And Sylvie finds nothing to say. She wishes to say, 'Walter, trust me. I have never let you down. I never will.' The tragedy of the human being's gift of speech is that he is never able to use simple words. Thought is too complicated for speech.

So that everybody keeps a stupid silence, and Walter slams in behind the wheel and starts the motor with much too much noisy revving-up, and drives too fast through the placid morning traffic of a pleasant, grey, slightly drizzly September day in La Rochelle and Miriam says quietly, 'Slow down till you get an open road: you do not want the police enquiring into a traffic accident' after a sudden squeal of brakes has put an old lady with a shopping bag in peril, with a great jump of her nervous system since the imagined perils are so much more frightening than the real ones.

Walter finds a main road and heads east. That much of the projected plan still exists: that if any curious somebody has picked up scent of their doings and goings, this direction will be the one least expected. Poitiers – tiens, hallo there, thinks Miriam haphazardly. Le Blanc – roughly: it's only a couple of hundred kilometres but the cross-country road is nothing famous. Nevers – another couple of hundred: at this point Walter thinks of a sudden turn and dart north or anyhow north-east; but one will see when one gets there.

Meantime this is some of the dreariest country in France, and all these places are symbolic of provincial dust, boredom, and nothing ever happening. It is the in-between land; south of the rich valley country of Touraine and Berry; north of the great mountain massif of central France. It is the area about which comedians make jokes. When Parisiens want an example of the never-never land where no thought and no action has ever been known to occur, and thus supposedly the perfect barometer for the country's doings and sayings, where poll-takers, statisticians and suchlike soothsayers come to 'take the political tempera-ture', a sous-préfecture in the Deux-Sèvres is the classic place-first-thought-of. Exactly as Hollywood studios are supposed to measure their projects and estimates by the likes and dislikes of Kokomo, Indiana.

Adulterous wives, jealous husbands, leading to nasty dramas; these do not exist in the departments of the Vienne, the Indre? Bank hold-ups, terrorists, liberation armies; are here unthink-able? The population is bovine, cow-go-to-market? It wouldn't do to be dogmatic about that. The name of Bourges, capital of this province between Limoges and Dijon, sounds reassuringly stolid. It was the capital of France once: there are fine buildings and a great cathedral: that was a long time ago. But France is an unexpected, deceptive place: at its dreariest and most anaesthetic capable of surprises. It doesn't do – a commonplace error in Eng-land or America – to denigrate or dismiss. There are bold spirits, and revolutionaries, in Bourges, who might just astonish you.

One can be forgiven for finding it boring. Stopping for lunch in Le Blanc – but surely nobody ever does stop for lunch in Le Blanc? The tourist guides probably do not mention it. Walter cannot be sure: he has no guides, to good food in particular. He has lived here long enough to have caught them out; rather too often.

So they stopped at some Café de Commerce, lacking paint both outside and in. There were few customers. It was quite unpretentious and very cheap: ignored by guides and therefore both as well as being good.

Everything was home made; everything was fresh; everything was generous. Bread and butter. Radishes and local sausage. Hard-boiled eggs with Russian salad, a huge pile of fresh vegetables and an extra sauceboat of mayonnaise: they stopped giggling when they tasted it. Calves' head vinaigrette: the waitress brought frites as well as boiled potatoes: sniggering broke out afresh until the thought struck them that they were tourists: tourists want frites with everything. Said the Reverend Francis Kilvert, in Radnorshire, in the eighteen-seventies, 'of all noxious animals the most noxious is a tourist; and the most vulgar, illbred, offensive and loathsome is the British tourist'. And of course in every other country they would say 'No no, it's us.'

And since the frites were there, they all ate them with their fingers, exclaiming upon their goodness.

Fernand (relaxed; Sylvie is sitting next him) says there's nothing nicer than calves' head: there is a chorus of assent as full-throated as Handel.

Miriam wins further praise, by going to the lavatory and coming back with a magnum of champagne. The price is in ancient francs, and dates from before the Oil Crisis, which is equivalent to like saying before the flood.

It became an occasion for loosening the belt and for startling utterances of wind. One is no longer 'too polite' to mention such occurrences but one doesn't generally bother. It's pretty unimportant. It was only important now because just as everyone in the car could have become tetchy and irritable, leading to something much worse, they were all contented in a vulgar, necessary way. With the lethargic somnolence of overeating comes tolerance. Somewhere exists a diary, written by an administrative gent in Nazi times, who had the misfortune to get posted to an extermination camp, was much shocked at the goings-on, and confided his distress to paper. One day a party of brass hats appeared, for inspection purposes – were the statistics being properly collected? – and a really good lunch got laid on in the officers' mess. Approvingly he gives the entire menu. 'Ate myself properly full at last. Felt much better.' And that afternoon's Special Action went smoothly.

*

Manuel had slept upon his uneasy mind, found that awaking had done nothing for tranquillity, and made up his mind to action, though the form this had to take was distasteful. He has no liking for the police. But they are necessary now and then. Very well, one must not be the kind of hypocrite that abuses an institution and runs screaming for its help as soon as a pinch is felt. Supposing a connection with a criminal affair, and further ramifications, this will have nothing to do with the urban police, and he addresses himself to the regional service of the Police Judiciaire, whose authority in criminal cases extends over the whole national territory.

The SRPJ is exactly like any French administration, meaning there is a shelf at waist height and a little glass cage, and behind this a hostile, rude and incompetent agent of the administration who views the public with unconquerable dislike.

The little wicket slammed open.

"I wish to see the duty inspector."

"Why?"

"Possibly I've been a witness to a crime."

"Wait." And the wicket slammed shut again. Beyond the glass can be seen the apparatus of computer terminals, telex machine and telephones. It is all exactly like a bank. Presently with heavy tread a chap appears, boosts him grudgingly up a gloomy stairway into the sort of dreary little office where they refuse you a loan. There is a table and two chairs. On the table is a large pub ashtray and a battered old typewriter. Table and chairs are of laminated plastic. For the rest there are some filing cabinets and an unaired smell. After a minute appears a youngish man, neither clean nor really dirty; neither polite nor really rude. The PJ has advanced a long way since the days of Maigret. The proof is that they no longer chain-smoke and no longer blow the ash off sideways (into the typewriter keybank) without lifting the fag off the lip. Otherwise the changes don't meet the eye a great deal. Number 36 Quai des Orfèvres looks

175

much as it always did. One thing doesn't change in France and that is official parsimony, and the deepest-seated conservatism of any country bar perhaps Russia. Perhaps because of this the French quite like Russians. In both countries there have been a lot of cosmetic changes, but there are strong grounds for belief that the one has not altered since Louis Quatorze, and the other since Peter the Great. This will be borne in upon the onlooker when he has anything to do with the police.

The youngish man was a quiet listener, and asked sensible questions at intervals. At last he said "Ce n'est pas évident", a phrase much used in France.

"No," agreed Manuel.

"Wait here a moment." Manuel waited ten minutes.

"Well – the commissaire agrees, on the whole. Not an awful lot we can do. Not really our pigeon either – belongs to the gendarmerie. Not that it isn't helpful" – the chronic lack of enthusiasm must not be too manifest – "this sort of thing is always useful and you're right to come in. We're glad of the information. The description of the car is handy – we could put that on the gendarmerie computer."

Besides the smell in the office, which is frightful, but banks are air-conditioned, the police isn't, there is a hint on the air of a certain absence of zeal towards cooperation between two law-enforcement agencies. Manuel realises that he has made a mistake. But having made a step . . .

"I didn't come without thinking it over carefully."

"Yes, we've lost a bit of time there," says Inspector Barbe – probably nicknamed Klaus by colleagues. "Tell me, you think the fellow might be armed?"

"No outward sign of constraint, but my father certainly had a constrained air."

"He owns a pistol? The idea is this fellow might have found it? Trouble is, this information's two days old. They could be anywhere – out of France."

"Look, I'm just a member of the public. I saw it in the paper, old then; got a notion – pass it on for what it's worth."

"Well, we'll pass it on. There is a warrant for interrogation, I checked that. We'll do what's necessary."

On the pavement, Manuel feels solid dissatisfaction. But the gendarmerie? – no, he's had enough policemen.

But he turns the car, up into the hills. Doesn't have much idea of finding anything useful up there. But one never knows.

'Up the hill' he finds Jesus. They get on well together. They are both characters from Stendhal. This writer has been dead a hundred and fifty years and is remarkably up to date. Much lip service is paid him in France, though it is hard to imagine anyone there has read him – too many home thrusts altogether. But in Spain or Germany, Holland or of course England, and naturally in Italy; much read, and much loved. Jesus agrees with most of Manuel's thinking.

He potters round the house unhappily, and it gives a lot of impressions, but no positive information. Things lie about untidily and plainly they left in a hurry. But where did they go? And lying on the kitchen table is Pa's precious and famous notebook.

Walter never goes anywhere without his notebook, which is neither notebook, diary nor agenda, but has elements of all three. It is a school exercise book and Walter uses it in a kind of permanent dialogue with himself: the fibres of his being are to be found in the written word. Manuel has known it from earliest childhood and regarded it with respect – indeed it is tabu, a juju. Looking in it would be like Noah's sons catching pa drunk and naked. Nobody can read Walter's handwriting anyhow.

But he looks in it now. Scraps of phrase concerning personages unknown, and presumably from Pa's current fictional efforts. Bits of shopping list and exhortations against forgetfulness, as 'Stamps. Scotch tape. Bank. Pay *phone bill*. Washer kitchen tap'. There are squiggles, doodles, aphorisms, and what can only be called graffiti. There are no drawings, for Walter has no graphic talent. There at the end is – what? Walter thinking? Symbolic of indecision? Across half a page are arrows. Equipped neatly with barbs and feathers, but forming a strange up and down zigzag pattern. And at the points there are words written in, scribbled out and replaced – pretty well illegible too. Anch? That is meaningless – a sudden longing for anchovies? But Auch? That means something. Place names! And if that were so one could make out three more: Bordeaux, Nantes, Bourges, and at the end something with an M, and a cryptic '4 ds'. If there were four stages . . . four days! Metz – Mulhouse was closer: could they be making for the German border? It didn't look quite right. Manuel stumped off to the studio where a half hour with the atlas gave him two that fitted almost exactly. Montmédy, on the Belgian frontier, or Malmédy right into Belgium: he would have to gamble. Because if they followed this pattern, and he was familiar with Walter's liking for following patterns, this was the third day and they might be somewhere near Bourges. Assuming they stuck to that. But it made some sense. To go slowly, to follow no predictable path . . . he would go and have some dinner. Something was taking shape in his head.

A pattern of that sort. Not just in Pa's writing in the sacred notebook. It did not mean that they had been carried off at gunpoint. On the contrary – it meant that the idea came from Pa. To get this chap over a frontier meant out of the reach of cops – and yes, Belgium obviously, they spoke French there, and disliked being dictated to, and in the Ardennes – didn't Ma used to talk about childhood holidays there? A countryside she knew. And he, her son, had been the one to give them to the police . . . He looked at his watch – nearly two! But perhaps there was no harm in having this tough steak and dried-out frites under his belt because when would he get another meal? Back to the shop, quick.

"What's the smartest wagon we've got, for a hill road?"

"Mm, the Lancia's got no silencer. There's the Scirocco, that's got a clean pair of heels. Or the R Cinq – that has a turbo motor."

"I'll be gone a couple of days."

"That's your affair," resignedly.

Anybody can tell you that when travelling it is a great mistake to eat a heavy meal and drink a lot in the middle of the day. The position of the body, sitting squashed in a car, makes for bad digestion. It gets very stuffy. One becomes bleary, tired and cross. Brief, accident-prone.

And of course even the most elementary psychology points out with an infuriating righteousness that eating and drinking too much, when already much fatigued by nervous strain, is an infantile comfort mechanism. Like sucking one's thumb.

Cramped and cross and beef-witted they all crawled out thankfully when Walter who had been complaining for some time said, "That'll do nicely," and braked to an abrupt halt the far side of a large shield painted in fancy gothic letting and saying 'Motel des Roches'.

"What Rocks?" enquired Miriam. They were in the upper Loire valley, a few minutes outside Nevers.

"What does that matter? We're all tired. Need some fresh air. And I don't want to go into Nevers – it's the sort of place where everybody notices everything."

"Beuh," said Sylvie, surveying the motel of supposed rocks, presumably a few boulders inserted in some raw landscaping together with hideous little suburban trees in an effort to disguise the wide bulldozed clearing. "Polyethylene beams."

"Who cares?" crossly. "A vulgar roadhouse, I agree, and one goes on, because you're feeling toffeenosed, and fares worse. It'll be comfortable." So typical of Walter, thought Sylvie; not just to be bullying but in total self-contradiction. If I'd made the suggestion we'd have had a tirade, about wouldn't-be-seen-dead in such a dump as you Perfectly Well Know. The food will be dollied deep-freeze and the prices idiotic. "Nobody wants much supper anyhow."

"Rather than make an argument of it," said Miriam sensibly, opening the door on her side. It decided them. At least the bathrooms would be modern. "I'm longing for a wash." She went round to the back for her case.

More than anything else, it was a personality clash that brought it about. And that, as usual, arose from a multitude of tiny things. Like the 'fussy little man' at the reception desk. Weasel-faced individual wearing a cherry-coloured blazer. Just the sort of thing to put Walter's teeth on edge. All together? Of course we're all together. And an irritable tone would be enough to irritate. A scruffy-looking crowd, and ill matched. One liked predictable customers. Business men.

Pretending not to know that he's three-quarters empty, thought Walter, catching sight of a large menu in curly script and making a face at it.

"Seventeen and eighteen then. I must ask you to pay in advance, please. Standard practice and I'm afraid I can allow no exceptions."

A loud sniff, and some decidedly ill grace.

"You'll be dining in the house, naturally." Walter now

grimacing openly at that precious menu. It was enough to tip the scale.

"The car registration, please?"

"I've no idea, it's a hired wagon. I'll look it up for you."

"Then some proof of identity."

"What's this then, East Berlin?" sarcastic.

That was more than enough, and as Walter tacked off, shovelling papers crossly back into pockets, the face tightened up nastily. It would be ridiculous to suggest that he had 'suspicions'. What of? The gendarmerie had the car, of course, on the computer. They had several. They didn't run about eagerly dishing out printed lists to petrol stations. It was a routine affair.

No, the little man was just being slimy. The hired managers of roadhouse chains live in terror of some – any – untoward happening that would put them in bad odour with the financial gentlemen in Paris, and between increasing the occupancy coefficient and cutting down staff their lives are a misery. There are often drunks and sometimes brawls; there are 'histoires' about drinks served to minors and peripatetic prostitutes; and there are sometimes hints and more than hints about drugs. One thus curries favour with the gendarmerie. One can't turn away customers, but one is quick with a lot of officious tale-bearing. Nothing to lay one's finger on, but something odd about that quartet. As well as dislikeable.

"No towels," Miriam was complaining. Oh well, Walter knew the way. Chambermaids! . . . The little sneak was telephoning.

"Hold the line a minute. Yes? Something you still wanted?"

"Towels." A small but gloomy triumph.

"Just a second. Sorry about that. And you won't forget the car number? It's the rule, I'm afraid; we do have to be careful." Defensive, because of the towels. Was that Turkish woman pinching them and blaming it on customers? "I just wanted to confirm those reservations," in a high voice.

"The usual bullshit," said the duty desk man, in the local gendarmerie, writing a note in the daybook. "Funny looking people in cabin seventeen, and he thinks . . . worth the trouble to check?"

"Where's Migeon on that bike – at the crossroads? Tell him

to check it out on his way in." It went out on the local frequency. The patrolling agent, standing beside his big BMW parked at the roadside was bored and stamping his feet. And it was only two minutes down the road.

In cabin seventeen nobody had got sorted out yet. Miriam was rooting about in her case – some washing-powder somewhere, screwed up in a plastic bag. And where had her hairbrush got to? Sylvie was reading tourist literature left on the table; Walter was lying on a bed with his eyes shut. Fernand appeared to be wondering what was meant by 'Sanitised for your protection'. At the back of every mind was a wonder whether the sleeping arrangements . . . Walter was comparing the inside of his head to a dustbin put outside for emptying. Overfull, so that one could hardly get the lid on, and beginning to smell somewhat of rotting fish. A slogan running 'See this through to the end' unwound itself in a monotonous ribbon crawling across his mind like the announcements on television screens superimposed on somebody else's pictures and dialogue. Miriam was seeing one of those composites of newspapers arranged in studied disorder so that one can compare the headings. 'Lawyer tells of nightmare journey. The dangerous hours relived. Forced at gun-point, she says. Tedium was the worst strain, says hijacked lawyer'. This was replaced by a dotty kind of 'anonymous letter' of newspaper cut-outs pasted together crookedly on a grainy background. 'Your dainty undies whiter and brighter still with Zappo'.

Sylvie, gazing blearily at gaudy colour-prints of swimming pools and beach umbrellas, noticed that the girl in the shocking-pink bikini trailed a jagged fuzzy shadow behind her as though on fire, like television where there is snow on the antenna. Sheer insanity to look without one's reading-glasses. Fernand had turned the television set on. Grace Kelly and James Stewart grappled luridly in what passed for Alfred Hitchcock's imagination. Fernand stared enrapt. The door-buzzer whirred twice, loudly. Walter remembered some time after that he'd thought something else had been forgotten, because he'd brought the towels with him, surely? Sylvie was nearest. She got up automatically and opened the door without thinking.

The gigantic figure was frightening. It was not really frightening – she was still not seeing very well and the lighting from the

181

walkway outside was feeble, casting a crooked sinister shadow. It was not really gigantic. But a motorbike cop appears still more corpulent in the bulky black leather jacket and gaiters, dramatised by the white crossbelt, the high white helmet, and in this case a large black moustache. Sylvie uttered a small squeak rather than shriek. The gendarme saluted politely with his gauntlet.

"Oh," she said. "You startled me," and everyone looked up, startled.

Day Four

You had need to be resolute, keyed well up; and in good physical condition. Walter, for example, found the two hours of pottering driving down the hill into Toulouse and back 'a day's work', and complained about the traffic on return. On the autoroute you fell into the pattern of things, drove on the rear-view mirror, found a rhythm at about a hundred and thirty an hour of letting the fast stuff go by while passing trucks, trogs and prudent old ladies, and one could manage around four hours before having one's belly full. Manuel thought little of the task in front of him, though he had been up the hill and back, and it was four in the afternoon. He was keyed up, and he was resolute: certainly; decidedly. As for physical condition he was twenty-four, built like a centre three-quarter, got plenty of hard exercise, had a health like the Pont Neuf, drank little and smoked hardly at all. He was also a good driver.

Even so, that was quite a programme. One could be glad of the turbo-engined car, small and agile, with power in reserve for any moment. For Manuel was going to take the direct road, slap over the mountain massif, the Auvergne, France's big central highland.

The first part was not too bad, up the main road from Toulouse to Albi and along the valley to Rodez, though there was a lot of traffic. The second stage, on the plateau to Le Puy, is sheer hell. The limestone is everywhere cracked by the little crooked river valleys, the way a windscreen will be starred by a flying pebble. One has the same impression of opacity. Up and down like a roller coaster. From Le Puy (a puy is a conical sort of mountain formed of an extinct volcano, numerous in this part of the world and we haven't time to stop and admire them if, like Manuel, we want to get to Lyon while the daylight lasts) it is a shorter stage to Saint Etienne, and one tells oneself it's 'downhill'. Still nasty. From Saint Etienne to Lyon is pie after what lies behind one, even if the traffic is badly congested; which it always is. At Lyon he got on to the Paris autoroute and stopped to tank, to rest, clear his head and think. . . . eat a hamburger, or whatever the hell he could find in the dreadful autoroute junkfood shop. Through the massif to Lyon had taken him something over five hours, and since from Toulouse it is well over four hundred kilometres this was very good going indeed.

And from now on, thought Manuel, using a paper napkin to wipe somebody's tomato ketchup off the table, it's easy: jam in fact. Lyon to Dijon an hour; rather better, on the autoroute. Dijon to Langres, plain road but straightish and by that hour fairly clear of trucks; north to Saint Dizier, much the same. Bar le Duc and up to Verdun. Another five hours; by night it might take more. But he had the night before him, or what was he doing here at all. Neither Dad nor Ma liked to drive at night: their eyesight wasn't what it was. If they could help it. From Verdun to the border was nothing, a matter of fifty kilometres. Crinkly road again though, there, the Argonne or whatever it was called. Battlefields. The Germans came that way in 1914. As they had done in 1870. As they would do again in 1940. Everyone has always come that way, since time immemorial. Couple of miles north, sixteen hundred and something, Condé at Rocroi stopped the Spaniards. Meuse valley, no? – running up towards Dinant and Namur. Sent them arse over tit if memory served. No, rather a good idea to get rid of invaders that way. Poetic justice. Idea that would appeal to Pa.

Would one risk another cup of this revolting coffee? He was half way. And well over the worst.

*

Everything had simply gone much too fast. And if that is a cliché, then so much the worse for the cliché because it happens: it just had.

183

Walter had not even got off the bed. Miriam had just found her little packet of detergent; how had she come to put it there? The gendarme was in the room, just inside the door, and Fernand standing easy, nicely balanced, smiling, in front of Alfred Hitchcock where the suspense was getting the screw turned, was pointing the gun at the large black leather stomach and saying conversationally, "Hands behind the neck, matey, and turn round." A big man, but he did as he was told, and quietly. Nobody wants to get gutshot at eight paces. "Now stay still." On the late night movie the baddy gets too close, and you do this very rapid twist, but not in real life you don't, especially in that big heavy autocoat. Your motorbike cop is a pro, and a pro is prudent.

The gun went deftly into the left hand; the right snaked out fast to the white holster on the gunbelt and came up with pro material. A .357 magnum revolver. A motorbike cop carries it loaded, and cocking it brings a round up under the hammer. "Now it's your gun, and you know what it'll do to your spine. Walter –" now he had two guns to point.

"Fernand, whatever you do –"

"Don't stand there like a silly sheep. Tear a towel. Tear a sheet. Pack that shit back in," at the bewildered Miriam. "Or leave it behind, I don't care." They were all like silly sheep. He was the one unflustered. The time of uncertainty, of halfhearted self-questioning, slipped off like an old jacket: the sight of the uniform acted on him like a fix. None of them could think; they could not summon any coherent reasoning. Tearing up a towel? Like Tarzan or something? "Take a razorblade, you stupid . . . Don't move, you." Wrenching the helmet off, digging the revolver barrel into the side of the thick neck. "Put the sheet over his head. Of course he can breathe . . . pull the knot. Hold it under the tap. Lie down on the bed there – no, belly down – stretch your arms and legs." It brought Walter back to the quiet firelit hour in his own house, being tied with strips of windowcurtain. And now he was tying the knots . . .

"Look, this is foolish, we can still manage to get –"

"Shut up, Walter." It was said viciously, like a trap springing but so quietly that the shock was the greater.

"I'm not standing here for this," said Miriam in sudden outrage. "You're killing him, I won't have it."

"What you'll have is a bullet in the belly." He set the automatic below her navel. "Here about right?" She put her hands over her eyes and recoiled. Sylvie, appalled, made a monstrous effort to bring her voice down to the level of this chilly, gentle violence.

"Fernand, it's true, he'll smother. Respect life – for me, please." When he looked at her she knew that this time she would not lose. But would there be another? There was no grip to be got with reason. She had only this emotional appeal, to the man she had slept with. It wouldn't serve a second time.

He pulled the sheet back, tapped the forehead with the foresight of the revolver, wrenched the wet towel down from the nose.

"Breathe, can you? Nod. Shout. Go on, shout. Shout your head off. He'll do. Just get your coats. Never mind the cases. Don't want them thinking we're skipping. Nobody's noticed him. Look, there's his bike. He hasn't been to the office." Quiet and reasonable, as to small frightened children. "In fact I'd bet he didn't even know." The radio on the bike, set to receive, was making blurry mumbling sounds, with no urgency in them. "He's just gone for a drink, see. Get in the car. You drive, Walter. Easy-like. Just going off to dinner. Down in the town. Don't fancy this dump. Now – now you can speed up. Don't lose your head, stick to the plan. No reason to change it. Now, how do we get out of here?"

"Towards Auxerre," said Walter. Perhaps it was true. Perhaps after all no signal had been made. Perhaps even if they had . . . but why should they have been signalled? Nothing had happened along the way. It wouldn't be Manuel, to say anything. Perhaps after all it had been a coincidence. But that man back there would be missed, and soon. The big police bike . . .

"Real quiet, at the crossing," ordered Fernand. "These bike patrols go in couples."

"Clamecy." Turning. No cops to be seen.

"How far is Auxerre?"

"Hundred and twenty. Give or take."

"Now speed it up."

Since autoroutes were invented Nevers is no longer the important crossroads point it once was. But there are still four main roads. The old National-Seven from Paris to Lyon, south

185

to Moulins and Roanne, north to Montargis and Fontainebleau. And the N. Seventy-six: west towards Bourges, east into the Morvan, Château-Chinon and Autun. The Auxerre direction, north-east up towards the bleak Langres plateau that is one of France's deserts, might be the least expected. If once one got past Auxerre – they might have an hour before an alert got properly organised. Fernand, who was in the front now, next to the driver, switched on the little map-reading lamp.

Because now the sooner in Belgium the better, and it had to be this night, and that clown Walter had understood because now he was making this old Alfa fly. Lucky it was dark blue and pretty dirty. At night that would show as black, or indeed as almost anything. And even raining this was a goodish road.

Yes, Auxerre was right. But from there out one could take two ways. Troyes, Chalons and Verdun. About four hundred kilometres, and autoroute the second half – no, one would travel quicker but those roads would be stiff with police. The other was through one-horse places, where cops were a lot thinner on the ground. Chatillon and Chaumont and Neufchâteau, say two hundred and fifty. And then about a hundred, straight up the Meuse valley. Empty roads at night, and a shorter distance. It could be done, and he would do it. If we've gas enough to get past Auxerre which is a danger-point: there might be road blocks, there. Yes, we tanked just a short way back.

Walter did not think – we use the word in such a loose sense that nine times in ten we mean no more than talking to ourselves; the vague interior monologue that passes for thought. Even this was limited for the most part to technicalities: one drives with an empty mind, but pushing the car as hard as he dared to the three limitations of darkness, an unknown road, and the sludgy little drizzle that had not stopped all day – this concentration, and the flow of adrenalin, took all the thought he had. The Alfa was a good car, by European standards a biggish one, solid, holding the road well. The strong yellow light bored satisfyingly into the blackness: the swish of the windscreen wipers and the soft rubbery thud at each return – a steady metronomic rhythm that comforted, consoled; though 'Comfort, Content, Delight ...' (what was this scrap of verse that fluttered weakly about in his head, moth attracted to the lamp?) – something about the years' slow-bought gain ... 'They vanished in a night' ...

186

Something else too, to do with the catch in the wiper blades – like an oldfashioned gramophone whose turntable did not stop at the end of the record; the needle went on freewheeling in an escape groove, swish and click at each turn infuriatingly until you went and stopped it. And a hideous popular songhit from those days, somewhere in the mid-thirties, that went on and on interminably, to nausea –

'And the music goes around and around, o - oh, o - o - o - oh'. It is no magic formula, alas, for opening the blocked gate out of the city of Walter's solitude. It is Open Barley, Open Buckwheat, Open Cornmeal, Open Peanut, Open Shredded Wheat, Open Frostyflake. No, he couldn't find it; the music goes around and around and it's still open Hambone, open Hitchcock, all useless. The illusion persists that you advance: third gear, fourth, fifth, and the responding high note in the motor – but it's just the same record going round and round.

Comfort, content, delight: not the years, it had to be a bisyllable – could it be 'the decades' slowbought gain'? . . . Three good things, fine things, and somehow always too dearly bought, and the first two not even worth it. Comfort and content, a very bourgeois ideal surely, and delight always comes unexpectedly, and free, and the dearer for being so rare, and so ephemeral.

It's not what we've ever looked for, surely. Comfort and self-love in all its vain manifestations; that is where that road leads. Honour: that is a word that has tumbled clean out of our vocabulary. Now only a literary word, as befitted a medieval concept. Went out along with troubadours. Or codpieces. Desuetude is the word I'm looking for.

Auxerre. Second to third gear. Gently. There is no one about. Not a sign of gendarmerie and road blocks. And now Auxerre past, miraculously – now that is a word we still use: we remain astoundingly superstitious beings. And now I really think we've a chance of making it. Fourth gear; fifth. But you are still a prisoner. It is that, which you and Fernand have in common.

Fernand thought. Or, at least, he day-dreamed.

That was the city. That was my city. They don't know it but I come from hereabout. I don't say it, I don't think it, I've long obliterated it. I saw that town two or three times when I was a little'un, and thought it the centre of the world. And then came the day when I made up my mind I'd never eat beans again. I found out that Paris existed. Right, there I'd go, if I had to walk every step of the way. And find the world. Did too. Knew it would be hard. Less hard than being up at four every morning and getting out to the stinking vines and the stinking beans on the stinking hills, I remember saying to that slut Anne – cold? You don't know what cold is. The way I got warm was getting my jacket tanned, and my breeches too. The peasants . . . I swore I'd never come back here. And now I'm back, you never get away. Fernand's your name. Couldn't find more of a plouc hick name than that: Christ, you might well as be called Jules or Léon: never found out till the boys asked what's your name and I said Fernand and they fell about laughing, well I stopped them laughing.

Belgium? All those jokes about frites, and being real dim. Long time I thought it really was like that. Thought I knew better when I'd seen a bit of the ch'timi country up north, bricks 'n' beetroot, coalmines 'n' potato fields, all black like Lens or Béthune. Full of Poles. Or the textile mills at Roubaix. Rather that, too, than the hills – and the beans, rather a good beer than that lousy donkeypiss wine. Gautier made me laugh – Walter's what they call him in the north, he comes from up here some place – going on about the Corton Charlemagne and the only wine that's drinkable comes from here. Yes, down south Beaune-way, at about three hundred francs the goddam bottle. Try our home growth some time.

South Belgium's different, she says, telling me in bed, good she was there too, good I mean good, what a stupid dimwit word. Forest country in the Ardennes, knew it when she was a nipper. Said I'd like that. Reckon she might not be far wrong at that. Hills not big, she said, so trees right up to the top, and valleys between, not so deep really but steep and sudden, and trees right down to the water. A tree's worth having: you can't make it, and you've got to wait for it, yes I can go for that. I liked the Pyrenees; not all that different, she says, not so open, you can't see far. But woods, and real little hill streams not polluted, with fish in them, hill farm with just a couple of cows, dead poor, I know all about it, I'm being sentimental she says, okay, but bit of cheese, bit of yoghurt, bit of fish. And there's boar in those woods, still. Bees. I'd like to have bees. I know how. I tell you, if I can find this ol' fella she says might be still alive, taught her how to set a wire for a rabbit when she was a kid – I'd give it a whirl. At the worst I can rest up, get in shape, and I can make a connection up there in Holland. Not Amsterdam, there's too many thinks of that racket, it's overcrowded. Go up there these towns on the Rhine, that bridge-too-far place in the war film on the German border, I know a fella there. But it'd be nice to be out of it all. A little hill farm. You've a country name, Fernand, she says, maybe you're a country boy and should go back. She could be right.

To surpass yourself: Walter pressed a little harder; got another ten kilometres an hour: it might make the difference by the time one made the border at Malmédy. Surpass yourself. You are just a man, so you are neither good nor bad. You are both, or you are neither. It's the Bernanos theme as well as Stendhal's: hell, it's the theme of any writer that's any good. Do not be mediocre.

Another sixty to Chaumont. And if we make that – then we've a real chance. Me and my hitch-hiker. Last time I took one it was that American boy. Even there at the side of the road you could see he was American! That great damn big smile! Laugh at it if you like – not to Grin is a Sin – but god it can warm our chilly European heart betimes; there are moments when it's good to have. So you ask straight off the inevitable classic question 'Where you from?' And damn if he didn't say 'Sun Valley.' Laughing his head off.

'Not so very long ago.'

'You know that tune?'

'Part of my youth. And reminds me of it. Dear ol' Glenn Miller.' Meaning – Manuela.

'You from round here?' making polite conversation as they always did. You couldn't say 'I'm from nowhere' – it sounded an affectation!

'Skier?'

'What, in Sun Valley! Didn't come for that. To see – and to learn some Catalan. My grandad, he was a sheepfarmer up in Montana; his folk came from hereabout. He could still just patter a few words.'

'This is the Cathar country. They used to practise transhumance; trek right up and over into Cataluña.'

189

'Sure. I've read it up. Professor Braudel, and Leroy Ladurie.'

'Then you know as much as I do,' said Walter good humouredly, 'and probably a lot more.' He envied this boy, who was on such easy terms with his ancestry, and came all the way from Idaho, to see it close up.

And the girls, together in the back seat? Sylvie had always had an enviable 'animal' (a word used pejoratively, when it ought to be a compliment) with ability to sleep in moments of strain, boredom or discomfort: in airports, on railway platforms, aboard cross-channel ferries. And was asleep now. The mouth slightly open. Small, and fairly ladylike snoring noises were heard from time to time. The big but still supple body was curled up in a feline position, rocked when the car took a more abrupt bend. She smelt nice, of herself which was clean and healthy, a warm natural smell like bracken on a hot day, as well as of a good and well-chosen perfume that married well with her skin. I should smell as good, thought Miriam a little sourly, aware of travelling too long in the same clothes; but no longer than Sylvie had . . . Take me out of my natural (which is unnatural) habitat and I'm nothing, thinks Miriam. Pitying herself and fighting against it. Maître Lebreton is always cool and clean; her white collars immaculate, her robe thoroughly brushed and aired (so unlike numerous male colleagues, intellectually distinguished and physically grotty – so often given to Hermès briefcases, but scurf on the shoulders). Take though Lebreton away from her book of words and that bright acute mind gibbers and stammers, mouthing and dribbling in a cerebral palsy. She could have got away out of this twenty times, and had been too feeble of mind and will. But plainly, mind and will were subconsciously, instinctively, bent in an altogether contrary direction.

I am an advocate. In Walter's eye the worst sort of parasite: he told me as much and I burst out laughing. I no longer laugh. I cherished the illusion of criminal practice as something worthwhile but I was admiring myself. Fast Fanny with her scarlet Porsche. I admired my cleverness, my skill in debate and repartee, my lucidity in argument. Worthless: I am a hypocrite no less than a coward.

The pistol barrel in my navel – it hurt me. What would a shot have done to me there? In my femaleness; it would have exploded those ovaries. I thought myself skilled at competing in a man's world; what have I done in my female world? I have interfered with these two lives, and provoked catastrophe.

This boy, Fernand – he said to me that he would not support prison, and I told him the truth, that however I pleaded the most he could hope for was some slight diminishment, for society would see him as a threat. What could he do? 'Escape!' I said, half-frivolously.

Walter . . . that richness of personality delighted me and what did I do? 'Amuse me, admire me, seduce me.' Provoking him I provoked guilt, and I provoked this fugue. The jeopardy in which we now all stand has been my doing.

*

Manuel had only arrived in Lyon around the time of the flight from Nevers, but he had made much better time, driving faster upon easier roads. Leaving the autoroute at Dijon, and again near Langres, he had noticed gendarmerie patrols with an unusually sharp eye upon the road, but had thought nothing of it; such things were commonplace. There'd been a hold-up somewhere, perhaps.

He is a person of fewer unnecessary words than most. Less talkative in company, he thinks more, and chats less, also inside his head.

Insofar as I think at all – little and infrequent – Pa and Ma have got into this extraordinary muddle without meaning to. They are prisoners, of themselves and their past. Their history, their ancestors: things it is not easy to escape from. I am very fortunate – I have no ancestors, no history. Well for me; I'm a freer man than most.

Poor Ma! She is an intelligent woman, or would be if she left herself alone, but no, she must always see herself as foolish thick-ead, the Belgian mare, whose centre of thought is in that stupid connasse, because that is what the men have always told her, from her father down. Because of that tremendous Flemish family-feeling she has always been very strongly Mum – and because of those little adulterous escapades the more close and clinging with the children. It certainly was never her fault that Pa has always been a tormented unstable man, but she didn't make things better! I always wondered why he married her: I suppose to get away from his background, all that upper class crap he hated so. He was looking for stability, I have always

191

thought; solid bourgeois values, roots and an anchorage, law and order and safety first – a sight too much of it in that family. She brought him a lot; too much of it material, perhaps: the nice comfortable house and good food and plenty of it, the pretty wife in nice clothes to be proud of. She protected him. Perhaps too much, too efficiently. It wasn't altogether what he wanted. Speculation all this: very little point in that. Least of all now. Tja, a road block.

*

The gendarmerie had in fact got upon its horse and gone mobile, rather belatedly. In the neighbouring departments to the Nièvre it was now a Thundering Herd – but the Alfa had reached Chaumont together with the news. One would never quite know how much of this delay could be attributed to a certain lack of zeal in the PJ services, who had not taken Manuel's information all that seriously, and might have gone about broadcasting it in sketchily or half-heartedly guise. The truth of this matter, mentioned reluctantly, admitted unwillingly, is that the Police Judiciaire and the Gendarmerie are at no time really cooperative, a fact deplored in law-enforcement circles, but more frequently skimmed over. The famous central-command-post for the whole national territory, near Paris at Rosny sur Bois, said later that the PJ had been a bit slow. The PJ said Rosny had been a bit slow – or maybe a bit garbled. As usual in bureaucratic circles, it was later said that it was all the computer's fault.

Once Rosny heard that another gendarme had been discovered tied up and gagged, at Nevers of all places, it said crossly that the author of these outrages was certainly the same. That's his trick. And now kindly get your finger out. One has to remember that the gendarmerie is a body under military discipline and is extremely competent. But it's human after all. It likes bed and dislikes drizzly rain. It was now rushing about north-eastern France anxious to efface humiliation. It questioned the occupants of several Alfa-Romeo cars pretty closely, amounting to persecution of a respectable German couple (happening to bear some physical resemblance to Sylvie and Walter) in a dark green one.

Its main trouble was being thin on the ground. The population of this huge area of north east France, a desert belonging neither to Bourgogne nor Lorraine nor the Champagne, and unwanted by all three, is sparse, and the forces of order are in proportion. Especially at night. One can call for auxiliaries, for the Republican Company of Security, but that is a weighty business. Nobody, said the Préfecture, had got killed. There is no riot.

True, the motorbike cop when found and unwound said, 'He's a killer,' but that was to cover his personal humiliation. It isn't a French vanity; that's universal.

Outside Saint Dizier was a road block. Not the aggravated sort, with metal crash barriers. Simply a motorbike cop in the middle of the road saying Stop, and an Estafette van at the side with the rooflight winking, and a cop on the shortwave radio, and another standing sternly demanding 'Papers'. Had he seen anything of a dark Alfa with three or it might be four occupants? There are few cars on the road at midnight in these regions, and those mostly on the road to Paris – naturally, it was on the Paris approaches that the search was thickest concentrated.

"Like to meet up with it myself." This involved Manuel in some unwanted explanations, and lost him a lot of time. But the road to Bar le Duc and Verdun is relatively fast. Walter, driving up the Meuse valley through Neufchâteau, was finding it very tedious going. The gendarmerie though had got the general idea. A gangster who had broken prison somewhere was now doing a conventional thing, which they well understood: making for Belgium, always traditionally thought of by gangsters as a haven. At Verdun, seat of the authority in the border department of the Meuse, hasty dispositions were made.

'Well,' (went the shortwave dialogue), 'if they're going for the border we can concentrate there, instead of trying to cover every piddling side road from here to Commercy. This fellow you've got there who says he's the hostages' son, is that right, he wouldn't be trying to take the piss out of us by any chance? Well, he might come in handy if it comes to a whatsit, a dialogue, send him on but make sure he's covered.'

Manuel found himself with an unwished-for passenger who sat stolid and chewed gum, but was otherwise harmless save for a faint reek of disgusting aftershave. It's something like a hundred kilometres from Saint Dizier to Verdun and the time seemed short. Manuel had a lot to think about.

193

(Walter, slogging through the night up the tiringly twiddly loops of the Meuse valley, felt cheered. Commercy, and not a whiff of gendarmerie anywhere. They would make it, now.)

One of Manuel's troubles is that he can see the other side and sympathise with an opposing point of view. Cops have a simplistic sort of mind. And pretty rigid.

"Now tell me this tale of yours," said the lieutenant, "and try and make it coherent," as to the simple-minded. "And above all be brief: we may have little time."

"I don't get this." Manuel wasn't allowing himself to be provoked, but was beginning to feel irritation. "I think I'm reading this right: it's the sort of thing my father does. To-morrow – today some time," it was two in the morning, "they're likely to try – what's all the big panic? This chap broke jug, okay, and he might just be armed, because I looked for my father's pistol and couldn't find –"

"He broke jug and he might just be armed," with heavy sarcasm. "Let me tell you, young man, that last night in Nevers this chap of yours attacked a patrolling agent and stole a service pistol. And escaped, forcing the hostages with him. Made off, we're by now pretty sure, in a northerly direction. Get maybe a cross-bearing any moment. Dirty night, visibility not so good but we'll have them spotted. Now if you tell me they were intending to cross at Montmédy –"

"I said it was possible."

"You were a lot more sure than that a while ago. Your father know this part of the world well, does he?"

"Fairly, I think. My mother was originally from over there round Arlon."

"Good. Hostages start to sympathise, and even try to help. Well known phenomenon. This note you found saying Mont-médy clinches it. They wouldn't risk going near Metz, especially now, and the next crossing's up near Stenay. Side roads are a rabbit warren up in the hills. Instead of trying to pin them down we leave everything open and we'll have him in a bag."

"Look, I want to try and avoid force. That's what I came here for – let me talk to him quietly and I'll –"

"What, fella loose with a big banger – boy, that thing's loaded. You stay still. I'll keep you with me, because there may be a chance of a parlay and we've got to cut him off from the hostages but I know that border crossing. Ideal place. He's got nowhere to go."

*

As everybody knows, Verdun is a fortress, and the home of the unyielding fortress mentality. Apart from that it is a pleasant town, built on a hill commanding the Meuse crossing. The old citadel is at the top of the hill. The gendarmerie head-quarters is up there too.

"Getting too tired to drive," said Walter, whose eyes were giving out.

"That's all right," said Fernand, unexpectedly gentle. "Move over, and I'll drive the rest. Trusting you, see?" It was as un-expected as the gentleness, after the nervous frenzy earlier, and it put heart into Walter. There would be no real problem, now. The last tricky point would be Verdun; a crossing point for the roads over the plateau and up into the hills as well as along the valley to Sedan. But their road ran along the right bank of the river. The town is over the bridges, "outre-Meuse'. A lot of traffic lights, but set to blink at amber at this time of night and with nobody much about. North and east of Verdun is the forest. The young trees have grown. The scars of the battlefield are hidden now, unless you go hunting for them along forest paths. The military cemeteries are quiet, peaceful places. The road meandered in large placid bends through the trees. Walter, his eyes giving out. Only another forty kilometres to go – nothing.

The borders of a country, so often absurd political abstrac-tions, lines drawn on a map, as can be clearly seen in Picardy and Flanders, are here a real frontier. The mentality of England (to take an obvious example) is shaped and hammered by the fact that when you take a step over the border you fall in the sea. White cliffs of Dover and what-have-you.

That this frontier is eminently defensible strikes the eye at once. The hills round Metz and Luxembourg are not high, but are jumbled and abrupt, steep-sided, full of gorges that bristle with cliffs of sheer rock. All the Moselle valley is like that, right down to Coblenz and even down the Rhine to Bonn. It was the rampart behind which the Romans sat for all those years.

Westward, the Meuse valley has narrow passages between cliffs of rock, as one sees at Dinant and Namur. But these, once forced, are the weak point, and all invading armies threw

195

their weight here. For between the rivers there is the massif of the Ardennes. The 'sensible' invading army tries for the easier ground, west of Charleroi. It is from Maubeuge on that the border becomes a nonsense, and the French begin to tell 'Belgian jokes' – identical to those told in Ireland about the Kerrymen. The border is only psychological and must be reinforced by legend.

The hillmen of the Meuse country know very well how to find paths across the 'frontier' and use them: there has always been a flourishing population of poachers and smugglers. But the official crossings are few and easily controlled in the narrow defiles.

This was the point of the gendarmerie tactics. Alarm fugitives by a lot of largely futile checkpoints on open roads, and they will turn and flee in any of a dozen directions and, alerted, will be the harder to stop. Lure them gently into a bag by withdrawing all the barriers short of the border itself, and . . .

Walter woke up at Bras-sur-Meuse, where they left the main Sedan road. The ten-minutes-kip had done him good. Wakeful, there was a moment of alarm at the village of Damvillers, where there is a gendarmerie post right at the roadside – but it was dark and still behind the milky, illuminated red-white-and-blue sign.

Sylvie had woken too, but was deliberately 'not thinking'. A familiar place to her, Montmédy. She had been there half a dozen times and was reconstructing from her memories.

A break from jail, Miriam was thinking. Relatively a venial offence and of no great penal consequence: thirty days or so of strict confinement; punishment conditions 'in the hole' – gone were the good old bread-and-water days. Revocation of privileges: no letters, no 'parlour'. Small punishments, and temporary. But resisting arrest, clonking a cop while on the run, stealing the official weapon (property of the state). Aggravated assault and highway banditry, the hostage thing, the rebellion – a prosecutor went to town on such meaty, biteable bones. However liberal the president of a tribunal judging that, the court could lay down a mighty stiff sentence. Five years, even seven, a thing like that might fetch.

Now what – she was trying to remember – was the possible maximum in California (and that was a place where a caper of this sort could send you up for half a lifetime) for distributing, i.e., profiting from, battening off kiddyporn? Nice movie, soundtrack and all, high technical standards, of little girls and boys being forced on camera by the 'eight is too late' gang? Four years? No more.

She would have to look it up in the California Penal Code. In the Department Assize Court of either the Garonne or the Meuse – whichever desisted in favour of the other – the Proc would not be in the least interested in California, and would say so, loudly, but one might find a key to pleading. She would plead, if she got out of this with a whole skin that is (Miriam's imagination, ever vivid, had her hobbling into court on crutches) – she would plead.' She would know what she was pleading ABOUT.

The village of Jametz. Everyone in the car made the little twitching movement, nervous as much as physical, of 'sitting forward'. The last lap: they had come after all the entire length of France; half as much again in road distances. This old car had come to resemble a kind of Noah's Ark. One had got quite attached to the faithful old dog. The motor went racing on, unperturbed and unfatigued. Fernand driving as correctly as though at school, hands at a quarter to three; impeccable gear-changes.

It's a pleasant little town, Montmédy, open and airy, sheltered in a hollow of the hills. Formerly the Seat of the Border (sous) Prefecture, which is as close as you can get in translation to Dien Bien Phu; another place in a hollow, whose garrison (it might be remembered) made the elementary and fatal mistake of not occupying the high ground. There's no risk of that here: seen by day the hill behind is crowned by a massive building with twin cupolas, so that one is reminded of some Spanish monastery. From closer by it is a church and one wonders what it can be doing up there on the hill before realising that it sits upon a foundation of massive fortifications. The citadel has guarded the hill pass since very early times, was given its classical shape by Vauban, locking the door against the Spaniards. A big church for a big garrison. Proving futile in 1870, but they were still pinning their hopes to forts in 1914. The railway line from Calais, skirting the frontier down to Switzerland and Italy, here actually touches the border. For the rest it is just a quiet little market town and in the square a pompous neo-classical town hall in the ochre sandstone of the region, looking much too important for the size of the place. As you drive out the road splits abruptly, going on to Sedan or, turning suddenly aside, to Arlon and Virton. One only sees it at the last moment: Fernand had to brake and the tyres squealed a little. A watcher by the railway line pressed the transmitter button on a walkie talkie.

The road is narrow, only two lanes, but quite good. Five kilometres out is the village of Verneuil. Just beyond Montmédy the railway line crosses over from left to right, running along the border before turning down to Longuyon and Metz, coming closer to the road as the pass narrows . . . The last village on the French side is a little, rural, shabby place called Ecouviez. And immediately beyond that is a dip and a bend, and that is the frontier.

Like all European frontiers now, there is no show and little fuss. There isn't even a barrier. Beyond is an unpretentious little red and white notice that simply says 'Belgique', and the circular disc to tell you that here too the legal speed is ninety kilometres an hour. There might be a customs agent, the douanier in his old-fashioned-looking blue trousers with the broad red stripe, lounging in the middle of the road. In a private car you slow down politely, for him to glance at your number plate, and unless it is from 'somewhere funny' the odds are that he will wave you negligently onward with a flip of the fingers. You would need to be simply stacked to the roof with whisky bottles and all a-clatter together, for his attention really to be aroused. Well, what is he there for at all? The answer is 'to persecute truck drivers'. Common market or no they must stop, and get down, and present their manifest, and a lot of declarations in triplicate; a mass of paper that takes a quarter of an hour to go through. And if the douanier is in a bad (or just zealous) mood, frequently a lot longer. To this end the road has been widened just before the crossing, with neatly painted parking signs on either side, room for three – or six – of the big thirty-tonners so as not to obstruct the roadway.

The customs office is in a pleasantly rustic little wooden house on the crossing, and opposite is a tiny shack. It carries an important-looking inscription saying Police Nationale des

Frontières, so that you should not be tempted into thinking it is a public lavatory. There is never anyone there. For the rest there is an ugly concrete blockhouse with barred windows, an entrepôt for wine calling itself Aux Caves de France. And that's all. Coming from France, on your right is the railway; on your left the hillside with little sheds and little fields, wired to keep the sheep, that are grazing among fruit trees, from straying.

As Fernand came into Ecouviez, slowing to the legal sixty-through-a-village, the road surface suddenly became very bad indeed and with no warning, all potholes and worn-out patching, so that he cursed and braked harder, down to thirty, and sailed through the sleeping ill-lit dorp at this inconspicuous gait. The border crossing is masked till the last instant, by the dip, and the bend.

There were no trucks at this hour of night. They knew better than to risk an even more tedious wait than usual, with a sleepier and crosser douanier, apt to suspicions of their carrying foot and mouth disease or something equally nasty. There was however a lot of Police Nationale des Frontières. The road was blocked with mobile metal barriers painted white. These are fairly flimsy, being used mostly for traffic guidance and crowd control. But there were also two Estafette vans parked in a V across the roadway. And there were half a dozen or more cops with varying weaponry. These did not look flimsy.

It should have been over then and there. You sit there stuck under the wheel of a car, with a semicircle of machine guns pointing at you. You're in the bag, and they have only to pull the string. It would have been over then and there but for the two factors, known but insufficiently considered; the bad road surface and the widened parking space. Fernand, in second gear, got well in to the right and made a screaming U-turn. The Alfa fled back up the village street.

There is a little potty stream that comes down from the hills. The street crosses it upon an antique, solid stone bridge. Upon this appeared another of the gendarmerie's blue vans. The lieutenant, with Manuel in tow and having taken his disposi-tions, wasn't going to hang about on the street in the rain in the middle of the night. Comfortable in the certainty that things were under control, he had stayed drinking coffee in the gen-darmerie barracks up the hill, in Montmédy. Waiting there for a buzz, and finding Manuel quite good company, but for this bee in the lad's bonnet about violence . . . He was now catching up.

And if the driver had simply slewed the van crosswise on the bridge . . . but a bit over-eager, he came charging down upon them. Hereabouts the street opens into a triangular space running down to the waterside, enclosed by a few houses, the village Post Office and a bus shelter placed there by courtesy of the Co-op Agricultural Bank. Fernand, quick of wit and wrist, dodged into this and out again as the van lurched past him. Before the clumsy thing could turn he was over the bridge at the village crossroads upon which stands a remarkably ugly village church. The main road itself is a cul-de-sac (as the lieutenant knew) since it simply leads back to Montmédy. And to the left there is no escape, for there lies the railway line. Remain two rough twisty little laneways past the church, up the hill. It is by instinct that the fugitive takes to the hills.

And the Alfa Romeo, built by Italian engineers with an eye to the tortuous and uneven hill lanes of Italy quite as much as to the autostrada, is the car to do it. True, the Estafette van, with front wheel drive and a high clearance, will do as much, but a lot slower.

These laneways might lead to another village, and be in quite good condition. And just as often they lead to nothing but an isolated farm, petering out beyond the cow shed. This one led straight uphill and turned abruptly to a cart track, unmetalled: the farmer's access to his fields. His tractor had worn two ruts into the sandy, stony hill soil. Rain, coursing down the slope, had worn the ruts into deep, nasty gullies. Just the width of the wheels. Fernand got the car out of the gully, balanced it between the hump in the middle and the ditch to the side. But too fast, and in the dark – nobody could have managed that. The Alfa skidded, went into the rut and out again, skidded afresh, hit the ditch just where the farmer had built a little culvert for drainage. The front wheel stopped dead on the obstacle, the back jinked sideways and the whole car turned over, on the edge of the stubblefield.

Walter was stunned. But his belt had held and he had hit nothing much – the padded sun visor. A car like that has a safety arch and can turn over two or three times – even at speed, on an autoroute – without much real damage. It was the culvert that broke the front suspension. He was stunned only by being suddenly turned upside down and having the breath knocked out of him. He was unaware of another racing motor, another tremendous bump, and a yell. That eager driver of the lieutenant's van – he was only a young chap – had come roaring up the hill and got into exactly the same tangle with the ruts. When the Alfa crashed he braked too late and too hard. He didn't hit anything, but the Estafette's off wheels went into the ditch, the whole topheavy thing slewed over; subsided, quite gently, on its side. Climbing out was complicated, and rather slow.

Walter got to his feet, tottery. The stubble was wet, but not soggy: the hillside drained the water off. They were on the slope below the track. A moment, to get one's bearings, in the dark. On the steeper hill, above the track, there was pasture. As one's eyes became accustomed to the dimness that was less dim above the skyline the outline of trees could be made out on the low, scraped summit. These hills are not high, are much eroded. It was a hump or hullock, rather than hill.

There was a scrambling activity of two or three people near him. He looked at the broken car. Miriam was still in it, and perhaps injured? – but Fernand was gone. And so was Sylvie. A muscular hand gripped his shoulder, and an extraordinary, familiar voice said quietly, "Hallo, Pa, I'm here." Manuel! Walter felt the whole monstrous crowd around him dwindle and vanish. He had been pulled and jostled; deafened and bewildered: frightened. A bellowing mob spitting in his face, snatching at his clothes, fingering and poking at his whole body: he was helpless; he had lost all sense of identity. He did not know whether it was friendly or hostile. And now Manuel was here. The howling, crass, gibbering hysteria vanished. The grip upon his shoulder was that of his own son.

"Hallo, son," he said. "But where's your mother?"

"Up there," said Manuel, pointing.

"We'll go and get her."

A roar and a clatter, differential whine of a motor, in low gear; gendarmerie reinforcements arriving. The lieutenant, cross and flustered (tipped in the ditch, his cap lost) was struggling with things that wouldn't work: spotlight, loudspeaker. Dashboard connection bust, or a battery terminal pulled – fuse? – but he had no time.

"Spread out, and don't shoot. Up the hill there . . ."

Uneven hill pasture, steep and tussocky. Walter was accustomed to it at home. His climbing was strong, loose. That middleaged and wearisome personage who overate and smoked too much, given to drinking and chatting, had been left behind on a cart-track. And with him was Manuel. Who understood, who needed no telling. He could see them now. They weren't far away; had not reached the tree-line. The light was enough. Sylvie was a good walker, but she was limping from some hurt, and as Fernand dragged her she stumbled, down on to one knee. Walter felt no indignation. It was all in the family.

"Fernand!" he called. But he had no breath; it came out flat and feeble. He had to stop; his legs had gone to rubber. But it was only a few more steps.

She had twisted an ankle on a tussock, could not walk. The man stood behind her, holding her arm. In his other hand he held a big pistol. But he was not menacing her. Manuel did not look to see, but he knew those cops would not shoot, for fear of hitting the woman. He could hear Pa, fighting for breath. Well, he knew the chap's name now. The thing was not to frighten him.

"Fernand," he said quietly. "It's only me – Manny." He could not have said why he used the old, child's name.

Fernand stood indecisive. He dropped Sylvie's arm. She had got her breath, clambered to her feet, stood at his side. He raised the pistol arm, but half-heartedly. It'll be all right, thought Manuel. He walked slowly, his hands dropped.

Three more steps, thought Walter, forcing himself.

"Fernand – it's only me and Manuel." He remembered thinking – shut up, you ass!

Two things happened. The powerful spotlight made suddenly its connection; probably more by luck than judgment shed the beam full upon the ragged little group. Family photo, one for the album. Giggles: look at us acting the goat there. Yes that's us – foothill there, somewhere on the edge of the Ardennes.

Good luck? Good judgment?

Sylvie, bewildered by the sudden light, saw the pistol. With her fist and forearm she struck, as hard as she could, at the hand holding it. Her man, her son.

There would be different accounts of what happened next: there always are. That the three shots came close together, or that there was an interval. Some saw one thing; some saw another. That the woman knocked the gun up and the first shot went wild. The lieutenant said, "Oh Jesus Christ," but this sentiment, however pious, was suppressed as irrelevant. The official report is what counts, and the lieutenant wrote it, as the senior officer present. The gendarme who said later that turning the light on was a mistake, that but for that nothing would have happened, was likewise suppressed for querying an officer's judgment. After the three shots nobody hesitated any longer. There was a volley from all sides of the field, and however many went wide there were enough to make an end of Fernand. He was just standing there: an easy target. Who had been shot first? The woman, while struggling with him? – it was by then an academic question. With great courage, said the report, the two men attempted to disarm or immobilise the criminal. Normal, since she was the wife of the one and the mother of the other but people do not always behave normally in face of such a threat.

We say, or better put we hope we would do as much, thought the gendarmerie captain, who when told on the telephone was not pleased, and said 'massacre' before adding, "Leave the press to me, you hear?" The lieutenant, uncomfortably aware that he had not handled the matter quite as well as he might have done, made much of the fact that this was a very dangerous criminal. Had he not mugged police officers on two different occasions? Fugitive from justice, no? Wanted for armed robbery and banditry as well as the breaking-and-entering. And the plan to capture him had been perfect: well, the best plans can go astray upon occasion. Yes yes yes, said the captain irritably and what about this other woman in the car?

Dead, poor thing; neck broken. "You see, Chief, when the car crashed it was with a violent jerk to the left. The other woman was sitting on the left and was thrown clear when the door sprang open. Whereas t'other – she turns out to be this missing lawyer – was on the right and no belt of course, and was rabbit-

punched by the impact. Can't make out how she came to be
with them at all. Some collusion or whatever possible there –
but since she's dead . . ."

"Are they all dead?"

"No, the young chap, the son – pretty badly hit in the chest
but they thought they might pull him out of it, in reanimation."

Manuel knew, but he was not saying.

He was forbidden to talk anyhow, because his lung was
punctured. His chest was a mess; he was immobilised. Large
areas of tissue and bone were badly torn and would have to be
put together bit by bit, said the young surgeon, tapping his face
with affection and reassurance. A good surgeon. Didn't know
much about gunshot wounds or he would have understood what
happened. Maybe he had, and like Manuel himself would keep
quiet. One respects the dignity of the dead.

My mother fought for the gun. She was fighting for her men.
She shouldn't have, and didn't need to. They were both
frightened, and shocked; by the crash, the fear, the flight, the
pain. The noise, the shouting, the lights. What does it matter –
they both lost their heads.

She didn't get the gun. She got him round the hips and clung
to him and that sent him wild. Without the light he would have
given me the gun. I was close enough to see the irresolution. And
perhaps it seemed to him that she failed him in the pinch when
he had counted on her, and that he could not forgive her the
frustration.

But that is speculation. There is no speculation, there is no
doubt, about what my father did.

Call him by his name – Fernand. He has a right to his name,
no? He blew my mother's head off with that big pistol. I don't
think he meant to, but that's what he did. And then he turned it
on me, and that would have been my lot.

Instead of trying to rush him, which would have been too
late, my father stepped in front of me. To take the shot for me.

There was a first shot, I think. It went into the sky when
my mother knocked the gun up. I think he was holding the
pistol out to me, but his finger was on the trigger and it was
cocked. Light pull.

A magnum revolver. The surgeon might not realise but the
police will. It was their gun. A three fifty-seven magnum . . . it

goes straight on through. It went straight through my father. Neither of them felt a thing and for that I'm grateful. I have pain, plenty of it. Doped or no. And for that also I'm grateful. Because my father could not know that a bullet like that will kill two people, standing close together. The bullet hit one of his bones, was deflected a bit. Tumbled, maybe, to have torn me up like this.

My father saved my life twice. With his blood; and with his bone. I have that, now, to carry with me.

The gendarmerie lieutenant went home, after a very rough night. His wife asked him whether he wanted coffee, and he refused with a shudder: his guts were awash with coffee. No no, the schnapps bottle, to settle his stomach; and his nerves too; Christ. Wouldn't get any sleep anyhow. He'd have to go into headquarters and get his head washed by an irritable chief. They hadn't come too well out of this – whole goddam episode from start to finish.

Better see it that way. An episode. That's all it is and now it's finished.

Routine, quoi?

"You oughtn't to take another!"

"Bastard won't smell my breath . . . Funny people. I'd like to see the young one pull through. Nice lad. I talked with him quite a lot while we were waiting." The lieutenant would not ordinarily have been talking to his wife like this. Business is business, and one keeps it at the office. Not always stuff the women ought to know; right? He too can be forgiven. Although an experienced officer he had not had an experience like this before. And to do him justice he was conscious of having failed. He took a third against her frown, waving an angry hand when she tried to take the bottle away.

"Remember that fellow who died? – the one who used to do the rugby matches on the television?"

"Vaguely. The one who used to roar? 'Allez les petits' – that one? What makes you think of him?"

"Used to talk something the same way. Phrases. About nobility, beauty, honesty, honour. Stuff like that."

"About rugby matches!"

"Yes, you don't see much of that about. In life neither. Not in our trade you don't. He was a dotty chap – one of the old brigade. Saw it all as a kind of medieval thing, whatsit, a tournament. You know, knights in armour. Bash, bash. Fellow two metres high, a hundred kilos, built like a bank's strongroom. Allez les petits! Living in a different world, what!"

Walter would have been pleased, with this much understanding.

"You be careful how you drive!" said the wife.